Peach Trees

JOHN DUNCKLEE

Other books by John Duncklee:

Quest for the Eagle Feather
Graciela of the Border
Genevieve of Tombstone
Coyotes I Have Known
Good Years for the Buzzards
Forced Journey

These are all available through Barbed Wire Publishing (website www.barbed-wire.net), Amazon, Borders, Barnes & Noble, and other great bookstores everywhere.

Peach Trees

JOHN DUNCKLEE

BARBED WIRE
PUBLISHING
LAS CRUCES, NEW MEXICO

Printed in the United States of America.

Published by Barbed Wire Publishing
1990 East Lohman Avenue, Suite 225
Las Cruces, New Mexico 88001 USA

Title font Aja
Text font Adobe Caslon
Book and cover design by Vicki Ligon

ISBN 0-9678566-8-X

1 2 3 4 5 6 7 8 9 0

As always, to my wonderful wife, Penny

Acknowledgements:

Continued friendship for Felipe, Dave and Schmedley; of an era.

Many thanks to Brian McTavish, without whose efforts this book would never have been written.

Sincere appreciation to Bill Buckmaster, host of KUAT-TV's "Arizona Illustrated," for his generous support of authors.

Jim Woolard for his valued friendship.

Por seguro- Talented Barbed Wire Publishing.

CHAPTER ONE

"Cheap weed," Pete had told him, but who do you hit up? Billy O'Leary strode the Haight-Ashbury pavement, watching the hippies who lounged in doorways or stood talking in groups. They laughed or sat vacant-eyed until he tripped their field of awareness. Then they went somber or glared, until he'd passed and the laughter would erupt again. He couldn't help his military buzz-cut, but at least the army boots no longer had a spit shine.

"Hey soldier. Whatcha got in your case? A stinkin' 'Nam uniform?" asked one of the doorway lizards. Black hair scraggled from the man's face and head. From his tee-shirt a Grateful Dead skull leered through strings of beads.

Billy paused. "Just my banjo."

The man grinned and nodded, then held up two fingers. "Peace, man." The unmistakable spice of hash smoke swirled around him, along with the stench of garbage that seemed to drift from the doorway.

Billy thought about stopping to talk, but kept walking. San Francisco fog hazed at the end of the street and shrouded groups of dopers and Hawaiian print tourists who seemed surreally out of place. It was like nothing he had seen in Illinois before he got shipped to the jungles. Two tours in hell and now everything stateside seemed to have changed. He knew he never belonged in Vietnam. Now he wondered if he belonged here either.

"Hey soldier! How many kids you kill?"

Billy kept his eyes focused on the sidewalk, and let the cracks slide past his feet. "To hell with it." He turned at the corner, heading for the line of trees that marked Golden Gate Park. There were other kinds of highs.

The fog seemed to grow more dense as he neared the green belt of shadowed pines and rhododendrons. Its salt tang reminded him of Fort Ord. God, he'd been glad to board the bus and leave the army behind. He'd climbed off in San

Francisco, found a Goodwill store, and traded his army issue for Levi's and a denim shirt. Nearby, in a pawn shop window, he'd seen the banjo and asked the clerk the price.

"Seventy-five," the old man had said, his double chin tilted against his chest as he inspected Billy over the gold-rimmed glasses that perched on his nose.

"I would like to see it, please."

The clerk had reached in among the other things on display and grunted as he lifted the banjo out. He handed it to Billy, and the feel of the wooden neck and the hard strings was the most familiar thing Billy had experienced since he'd come back.

Billy slipped the strap over his head, let the body rest against his hip and fingered a C chord. He strummed and plucked. A smile spread through him. Head bent, he listened to the tone as he adjusted the tension on the strings. Then he strummed again, enjoying the sound and the vibration. Even after three years without holding a banjo, he could tell it was a good instrument. It had to be; it was a five-string Gibson.

"You gonna buy it or play it?"

Billy recoiled, irked at the man's impatience. "I need to try it first." He took his time tuning it.

With an eye on the clerk's reaction, he began playing "Camptown Races," one of his favorites. For an instant, he wasn't standing in a cluttered pawn shop, but felt the warmth of stage lights and the attention of the crowd. The banjo's tone was true, and it had the right proportion and feel. He plucked out the melody and hummed along, emphasizing the beat and noticing the clerk's attitude soften. Before the man fully relaxed into the music, Billy stopped. He slipped the strap and put the banjo on the counter.

"I guess I'll have to buy it, Mister."

The clerk sobered. "Ten dollars more da case."

Cheap shit, Billy thought. "Then I guess you can keep your banjo and the case," he said and started for the door.

"All right. I vill trow in da case."

Seventy-five wouldn't put much of a dent in his twelve hundred mustering-out money, and the pleasure was worth it. Billy put the banjo in its scuffed case and counted out his greenbacks. He didn't wait for a receipt.

Leaving the pawn shop with the black case on his shoulder, he had headed for Haight-Ashbury and the promise of cheap weed. The resentment he'd found wasn't the company he had in mind for a good time. His banjo offered more groove than the hippies on Haight-Ashbury. Remembering Pete's recommendation, he wondered if his buddy had made it after the helicopter had taken off from the jungle clearing with Pete inside with his leg half blown off.

Billy reached the park and settled onto a vacant iron bench, still damp with fog. A chipmunk darted toward him and froze, unblinking, eager for a handout. "Sorry fella. Wish I had something for you." In the distance, groups of flower power sat on the lawn or leaned against trees. A barefoot girl swirled with arms extended, and Billy heard the distant clink of a tambourine. "Go check them out."

The animal scampered off as Billy opened his case and took out the banjo and metal picks that fit over his thumb and first two fingers on his right hand. With the case open on the ground in front of him, he launched into a full round of "Camptown Races." Exhilaration surged through him. Just like riding a bicycle. You never forget. The park and the people seemed unimportant as he slipped into the music and the feel of the banjo in his hands. It was like an old friend, come to talk with him of good times and mellow days before things had gone crazy. He played the songs he'd learned as a boy, sitting on his bed at home or under a willow tree by the river, or songs he'd polished with his friends in high school. Some songs he vocalized. Some he just picked the melody.

He drifted on the rhythm of the music, and the hard ridges of the strings against his fingers. With a whiff of stale perfume, he glanced up to see a stooped, white-haired lady step forward.

In surprise, he watched her put a five dollar bill into the open banjo case in front of him. Thank you very much," he said as she retreated and stood as if waiting for another song.

"I enjoyed your music very much, young man," she answered. "It is pleasant to hear real music instead of the horrible noise they are making these days." The woman smiled and the toe of her shoe kept time with the beat. When she finally left on one of the sidewalks leading away from the park, her gait even had a little swing to it.

That pleased Billy. He played another song, followed by "Golden Slippers." An older gentleman, wearing a Homburg hat and trailing behind a brown and white terrier on a leash, came to a stop in front of him. The dog tugged at the leash as he dropped a five dollar bill in the case, to join the first. The man touched the brim of his hat, and nodded respectfully, then walked away.

Billy stared at the money. It had appeared without asking, and the people had seemed happy to give it. Clearly, Billy wasn't the only one who felt better for the banjo music. What a great way to make a livin', doin' what I love doin'. The hostility that had plagued him had disappeared when he played. But sitting in the park, strumming to make himself forget the last three years and the weirdness of *hip America* was one thing. The park gig was bound to grow thin. Maybe he could get a spot in a bar as live entertainment. Maybe he'd even be able to stay with it long enough to build up a reputation, but he doubted it. If it ever started wearing on him like military slavery, at least there were other places and other towns to play in, and he'd be his own master from now on.

Billy picked up the two fives and stuffed them into the pocket of his jeans. He snapped the lid over the banjo. Hefting the case to his shoulder, he left the park in search of a bar. And a beer.

Two blocks away, Leo's Bar and Grill caught Billy's eye with its blinking neon Budweiser sign in the window. Too early for the evening crowd, one customer slumped over the time-worn bartop with his head resting on his folded arms. On the wall behind the serving aisle, a row of assorted bottles stood in line, showing customers their choice of brands. Centered on the wall, a large, framed print of a reclining nude gazed aimlessly from her position on a velvet couch.

Billy chose one of the twenty stools, leaned the banjo case against the bar and sat down. The rotund bartender, with a frayed, stained towel clutched in his stubby fingers, stood with arms braced on the inside edge of the bartop. "What'll it be?"

"Budweiser," Billy answered.

"Bottle or can?"

"Bottle."

"Glass?"

"No thanks."

The bartender reached down, and in one fluid movement opened the battered metal top of a cooler, took out a bottle, popped the cap off and put it on the bar in front of Billy, with a cardboard coaster advertising Heineken's. The entire operation had the well-oiled practice of a drill maneuver. "Army?" the bartender asked.

"Just got separated," Billy said, and tilted his head. "How could you tell?"

"Boots."

"I guess I ought to buy some sandals."

"What's in the case, a guitar?"

"Banjo."

"How long you been playing?"

"Since I was a kid. I saw this one in a pawn shop and just had to have it. Makes me feel like I'm a civilian again."

"Been in 'Nam?"

"Yeah." Billy took a pull on the beer.

"I almost got drafted for Korea, but ended up 4-F. The ticker," he said, touching his chest over his heart. "Why not play me a song?"

"I'd be glad to," Billy said, and reached for the case.

Billy raised the strap over his head and got into position. After putting the picks on his fingers, he began to play "Wabash Cannonball." The words hummed in his mind and he could feel the rhythm of the chugging locomotive. He finished with a flourish, then grabbed the bottle of beer and drained it.

"You're really good," the bartender said.

"Thanks," Billy said. "I need to practice. I haven't played banjo in three years."

"Sounds good anyway."

Billy took one of the five dollar bills out of his pocket, and put it on the bar. The bartender waved his hands. "'Cannonball' was worth the beer."

Billy strummed a few chords and broke into "Sweet Betsy."

"What are you figuring to do, now you're out of the army?" the bartender asked when Billy had picked the last too-ra-lei-ay.

"I've been thinkin' of findin' gigs and playin' banjo."

"I'm sure you can find a gig or two here in 'Frisco."

"Big cities bug me. I'm thinkin' of some smaller burg."

"Before Leo made me manager here, I used to go to Jackson, Wyoming summers. Lots of Californians go there, and there's plenty of college gals working in the resort hotels." The bartender showed a lustful grin.

Billy couldn't imagine how any college girl would be attracted to the manager of Leo's Bar.

"I stay here year-round now, but every spring I think about Jackson."

"It's pretty late in the season, isn't it?"

"It runs through September. Slacks off some after Labor Day, but there's still action until it gets cold in the fall. Then there's skiing after it snows."

Billy finished the last drops in the bottle and put it back on the coaster. "I'll have another Bud. Then, I think I'll mosey on down to the bus station. Maybe there's a bus leavin' for Jackson. The college girls sound interesting. Maybe I could teach those college girls a thing or two."

The bartender put the empty into a box on the floor, and replaced it with a full bottle dripping beads of condensation on the cardboard coaster. He slid the five dollar bill toward Billy.

"This one's on me, too. Welcome home."

"Thanks. That's nice to hear. The people around Haight-Ashbury didn't seem to like my army boots."

"Bunch of pot-heads. I stay clear away from there."

Billy played another song during which the slumped over customer lifted his head, stared blankly around the room, left his barstool, slid a dollar bill next to Billy's beer and shuffled out the door.

Replacing the banjo in its case and stuffing the six dollars back into his pocket, Billy finished his beer.

"What's your name?" the bartender asked.

"I guess I'll go by what they called me back home, Banjo Billy."

"I'm Randy. Good luck in Jackson."

"Thanks, Randy," Billy replied. "And, thanks for the beers."

Ambling over the sidewalk, he saw two men and a girl in the distance coming toward him. The long-haired, bearded men in jeans with gaping knees walked hovering over the girl with long brown hair, wearing a tie-dyed skirt and a soiled, sleeveless tee-shirt with a peace sign on the front. Billy watched her prominent nipples sway across the underside of the tee-shirt. *I'll bet both those dudes are getting in her pants, but she probably doesn't have any pants on underneath that skirt.* They laughed occasionally as they made their way. Within ten feet of Billy, the three hippies glanced at him. He followed their eyes from his boots to his buzz cut. Their smiles and laughter turned quickly into sneers. Billy paused to let them break into single file to pass him. His mellow mood since leaving Leo's Bar and Grill turned to anger, but he kept it under silent control.

Moments after the trio had passed, Billy turned to look over his shoulder at them. They had stopped and faced him, each giving him the "finger." Still controlling his anger, Billy turned back with a determined pace toward the bus station. *Why has everybody copped this attitude? What's this feeling like I don't belong in my country anymore. For three years the Army told me what to do; what to eat; who to kill; where to sleep; how to think. I lived with death hangin' over me for two tours in Vietnam, scared shitless for two years. Everything has changed. Now, I'm a civilian again. Lost. Alone. Different. A stranger in my own country. Is it still my country?*

Luck followed Billy to the bus station. A bus, destined for Salt Lake City, was due to leave in a half hour. After buying a ticket, he went to the locker where he had left his olive-drab duffel bag. He had two blankets, a foul-weather jacket, socks, underwear and toilet articles in it. He had given all but one of his uniforms to another soldier. After buying the denim shirt and Levi's, he had changed clothes in the dressing room, and left the last of his army issue hooked on the wall.

Stowing the duffel bag in the luggage compartment, he took his banjo with him into the bus, and lifted the case up to the rack above his seat. Passengers crowded the aisle as he settled in, but no one claimed the space next to him. He sucked in a deep breath and sighed as the bus began moving out of the terminal. The bus inched its way through the streets full of traffic toward the interstate on-ramp as dusk settled over the city. Heading east toward Sacramento, the bus droned steadily as Billy watched golden hills with rows of houses give way to scattered farms. When darkness obscured all but the lights from houses, he managed to curl his six-foot frame onto the seat and fell asleep. Except for waking suddenly after a bad dream about VC snipers, he slept until the bus braked to a stop and the driver shut off the ignition switch.

The coffee in the Salt Lake City bus station tasted old and bitter, but Billy stirred four packets of sugar into the dark, murky brew to make it tolerable. Buttered sweet roll and the coffee finished, he bought a ticket to Jackson via Idaho Falls. He had an hour to wait. Finding a vacant seat in the waiting room, Billy picked up a well-read newspaper before sitting down. An article on the front page, captioned "Anti-War Demonstration At Columbia," caught his eye. He dropped the newspaper on the floor.

I spent two years in those goddam jungles risking my life for what? These anti-war demonstrations make me wonder why we got sent there in the first place. Defending who? Goddam politicians.

The bus from Salt Lake City arrived in Jackson, Wyoming just after sunset. Billy put his duffel bag in a locker before taking a stroll through the town. Mostly two-story buildings decorated with barnwood siding used as boards and battens hugged the sidewalks still full of tourists looking into shop windows, going from bar to bar, or just ambling along for an evening walkabout. The strangeness he had felt in San Francisco still lingered in his mind, but he found no one giving him derisive looks.

The noise from inside The Cowboy Bar piqued his interest enough to go inside. People, with drinks in hand, stood behind the seated patrons. Some occupied the tables throughout the rustic lounge area. The smell of stale beer met his nostrils, and the loud music from the juke box mixed with the noisy conversations among the bar patrons. Billy found a small round table in a corner, leaned the banjo case against the wall, and sat down.

A red-headed cocktail waitress came over carrying a tray. "May I get you a drink?" she asked. She wore a short denim skirt, a red bandanna patterned shirt under an open denim vest, cowboy boots and a bright red wide brimmed felt hat that made her hair look more copper than flame. Billy liked the way she gave him a teasing smile.

"I'll have a Budweiser," he answered, wondering if she was one of the college girls Randy had mentioned. She looked young enough.

"One Bud, comin' up," she said, and went to the brass railed space at the bar used by the table waitresses. *I wonder if she has a boyfriend.*

When she returned with the beer, Billy asked, " Do you know any place in town that could use a banjo player?"

"There's a man at the bar who has a small joint a couple of blocks off the main drag. Musicians play there sometimes. I'll have him come over to see you."

"Hey, thanks," Billy replied.

He watched the red-head tap a man on the shoulder, leaning close to be heard above the noise. The man turned and stared at Billy as she talked. He wore a leather vest, Levi's, and cowboy boots. Patting the red-head on her shoulder, the swarthy featured man ambled over with his drink in hand. Billy noticed his clothes that looked like a costume from some cowboy chic catalogue. "Myra told me you're looking for a gig. All right if I join you?"

"Sure, have a chair," Billy answered.

"What do you play?"

"Banjo."

"By the way, I'm Mort Abrams. I have a small place called The Golden Spur two blocks south and three blocks west of here. Once in a while I get bored over there, so I come over here for a break."

"I'm Banjo Billy. I just got to town and I'm lookin' for a gig."

"I had a guitar cowboy until three days ago. He got tired of town and got himself a job wrangling dudes. Do you sing, too?"

"Oh yeah, most songs need singin'."

Listening to Mort's accent, Billy could tell that the man had come West from somewhere East. But where, he wasn't sure.

"Where are you from, Mort?"

"Manhattan. I came out here on vacation six years ago. When I got back home, I sold my joint and came back to Jackson. Now I wear cowboy boots, Levi's and this vest over my pearl snap shirts. I got a cowboy hat, but I only wear it at The Golden Spur. It's just for looks. All the tourists wanna see here are cowboys."

"When do you want to listen to my banjo?"

"Come over to the Spur in the morning around ten o'clock. I'll be there stocking beer."

"Sounds good to me," Billy said. "I need a place to stay tonight. Is there a cheap hotel anywhere in town?"

"Go four blocks north on the main drag. Turn left for two blocks. Name's 'The Bison.' It's a little run down, but it's cheap."

"Thanks, Mort. I'll see you in the morning."

Mort left to return to the bar. On the way, he spoke briefly to Myra. Moments later she came over to Billy's table with another Budweiser. "This one's on Mort. Did you do any good?"

Billy shrugged. "I'll see tomorrow after I play for him."

"He'll hire you. He doesn't pay much, but I hear he has a bunk in his storeroom he lets his musicians use as part of the pay. He gets enough people in there, and I heard that the tips are not bad."

"Thanks, Myra. Looks like I owe you one."

"Glad to help out. What's your name?"

"Banjo Billy."

"Banjo Billy. I like that," she said, smiling as she tilted her head teasingly.

Finishing his beer, Billy left two dollars on the table, picked up the banjo case, and waved at Myra as he left to find The Bison Hotel. With the prospects of a gig and meeting a good looking woman like Myra, he felt optimistic about his arrival in Jackson, Wyoming. Reaching The Bison, he noticed the old flaking paint on the sign matched the condition of the outside of the building.

Entering through the old, flower-etched glass door, he tapped the bell on the counter. A middle-aged woman with bleached blonde hair waddled her bulk down the hall from a room in the rear. "I expect you're wantin' a room are you?"

"If you have a vacancy."

"It's twenty bucks for a room with a sink, or ten bucks for a cot in the basement."

"The cot in the basement will do fine," Billy said.

"The bathroom's here on the first floor, down the hall to your right. Pay in advance."

Billy gave the woman ten dollars. She showed him the stairway to the basement and flicked on the light. "There's no key, but nobody's going to bother you. Good night," she said, and waddled back to her room.

Billy found the cot. He sat down to take off his boots. Without removing the rest of his clothes, he pulled the covers back, and got into bed. After thinking about how far he had traveled since leaving the army, and the prospect of a gig playing his banjo, his thoughts turned to his father in Springfield, Illinois. *The old man would have a cow if he knew what I was doin'. Playin' banjo isn't his idea of makin' something of oneself. But, playin' banjo in Jackson, Wyoming beats hell out of sellin' farm machinery in Springfield. Beats hell out of tryin' to stay alive in the 'Nam jungles, too.*

Billy comforted himself with the thought that his father would have no way of knowing what he had chosen to do instead of returning home to Springfield. He had enlisted in the army to get away from the cold, distant man who was married to his business, had little time for his son and insisted on having his own way. Back in the jungles of Vietnam, Billy had decided that if he ever came out of the war alive he would not return to his former home. Every time he thought about his stubborn old man he felt his stomach tighten as if something inside pulled the ends of a rope into a knot. Billy turned his thoughts to his music and what songs he would play for his audition at the Golden Spur.

After a breakfast of bacon and eggs, Billy found a bench in the town square where elk antlers decorated street lamp poles and anything else where the antlers could be stacked. There were few people around at the early hour. Taking his banjo from the case, he began strumming chords. He could feel the tenderness of the fingers on his left hand. They would grow calluses in time, but he knew he would have to tape the tips to get through an evening's playing.

Sitting on the bench, he went through the songs he had

planned. When the big, round clock on the side of an old building across the main street said nine forty-five, he started for the bar, following Mort's directions. Without the neon beer advertising blinking, the Golden Spur looked like a vacant building. Peering through the small window in the door, he saw that the lights inside were on. He knocked on the door. A muffled voice called out, and soon Mort opened the door and let Billy in. "I see you found the Spur all right," Mort said.

"No problem at all."

"I'm almost finished stocking. You can go sit on that stool in the corner and get ready."

Billy put the case on the floor after taking out the banjo. As he sat, the maroon Naugahyde seat swiveled easily. Strumming a few chords first, he began picking away on the first bars of "Wabash Cannonball."

Mort finished stocking the beer cooler, popped the top on a Coor's can as he came from behind the bar and took a seat on one of the bar stools. Billy went back to the beginning of the song and sang the vocals. After playing two more songs, he felt his fingers on his left hand getting sore. Hoping Mort had heard enough, he stopped and bent over slightly.

"You're good at that banjo," Mort said. "I like the way you sing, too. Here's the deal. Twenty bucks a night, from eight until closing. I have a cot in the storeroom where you can sleep. That is part of the deal. By the way, the twenty a night is under the table; I don't want any more paper work than necessary."

"Sounds good enough to me," Billy said.

"Now wait a minute. There's more if you want to do it. You can go out to the park in the square, play music for tips and give handbills out to people who stop to listen."

"I don't know what you mean," Billy said.

Mort went behind the bar, grabbed a stack of handbills printed with black ink on bright yellow paper, and put them on top of the bar. "Come here," he said. "I'll show you."

Carefully, Billy put his banjo back in its case, and sat next to

Mort at the bar.

"I get these printed cheap at Insty Print. These are for Horse Thompson, that cowboy who quit me. I got stuck with all these. I'll have it changed to Banjo Billy. See, there's a map to show them where the Golden Spur is located and on the bottom it says 'Bring this in for a free margarita.' Usually couples come in with one handbill. Make sure you don't give out two handbills to a couple, 'cause then they can get two free margaritas. One, I can handle, 'cause the other goes for three bucks."

"Suppose they ask for two handbills?"

"Just tell them that you can only give out one per family. Now, here's where you can make some extra bucks. When a handbill comes in to the bar and the couple sticks around for three rounds, you get a buck."

"What if you are over at the Cowboy Bar when they come in?"

"Whoever is bartending knows the deal."

"That sounds like a heap of banjo pickin'," Billy remarked.

"You'll be surprised how much you'll make in tips out there, plus the bucks for the three round deal."

"All right, Mort, I'll go for it. Where's the storeroom?"

Mort showed him the storeroom and the cot that looked more comfortable than the one he had paid ten dollars for at the Bison Hotel.

"I'll get my gear at the bus station and be back in a while."

"Have a beer first. It's on me," Mort said, and went to the cooler.

He took out a bottle of Budweiser, opened it, and placed it in front of Billy.

"See, I even remember what you were drinking at The Cowboy Bar."

"Thanks, Boss," Billy said.

"I don't know your repertoire, but some Dylan, Peter, Paul and Mary, a little Creedence Clearwater, and Crosby, Stills and Nash will work well in here for the younger people. Lots of the tourists are your age. I don't know where they get their money, but they spend it."

"Is there a used bookstore in town?"

Mort gave him directions to find The Well Read.

"You might think about getting a cowboy hat and a pair of cowboy boots."

"Mort, if it's all the same to you, I can do without wearing a hat, and cowboy boots are too expensive for a banjo player makin' twenty bucks a night."

"But, you'll be getting tips, too."

"Have to be a whole lot of tips to buy cowboy boots."

Billy finished the beer, retrieved his duffel-bag from the bus station locker, and stowed it in the Golden Spur storeroom. Then, with the banjo on his shoulder, he followed Mort's directions to the The Well Read bookstore. Finding the shelf containing music books, he looked through the limited selection until he came to a dog-eared copy of "Sounds of the Sixties." It was just what he needed to add songs to his repertoire, so he bought it, and went back to the square.

Billy had heard most of the songs and knew a lot of the words in the book. What he was looking for were the chords. With the music at his side on the bench, he began going through several songs, smiling as the pleasure of playing filled his senses with joy.

Soon his still tender fingers started to hurt. At a drugstore, he bought a box of skin-colored Band-Aids and a pair of cheap scissors. Back on the bench, he cut round patches from the tape on the Band-Aids, and stuck them on the tips of his fingers. Playing with one layer still bothered the tenderness, so he proceeded to cut four more patches and stuck them on. That accomplished what he needed until they ripped off. He planned to put another layer on his fingers before starting his first gig that night at the Golden Spur.

By three o'clock that afternoon, Billy had learned the chords and melodies to six songs from the book. Without looking at the music, he began going through them, singing the words and concentrating on the chords. The banjo case lay open at his feet. One after one he practiced the songs until he was confident that he could perform them at the Golden Spur.

He had just finished "Proud Mary" when Myra's husky voice made him look up. Dressed in her waitress attire and in the outdoor light, Billy noticed the slight freckling on her face and how the freckles extended from her neck into her cleavage. Billy thought she was a whole lot prettier in the daylight than under the dimmed lights in the Cowboy Bar. "Did you get the gig, Banjo Billy?"

"Hi, Myra. I sure did. I'm tryin' to learn a few new songs to play."

"You sound real good. Is Mort going to have you passing out his advertisements?"

"Yeah, he is gettin' some printed up today."

"My day off is tomorrow. I'll go over to the Spur and listen to your songs."

He grinned. "Hey, Myra, I would like to see you there."

"When do you start, eight, as usual?"

"Eight until they close."

"See you tomorrow, Banjo Billy."

"I'll look forward to it, Myra." Everything seemed to be falling into place. He had decided to give Myra a try, but now she had made it almost too easy.

Myra turned toward the street corner. Billy watched as she crossed the main street, and went to the middle of the block where she walked through the Cowboy Bar's open front door. *Now there's a damn good lookin' chick*, Billy thought to himself, and began playing another song.

He had "salted" the open banjo case with a five dollar bill. He looked down and noticed another five and several ones. "And, we are just practicin'," he said to the banjo.

Before returning to the Spur, Billy stopped at a cafe for some supper. Eating the meatloaf special, he read through the songs again to make sure he had them all in his mind.

As he passed by the bar on his way to the storeroom, Mort handed him one of the new handbills with "Banjo Billy" printed in the same place where "Horse Thompson" had been. "You can start with these tomorrow afternoon," Mort said. "The stack will be here, next to the cash register."

"Sounds good, Mort. I'll be ready to play in a few minutes."

"Take your time, Billy, you have twenty minutes."

A thirtyish looking woman stepped to Mort's side. Dressed in a short skirt and a white blouse that was cut low to show her ample cleavage, she fingered the ringlets that hung down in front of her left ear. "Billy, this is Belle," Mort said. "She tends bar here five nights a week. Belle this is Banjo Billy."

"Nice to meet you, Belle," Billy said, and smiled. Belle looked like she had been bartending quite a while.

"Hi, Billy. It's a pleasure."

Billy sat on his cot, cut out four more round patches for his fingertips, and stuck them on.

More than half of the bar stools remained empty as Billy got himself settled on his stool in the corner. He left the banjo case open on the floor next to him. Testing once to hear if the banjo had held its tune, he draped his arm over the instrument and looked up at the customers. "Hi, everybody. I'm Banjo Billy and I hope you like my music." He began the first set with "John Henry."

After the first bar of the song he saw the bar patrons look up toward him. Throughout the song he kept their attention and they applauded when he was finished. Billy went right into his next song, "The Times They Are Changing." Again the people at the bar directed their attention at the performer. In the middle of the song, Belle came out from behind the bar with a Budweiser, and put it on a small round table next to Billy's stool. She pointed toward the bar and a man in a western suit and black cowboy hat waved. Billy nodded and continued the song.

As the people applauded again, he reached over for the beer, and took a swallow. *I reckon I must be playing well. All that worry was for nothing. I suppose I ought to talk to the customers some, but I'd rather just play and sing.* Another swallow, and he began another song.

Three songs later, Billy noticed that the fingertip patches were gone. As the applause began he smiled at the patrons, leaned the banjo against the wall and headed for the storeroom to cut out more Band-Aids for his fingers.

Returning to the stool he glanced down at the open banjo case and saw that several bills had been tossed into it. Picking up the instrument, he got settled and began playing again. More people had come into the Spur keeping Belle busy with their drink orders. But in a few minutes she came out to the small round table with another Budweiser.

After the second song of the set, the man in the western suit and black hat came forward, tossed a five dollar bill into the banjo case and told Billy he had enjoyed his music. Billy thanked the man and watched him leave the bar.

Shortly after midnight most of the customers had left. Only one middle aged couple and two authentic looking cowboys remained. Mort, who had been listening to Billy's music all evening, came forward. "You did really good stuff, Billy," he said. "Might as well call it a night. Belle's gonna announce 'last call.' Here's your twenty."

"Thanks, Mort," Billy said. "I'll start on those handbills tomorrow afternoon." *This joint isn't much of a place to play, but I reckon it'll have to do until somethin' better comes my way.*

"Those handbills will fill the place, believe me."

Billy put the banjo away, and took it into the storeroom. Sitting on the cot, he opened the case again, and took out the tips that had been tossed in. Taking stock of his day's earnings, he counted twenty dollars from the case, twenty from Mort, and eight dollars while he was practicing in the square. Forty-eight dollars and six Budweisers seemed like a good day, especially when he didn't have to pay for a place to sleep.

Leaving the storeroom, he saw the last of the customers

leave. He wanted to see if Myra was still working at The Cowboy. "Mort, I think I'll need a key to get in and out," he said.

"By golly, I forgot about that."

Mort went to the cash register where Belle was counting the nightly receipts, and reached around her to get the spare key to the front door. "Don't lose it, and I'm trusting you to not have a duplicate made."

"No problem, Mort. You can trust Banjo Billy."

"I figured that, or I wouldn't have hired you to begin with."

The Cowboy Bar still had a crowd. Billy made his way to the small round table he had occupied the night before. It was vacant so he sat down. Myra spotted him immediately, and came over. "How was your first night at the Spur, Banjo Billy?"

"I have to say it was great, but I am one tired banjo player."

"I'm one tired cocktail waitress. Can I bring you a Bud?"

"I reckon I'm good for one more."

"Be right back."

Billy looked at the worn out patches on his fingertips, and ran his thumb over them. They were sore, but not nearly as sore as they would have been had he not put the patches on.

"What do you have on your fingers?" Myra asked, putting the bottle on the table.

"I put pieces of tape on them. Otherwise they'd get too sore to finger the chords on the strings."

"I thought all you banjo players and guitar players grew calluses on the tips of your fingers."

"I haven't played in a long time. It takes time to get the calluses back."

"I hope it doesn't take long. Anyway, I will be off by the time you finish your beer. I know a cafe that is open until two. How about if I buy us both a cup of coffee."

"You're on, Myra." There was something in Myra's husky voice that intrigued him. He wondered how she would feel in his arms. It seemed like a long time since Saigon.

Most of the tables had emptied. Myra stopped at three that

were still occupied to tell the people she would be leaving. Billy watched as Myra collected her tips. Then she checked out with one of the bartenders. Billy tipped the bottle up for his last swallow as she came over. "I'm off, Banjo Billy," she said. "Let's boogie."

The Totem Cafe, located a block and a half off the main drag, had one empty table and a vacant booth. Myra headed for the booth. When they had seated themselves across from each other Myra sighed, then said, "Wow, is it ever good to sit down."

"I've been sittin' all night, but that stool they have me on isn't the most comfortable place."

A buxom waitress, with an order book in one hand and a pencil in the other, came to the booth. "Hi Myra, what'll it be tonight, your usual?"

"No, Betsey, just a coffee, please."

Betsey turned toward Billy with her pencil poised.

"Coffee is fine," Billy said, and returned his attention to Myra.

"Well, how come you haven't been playing banjo for a while?" Myra asked.

"I just got out of the army about a week ago. I bought that banjo in 'Frisco before I came up here."

"Let me see your fingers."

Billy extended his left hand across the table. Myra took his hand in hers and softly touched his fingertips. "Does that hurt?"

"You could do that all night, Myra."

She bent over and kissed his fingers. "There, they are all better," she said, and laughed. "Where were you, Vietnam?"

"Yeah, I pulled two tours in that godforsaken jungle."

"That must have been tough."

"Tougher on those guys who got wounded or didn't make it back."

Betsey brought the two mugs of coffee.

"I got involved with the anti-war movement while I was getting my master's at U.C.L.A.. It got out of hand when everybody started blaming the servicemen for the war, instead of realizing that the politicians and industrialists were the ones to blame. Did you ever know a soldier over there who was in favor of going out and getting shot at?"

"None that I knew. We just stayed halfway stoned most of the time. Some guys got into the heavy crap. Me? I just burnt weed." He wished they would talk about something other than Vietnam. The only pleasant memories he had about his two tours in those jungles were the occasional times he had spent in Saigon.

"One time I got up on the steps of the administration building during a demonstration and flashed my boobs. Except I didn't just flash, I held up my sweatshirt and let them get a good look at my freckled tits. We all did some crazy things there. I just got caught up in it all."

"I sure wish I had been there," Billy said.

"I know you are curious, Banjo Billy. Yes, the freckles go down to the nipples."

Billy blushed. He had been glancing at Myra's cleavage off and on wondering how far the freckles went, but he did not think he had been so obvious.

"Hell, I don't mind. I've been looking you over too. That's a nice bulge you have in the crotch of your Levi's."

Billy blushed again. He had never met a woman as uninhibited as Myra Paxton. She told him about growing up in Santa Barbara, California. Her father was a prominent lawyer and her mother lived for social events and the country club. "After finishing my bachelor's in geography at U.C. Santa Barbara, my parents wanted me to marry this up and coming lawyer in my father's firm. I dated him a few times at my parents' insistence, but he was boring as hell. I went and started grad school at UCLA."

"I never went to college. I enlisted right after high school. My father wanted me to get deferred and go to college since he had only gone through the eighth grade."

"When did you start playing banjo?" Myra asked.

"I started in junior high. I really got goin' with it in high school. I won the talent competition as a freshman. Then, a group of us started playin' dances. My father thought I should have been playin' football. I hated football."

"What does your father do?"

"He has a farm machinery business in Springfield, Illinois. I never wanted to work there, but he made me work summers. I wanted to play banjo. I guess I disappointed him."

"Someone who can play banjo as well as you do shouldn't be trying to sell farm machinery."

"Why did you come to Jackson?" Billy asked.

"When I finished my master's, I applied for an assistant professorship at Tall Pines State in Arizona. They called me for an interview and paid my airfare. The president is an old ex-farmer from Nebraska. He has one of those Ed.D. degrees, all teaching theory and administration. He offered me an instructor's position and eight grand a year. Before I signed the contract I moseyed over to the geography department and found out he had hired a man for ten grand as an assistant professor. The dude had the same degree as I do and also was a first-year teacher."

"Did you sign the contract?"

"Hell no. Just because I'm a woman I got offered less. It was poverty level any way you look at it. I finished with academia before I even started."

"Did you go back home?"

"Since I was that far, I did some fare switching and flew to Jackson. I've been here since."

"Why Jackson?" Billy asked.

"I heard that cocktail waitressing was good here. I did field work around here for my master's thesis. I needed a job to support myself while I write. And, there are a bunch of writers here."

"So you are really a writer?"

"I'm doing fairly well. I've had five short stories published, and I am working on a novel."

"What is the novel about?" Billy had no idea about writing or even reading novels.

"It started out to be about a fur trapper who falls in love with an Indian girl, but I'm not happy with writing in first person from the point of view of the girl. So, right now, I am rewriting it in third person."

Betsey came by and filled their mugs with fresh coffee.

"Where do you live?"

"I rent an old dilapidated trailer. It's cheap and it keeps me relatively warm during the winter. I don't have a car so I have to live within walking distance of the Cowboy Bar."

"Can you make enough money in the summer to last all winter?"

"I make a hundred a night during the summer. After Labor Day there's a slow period until it snows. Then, the skiers arrive. I worked one winter at the Mangey Moose Saloon, in Teton Village where the ski runs are, but it was too much of a hassle getting rides to and from work. Now, there's a bus."

"Maybe I would be better off as a cocktail waitress than a banjo player."

"You don't have freckled tits."

"But, you said I had a nice bulge in the crotch of my Levi's," he said and laughed.

Betsey came to the booth. "We're closing," she announced. "You done with your coffee?"

"Sure." Myra glanced at Billy. He nodded.

Billy and Myra got up to leave after Myra left enough money on the table to cover the coffee and a generous tip for Betsey.

Outside on the sidewalk, Myra stood on her tip-toes and quickly kissed Billy on the lips. "I'll see you tomorrow at the Spur," she said. Her kiss startled him, and he felt a surge of desire. He tried to take her into his arms, but she backed off, pushing her hands against his chest.

"I would sure like to see your trailer tonight, Myra," Billy said, and grinned.

"Not tonight, Banjo Billy. I'm too tired. Besides, the freckles won't disappear overnight."

CHAPTER TWO

Billy let himself in the Spur. Extracting the key, he closed the door, and secured the dead-bolt. Before going to the storeroom, he stopped in the men's room to drain his bladder. Looking in the barnwood framed mirror over the wash basin, he reached up to his face and felt the reddish growth of stubble. In spite of the itching feeling, he decided to grow a beard and let his thick, auburn hair grow out. He inspected his slightly bloodshot hazel eyes, rubbed them and ran a thumb and index finger down his thin, angular nose. Yawning in front of the mirror, he began unbuttoning his shirt.

Stretched out on the cot in the storeroom, he felt good. As tired as he felt, Billy could not fall asleep because his thoughts jumped around from the jungles of 'Nam to Myra Paxton. He remembered the last woman he had slept with. She was a little Vietnamese whore in Saigon. She had known her business well, and he had gone to her two nights in a row while he awaited transportation back to the States.

Just as he was wondering what Myra's breasts had looked like when she had flashed them at the demonstration, he heard a muffled knock on the door of the Spur. Wondering who would be there at that time, he turned on the dingy, fly-specked light, pulled on his Levi's, and trotted over to look out the small window in the door. It was Myra. Just as she knocked again, he twisted the handle on the dead-bolt and opened the door. She slid inside. "Billy, I couldn't sleep. I kept thinking about you and wanting to see you."

"I can't sleep either."

Closing the door and locking it Billy took her by the arm and led her into the storeroom. She wore a loose-fitting, faded, chambray shirt over a pair of equally faded Levi's. "Goddam, I'm glad you're here," he said, taking her in his arms and kissing her.

She put her arms around his neck and pulled him closer. "Wow, that's quite a bulge you have down there." Releasing Billy,

Myra kicked off her sandals, unbuttoned her Levi's and let them drop to the floor. Stepping out of them as she unbuttoned the shirt, she stood naked, smiling as Billy took off his Levi's while he looked at her firm, freckled breasts with their hard, pink nipples. She sighed as he cupped them in his hands and stared into her sultry, emerald green eyes. He felt himself fully aroused.

Myra reached down and took his hard, throbbing member in her hands as he kissed her again. In the dim light they moved toward the cot and were quickly joined in a passion they both wanted to last forever.

Spent from their love-making, Myra, still lying on the cot, watched as Billy pushed himself up to a sitting position and reached for his banjo. She listened as he played and sang a sweet and sexy love song he composed as he played. The song finished, he put the banjo back in its case, and squeezed himself next to Myra. "Do you think we can sleep on this little cot?" Billy asked.

"Who wants to sleep?" she answered, grabbing his left hand and putting it on her right breast.

She began fondling him and kissing him. Billy responded passionately and they were soon joined again. Myra groaned in ecstasy as Billy continued until they exploded together in an orgasmic fury.

"You are quite a woman. I'm ready to flake out."

"Let's go to the trailer," Myra suggested. "My bed is a double and we might sleep now."

"Sounds good to me. If I don't get some sleep, yesterday might be my first and last night playing banjo at the Spur." He yawned at the thought of sleep.

They put on their clothes, and walked arm in arm through the empty streets of Jackson, Wyoming. Billy felt lucky to be next to Myra, and remembered the conversation between him and Randy, the bartender at Leo's in San Francisco. Randy had been impressed with the college girls in Jackson. Myra was not a college girl, but she was more than Billy had reckoned on.

Once inside the trailer, they went quickly to bed, and fell asleep in each other's arms.

Groggily sitting on the side of the bed, Myra looked at her alarm clock. She turned and shook Billy by the shoulder. He came awake with a lurch and a yell.

"It's okay, Billy, you're here with me, Myra." She reached over to the bedside table, and switched on the lamp.

Billy sat up holding his head in both hands." Damn, I was dreaming," he said, blinking his eyes "I keep having the same dream. I'm out in the middle of a clearing in the stinkin' jungle with a hundred Viet Cong comin' at me laughin' their asses off, pointing their rifles at me. Just as I pull the trigger on my M-16, they all disappear."

"It is one-thirty in the afternoon, Billy. You have to begin handing out Mort's advertising pretty soon."

"I forgot about that bullshit."

"Let's take a shower, and I'll walk you over to the Spur."

"What about your writing?"

"I think it'll wait for me."

The shower stall was barely large enough for the two of them to fit into, and when Billy began soaping Myra's breasts she began washing his manhood. The feel of the firm, slippery breasts and her hands gentle around his member, brought him up to a hard, throbbing arousal. Myra turned off the water as they left the shower for the bed. Their wet bodies slid against one another as they joined again in passionate lovemaking.

The afternoon sun warmed them as they left the trailer. The white clouds seemed to be motionless against the azure sky as if moored in their positions.

Entering the Golden Spur, they found Mort behind the bar serving customers. "Give me a stack of those handbills, and I'll be goin' to the square," Billy said, trying to sound eager to work.

Mort reached over next to the cash register and separated a stack of the bright yellow paper. Noticing Myra with Billy, he smiled with understanding.

"I didn't know if you had forgotten or not," he told Billy. "You were good last night. See how many people you can send over here."

"I'll see what I can do, Mort. See you around eight."

Before setting up in the square, Billy and Myra had a sandwich in the Totem Cafe where they had had coffee in the wee hours of the morning. The foot traffic in the center of Jackson crowded the sidewalks so that people passing each other had to turn sideways to keep from jostling each other. After finishing their coffee Billy and Myra weaved their way to the square and found an empty bench. Billy put the yellow handbills in a stack next to him, and took the banjo out of the case. "You can pass these things out while I'm playin'," Billy said.

"You're going to have to do that. I'm going back to the trailer and write."

"Are you goin' to the Spur later?"

"I'll be there," Myra answered, then leaned over and kissed him.

Billy watched her as she made her way onto the crowded sidewalk wishing he could go with her to the trailer. After tuning the banjo he began picking out a song. Watching the crowd on the sidewalk he saw a few people look his way but they continued without stopping to listen further to his concert. Several songs later a group of eight young people stood in a semi-circle in front of him as he sang "Proud Mary." At the end of their applause he took some handbills from the top of the pile.

"Here," he said. "I'll buy all of you a margarita at the Golden Spur. I start there at eight."

He was greeted with eight "Gee, thanks," and as they began leaving, "See you there, Banjo Billy." To accompany the five dollar bill he had put in the open case they had left a dollar.

More people stopped to listen, a few leaving some money. He gave everyone who stopped one of the handbills. Some folded them and put them in a pocket. A few, going back to the sidewalk, dropped them into the waste barrel at the corner of the square. Half the stack remained when Billy put the money from the case into his pocket, and headed for a small bar where he had seen chili-dogs advertised in the window.

Washing down a chili-dog with a bottle of Budweiser, Billy pondered the value of playing all afternoon in the square. He had made twelve dollars and some change. He concluded that if he had lured at least six people to the Spur and they stayed for at least three rounds, it might be worth it. Thinking further, he decided that he might as well continue the playing in the square, because there wasn't much else to do in the afternoon with Myra occupied at her typewriter.

Wandering around the town before going to the Spur, Billy found a store featuring used clothing. He found two shirts, one denim, the other a cotton plaid. He also bought a pair of Levi's with the left rear pocket partially torn.

At fifteen minutes until eight, Mort met him at the door of the Spur.

"How did you do at the square this afternoon?"

Billy handed him the leftover handbills.

"All right, I guess," Billy said. "It seems like an awful lot of playing for just twelve dollars. Maybe some of the people I gave handbills to will show up for their margaritas."

"It may take a few days until people get used to you there."

Billy put the denim shirt and Levi's into his duffel bag in the storeroom and changed into the cotton plaid. Then, cutting eight patches from the Band-Aids, he stuck them on the tips of his fingers.

The eight young people, to whom he had given handbills in the square, filed into the Spur after Billy had played his first set of songs. Filling all the remaining barstools, they sat down and gave the handbills to Belle. Billy took a short break. He waved at the young people as he finished a beer one of the customers had sent to him. At least someone had brought in some handbills. By the time Belle had served the eight free margaritas,

Billy began playing again.

Scowling, Mort stood at the end of the bar nearest where Billy played. He had watched Belle serve the eight free drinks. Another couple came in with a handbill, and ordered two margaritas. Mort showed them to a small table.

Halfway through his third set, Billy noticed that all the small tables had occupants and there were people standing while drinking their free margaritas. Several of the patrons had dropped bills into his open banjo case. He searched the crowd for Myra as he played.

The same one of the eight who had given him a dollar in the square came up, put another dollar in the case, and requested "Proud Mary." Before beginning the song, Billy looked over at the group and nodded. He noticed that all eight sat on the barstools with empty margarita glasses in front of them on the bar. *Mort is probably pissed off, but what the hell, he's too damn greedy.*

His rendition of "Proud Mary" brought a long round of applause from the patrons, and five of them dropped money into the banjo case. To keep up the pace he played "Wabash Cannonball" at a faster tempo than usual.

After the fourth set Billy took a break and headed for the storeroom to renew the patches on his fingertips. He wished Myra would show up, and the people would leave so he could collect the twenty dollars from Mort.

Some of the customers had left when he took his place on the stool again. The group of eight remained with their empty glasses. Billy kept his eyes on the door hoping to see Myra arrive. He saw Mort go behind the bar and speak to the eight free-loaders. They stood up from their barstools, waved at Billy, and left. Those customers still standing sat on the empty stools as Belle stood behind the bar, ready to serve them.

He felt relieved when he saw Myra come in the door during the last song of his sixth set. There were only seven people still drinking at the bar. Mort waved at Myra as she seated herself. Billy left off the last chorus to end the song, lifted the banjo strap over his head, and leaned the instrument against the wall. He sat down next to Myra. "Hi, Billy," Myra said. "I'm sorry to be so late getting here, but I got on a roll, and couldn't tear myself away from the story."

"I was beginning to wonder if you had forgotten."

"I would never forget Banjo Billy," she said, and leaned over to kiss him on the cheek. "When the words start flowing, I can't seem to stop for anything. Hey, I see you have a new shirt."

"Yeah, I bought two and another pair of Levi's."

"You must have done well in the square after I left."

"Twelve bucks," he said, shaking his head slightly. "I don't call that doing well."

"That's probably why Horse Thompson quit."

"I'll give it a few more tries," Billy said. "Do you know of a better spot?"

"That's the only spot in town," Myra answered. "How much longer do you have to play tonight?"

"I don't know. As soon as these people leave."

"Take a long break, and they'll think you're done for the night."

"I don't want to piss off Mort. Do you want a drink?"

"I guess a gin martini would taste good."

"Belle," Billy called toward the bartender. "Give Myra a gin martini on me, please."

"I'll go back and play another song or two."

By the time he had sung two more songs, there was a five dollar bill on top of the singles, and, besides Myra, only two customers were left on the barstools. Mort ambled over. "Might as well call it a night, Billy," Mort said. "Here's your twenty and here's two bucks from the other deal."

"Thanks, Mort."

"Billy, you gotta be more careful with those handbills. Those eight goddam free-loaders sat on their asses half the night for free margaritas and free music. All those people standing up might have bought more drinks. They didn't even tip Belle, the cheap-ass bastards."

"Out there in the square I have no clue if those people I give handbills to will even show up, much less if they will just come over here and free-load."

"Try to be more careful, Billy."

Billy took the money from the case, counted twenty-eight dollars, and put it in his Levi's pocket. Snapping the case closed around the banjo he returned to sit next to Myra.

"Belle, give Billy a Budweiser," Mort said, and ran a comb through his slicked-back hair.

Before leaving, Billy paid for Myra's drink, and left the change on the bar for Belle. Once outside they decided to forego going anywhere else and walked arm in arm to Myra's trailer. Before following Myra into the bedroom at the rear of the trailer, Billy put the banjo on the cushioned seat of the dining booth. Less than a minute passed before they were naked on the bed.

The next morning, Billy awakened to the smell of freshly brewed coffee. The muffled tap-tap-tap sound of Myra's Smith-Corona portable typewriter came from the other bedroom that she had made into an office. Billy sat on the edge of the bed, rubbing the sleep from his eyes. Then, hoisting his Levi's up over his trim buttocks and buttoning up the front, he ambled into the front room. Filling the chipped, light-green ceramic mug from the electric coffee-pot, he sat down on the seat across from the banjo.

Halfway through the coffee, he stood and reached over to get the banjo out of its case. Sitting back, he strummed on the strings and began to tune them. Just as he began playing a song, Myra opened the door to her office, and came down the hall into the front room with her coffee mug. Seeing her clothed in nothing but panties, Billy grinned.

"Good morning, Banjo Player," she said, re-filling her coffee mug. "In case you are wondering, I like to be comfortable when I'm writing."

"You sure look comfortable."

"I must get back to my story. Sorry, there's nothing for breakfast. I rarely eat anything in the morning. Writers are kind of weird."

"I'll mosey out and get somethin' later."

"Why don't you go out now, Billy. I love your banjo-playing, but it's distracting when I'm trying to write."

"Do you want me to bring you anythin'?"

"No, thanks. It will be noon before I'm ready for nourishment. Come back then, and we can grab lunch somewhere."

"Good luck with your writin', Myra."

"Thanks," she replied, and returned to her typewriter.

Dressed and ready to go, Billy picked up the banjo, and quietly slipped out the door. Having had nothing to eat since the chili-dog the evening before, he was hungry and ordered a full breakfast at the Totem Cafe. As he ate the eggs and sausage patties he thought about the situation in which he found himself. He enjoyed Myra's passion, but she had an aloofness that made him wonder about her. Having to leave the trailer to accommodate her writing seemed reasonable, but he felt like she wanted him only for sex.

Enjoying the freshness of the eggs brought back contrasting memories of the "catch as catch can" meals in the Vietnam jungles. Now he was back in the States, but couldn't explain the constant restlessness he felt. Here in Jackson, Wyoming he could go and come much as he pleased except for his obligation to the gig at the Spur and when he had to leave Myra with her writing. No more regimentation. No more plodding through the jungles with the constant fear of being killed by the enemy who was expert at blending into the foliage like a chameleon.

The afternoon playing in the square bored him. Not only did he find it a frustrating waste of time, the open banjo case did not seem to attract much currency. If more people would listen to his music, he would enjoy performing.

The next morning, shortly after ten o'clock Billy sat at the bar in the Golden Spur, watching Mort restock the beer cooler.

"Mort, I would like to talk to you about playin' in the square and handin' out those flyers," Billy said.

"What's there to talk about?"

"I am not makin' any money out there," Billy replied.

"I can't help that."

"I was thinkin' that if you could just pay me to play and hand out the flyers, instead of me countin' on tips and the deal based on how many drinks after the free one..."

"I've never done that with anyone."

"Then, I think I would like to stop playing in the park and doing that handbill business."

"For chrisakes, Billy. I got all those handbills printed up, and now you want to quit handin' 'em out. That's a helluva note."

"OK, Mort. I'll continue until I get rid of all the handbills you had printed."

"Just make sure you don't give any out to the likes of those cheap-assed pukes who were here night before last."

"I'll do my best, Mort."

After changing his shirt in the storeroom, Billy stopped at the bar to pick up the handbills for his afternoon stint in the square. Mort put them on the bar. "I think you're just wantin' to spend your afternoons with Myra, aren't you, Billy?"

"She is busy writin'. Like I said, I am not makin' beans out there and gettin' tired out doin' it."

"It takes a while to get known around here. I'll bet it will pick up in a few days."

"We'll see," Billy said, and left to meet Myra for lunch.

They went to the Totem Cafe where Billy told Myra about his conversation with Mort.

"He is such a cheapskate he can't keep anyone there. Belle told me once that he puts about half the tequila in his mix that a decent margarita calls for."

He grimaced and sighed. "I just hope I can hand out most of those handbills this afternoon."

"Just dump the damn things. Then you won't have to worry

about playing in the square."

"I'll give it one more afternoon," Billy said. "But I would rather spend the afternoon with you."

"I have to get back to my story, Billy. Otherwise, there is nothing I would rather do than crawl into bed with you."

Finished with lunch, Myra gave him a quick kiss and left for the trailer. Billy watched her go, appreciating the spring in her step as she strode through the river of tourists that filled the sidewalks. With a sinking feeling, he thought about the town square and hours of strumming for people who only wanted free drinks and free entertainment. At least I can be learnin' some new songs out in the square, he thought to himself and made his way to the book store for more sheet music.

Sitting on the same bench in the square, he leafed through the collection of songs and chose "Raindrops Keep Fallin' on My Head." He played around with the chords, letting his fingers pattern the transitions, feeling the moves. A shadow fell across the pavement in front of him and he looked up. A tall man stood beside him, appraisal glittering in his eyes. He had a careful smile that seemed calculated to be friendly but not fawning. A maroon tee-shirt was tucked neatly into his dark jeans. The silver concho on his belt was embossed with the same logo that adorned the shirt: The Mangey Moose Saloon.

He stretched out a hand, "Hi, I'm Joe Spencer."

Billy slid the pick into his left hand and reached out. "Banjo Billy. Would you like to try a free margarita at the Golden Spur?"

Joe's smile widened, "Mort would dock your pay if I got a free drink. I manage the Mangey Moose over in Teton Village."

"I've heard of that place," Billy said. In his mind's eye, Billy could see Myra's face as she told him about it. "How's business?"

"Pretty good, but I'm thinking your music could make it even better."

At the praise, Billy tensed with anticipation.

Joe idly picked up one of the handbills and glanced at it. "I was over at the Golden Spur last night and heard you play and sing. I liked it."

"Thanks. I try my best."

He set the bill down. "I've got a guitar man out there now, but his gig is over Friday. Folks like a new face. I'd like to replace him with you."

Billy hesitated. Teton Village was miles out. "I'd have to figure out some way to get there."

"There's a bus that goes to The Village about every hour."

"How late is the last trip back to town?"

The smile dropped and Joe grew thoughtful. "That I don't know, but we can find out." He seemed to be measuring his next words. "I can always give you a ride back after closing. I manage out there. I don't live there."

"I'd be obliged." Mort's low scale and the back room cot that was part of his wage came to mind. "What do you pay?"

"Fifty a night. You play seven to close. Generally that's one o'clock in the morning. Tips are pretty good too."

Relief flooded him. "Sounds like you have got yourself a banjo player." Billy nodded for emphasis and strummed an A chord just for the pleasure of it.

"Good," Spencer said. "You can start Saturday night."

"You can count on it."

"Get there a bit early and get the feel of the place. I'll introduce you around."

"Sounds good," Billy said.

"Saturday, then." Joe reached out to shake on it, then turned to walk away.

Billy watched his retreating form and launched into a spirited rendition of "Raindrops." It felt more like sunshine was fallin' on his head. Things were definitely looking up. Too antsy to sit still any longer, Billy put his banjo back in its case, found a rock to put on top of the handbills, and hurried to the trailer to tell Myra. Hey, as long as he was on a roll, he might ask if her double bed had been empty too long and did she need a hand with the dishes. How about another paycheck to help out with the rent? Moving in with Myra would be the pretzels with his beer.

Myra answered Billy's knock on the trailer door. "I have a gig at the Mangey Moose," he said. "Fifty bucks a night!"

"Wow, that's great, Billy. When do you start?"

"Saturday night."

"Have you told Mort?"

"Not yet. I came straight over to tell you first. When I tell Mort, he will probably kick my butt out of his storeroom."

"You're not sleeping there anyway. Bring your stuff over here."

"Thanks, Myra," Billy said. "I can help with your rent."

"Don't worry about the rent. I have that covered just fine. All I ask is that you don't pick on that banjo when I'm trying to write."

"I won't, Myra. I'll find some place, maybe down by the river. I'll come back with my stuff once I've dealt with Mort."

"Good luck. I'll be here."

Billy put his banjo on the dining booth seat, and left for the town square to pick up the stack of handbills. The stack was gone when he arrived. Oh well, they aren't any good with me leavin'.

With a smile and a new light to his eyes, Billy strode purposefully to the Golden Spur. When he opened the door, Mort looked up from the sink where he was washing glasses. A look of surprise flashed across the bar owner's face when he saw Billy entering in the middle of the afternoon. "Did you run out of handbills?"

This dude is a real weasel, Billy thought to himself.

Billy frowned until the furrows in his brow were like rows in a freshly plowed field. "No, I put them on the bench while I went to see Myra, and they were gone when I got back."

"What the hell are you doing seeing Myra when you're supposed to be playing in the square, handing out the flyers?"

"I had to tell her about gettin' another gig."

"What do you mean, another gig? You've got a gig here."

Billy took Mort's key out of his pocket, and handed it to him.

"Here's your key. I guess I'm quittin' this gig, Mort. I start my new one Saturday night."

"What's wrong with playin' at the Spur?"

"Not enough money and that playin' in the square. I already told you about that."

"Where's your new gig?"

"Mangey Moose"

"I saw that bastard Spencer in here last night. So that's what he was here for; stealing my banjo player."

"You'll find someone else, Mort. I saw a guy carryin' a guitar. He looked like he just got to town. I guess I'll get my stuff out of the storeroom."

"What am I going to do with the rest of the flyers?"

"There's not many left, Mort." Billy wanted to get away from the angry bar owner. There was nothing Mort could say to change his mind about leaving. He went into the storeroom to get his things.

"Shit!" Mort exclaimed, and slammed his fist on the bar.

Billy picked up his duffel bag. Passing back through the bar, he glanced at Mort glaring at him. "If I see that dude with the guitar, I'll send him over."

Mort said nothing.

On his way back to Myra's he passed a laundromat. Once inside the trailer, he put his duffel bag on the floor. "Myra, do you have any laundry?" He asked. "I'm goin' to the laundromat."

"Hang on a minute while I finish this one sentence."

Stopping her typing, Myra got a laundry bag out of her closet, and handed it to Billy. "There's soap under the kitchen sink, Laundry Man. You are really going to come in handy here."

After finishing the laundry, Billy returned to the trailer to find Myra sitting on the bed, naked and smiling. "I've been writing a really sexy scene between my two main characters, and I am all hot and bothered," Myra said.

"Then, I reckon it's about time to get sweaty," Billy said, and began unbuttoning his shirt.

The gig at the Mangey Moose Saloon proved to be a good move for Billy. His finger tips had callused enough so that they were no longer tender, and he had stopped having to cut out patches from the Band-aids. His wiry, red beard and lengthening hair made him look more like a banjo player than the way he looked walking through San Francisco. But, in his thoughts he continued dwelling on the war and all the death and destruction he had seen.

He found a music store and bought two new sets of strings, one to replace those that had been on the banjo when he bought it, and an extra set in case any snapped while he played at the Mangey Moose.

The customers were younger and seemed to enjoy his playing more than those who frequented the Spur. Weekends he made at least fifty dollars in tips each night. Weeknights he never found less than forty dollars in his opened banjo case. Some nights Myra would arrive at the trailer before Billy. Occasionally, during the week, the Mangey Moose would close earlier than the Cowboy. On those occasions, Billy went to wait for Myra at the Cowboy Bar.

Every morning Billy practiced his banjo at a grassy spot near the Snake River, learning new songs and perfecting those he knew. Back at the trailer Myra continued writing her novel. Meeting for lunch at noon became something they both looked forward to.

While enjoying lunch together the Monday before Labor Day weekend, Myra talked about a place near the Tetons that she wanted to show Billy. "It is one of the most beautiful spots I have ever been to. I'll ask Betsey if we can borrow her old pickup. I want to take you out there and show you the place."

"When does Betsey come in to work?" Billy asked.

"About an hour before I'm on at the Cowboy Bar. I'll stop in before I go to work."

Betsey's pickup turned out to be a 1964 Chevy that had been refurbished after being worn out by a logging company.

The faded yellow paint had scratches everywhere and the fenders showed proof that it had seen hard use. However, the motor had been re-built six months before by Betsey's then boyfriend.

Leaving early in the morning with Myra driving, they traveled north, parallel to the Grand Tetons. The snow-caps and glacier masses on the rugged, steep slopes made the mountains a wonderland of viewing from the highway. After thirty miles Myra turned onto a secondary road, and followed it for three more miles before braking the Chevy. She turned left onto a narrow two-track driveway through the forest of spruce and fir.

Just before coming to a narrow gurgling creek, a locked gate barred further travel. Myra turned off the ignition and put a heavy woolen blanket under her arm. "Well, we're here," she said. "Almost, anyway. From here we walk a hundred yards to a cabin."

They stepped through a pole fence, got back on the driveway, and crossed the narrow wooden bridge that spanned the creek. Holding hands as they trudged along the rutted road, they spotted the log cabin nestled against a grove of white-barked aspen, green leaves fluttering in the gentle breeze. Behind the cabin and in front of the Snake River, a meadow with an occasional clump of bushes or young spruce and fir saplings gave the place a magnificent view of the Tetons. The cabin looked old with its faded, red-painted logs and gray chinking. The wood-framed windows had not been washed for a long time.

"There is quite a story to this place," Myra said. "It once belonged to the Rockefellers. When they donated the land that is now Teton National Park to the government, they gave their lawyer and trusted friend, who handled all the legal stuff, a lifetime trust to this cabin and the surrounding land. I don't know how many acres are involved here, but enough for privacy."

"Does this lawyer still own it?" Billy asked.

"His wife still has the lifetime trust. As soon as she dies, the place reverts to the Teton National Park. A ranger friend of mine told me the story, and he says the Park Service will demolish the cabin and outbuildings, and let it all go back to nature."

"It sure is a beautiful place," Billy remarked.

"It is also historic. Many heads of state and dignitaries from all over the world have stayed here and discussed world problems. It's mind-blowing to me that we are standing where decisions that affected the whole world were made."

"Maybe it was here that they decided we should go into Vietnam," Billy suggested.

"That was too recent. My ranger friend showed me a collection of old-fashioned, wooden clothes pins in the dining room. They used them like napkin rings. Whoever visited had a clothes pin with his or her name written on it. I remember one with Winston Churchill's name on it."

"This is an important place, for sure. Why are they going to tear it all down when such significant things happened here?"

"That's the government, I guess. My ranger friend would like to see this place preserved for its history, but he doesn't have much say about such policy matters."

"How did you meet the guy?" Billy asked.

"My master's thesis was on the effects of mountain roads on soil creep. I did some of my field work around here. He helped me locate observation sites. We also went canoeing. He was nice. When I came back to Jackson, I hoped he would still be here, but he got transferred to Oregon."

"That's beyond me," Billy said, raising his eyebrows. "I thought geography was capitals of states and countries,"

"Geography is concerned with everything on the face of the earth. It is too bad they don't teach it in the schools like they used to."

"That's pretty heavy stuff," Billy said.

Ambling toward the river through the meadow, they spotted some elk grazing in a small ravine. Seeing the humans, the elk trotted off to take cover in a grove of aspen. Arriving at another grove next to the river, Myra led Billy through the trees into a clearing. Unfolding the blanket, she spread it on the grass. "Ever since I first saw this place, I have wanted to make love here," she said.

Billy reached for the buttons on her shirt. "I'll make love with you anywhere, Myra."

After Labor Day weekend the foot-traffic on the sidewalks in Jackson diminished substantially. The once crowded bar had mostly empty bar stools. The tips in the banjo case became less and less every night. Two weeks after Labor Day, Joe Spencer told Billy that business at the Mangey Moose would not warrant nightly entertainment.

"This happens every year, Billy. As soon as we get enough snow to open the ski-runs, business will get back to normal. Are you figuring on spending the winter here?"

"I don't know, Joe. It all depends on what work I can find." But in his mind Billy wanted to wander south to Arizona. Mild winters and new places to experience seemed better than waiting in Jackson for the skiers to arrive.

"I'll keep you on until after next weekend. Then, if you're still around, I'll call you back after the ski season starts."

That night, when the Mangey Moose closed earlier than usual, Billy met Myra at the Cowboy Bar. She had but one table left to serve, so she checked out and they went to the Totem Cafe for a cup of coffee. Billy told Myra about the Mangey Moose manager laying him off after the next weekend.

"That happens after Labor Day around here," Myra said. "Business is down at the Cowboy too, but I'm still doing all right."

Sipping his coffee, he didn't express his thoughts about heading to Arizona for the winter. *I'll miss making love with Myra, but I'm beginning to feel tied down and anxious. Dammit, I wish I could figure out why I'm this way. I just need to get on the road to see new places and play banjo for other people.* Besides Arizona, he thought about trying for a gig in Las Vegas, but he knew, from talking with a soldier in his company in 'Nam, that southern Arizona had warmer winters than most places.

The following morning he left for his place next to the river right after having coffee in the trailer with Myra. Even though she was deep in thought about her novel, Billy could tell that she sensed his restlessness. Sitting on his favorite log as he aimlessly picked out a slow moving tune, Billy wondered about leaving. In many ways he loved Myra, but he felt that she was too much of an intellectual for him with all her thoughts about world happenings and her interest in geography. "I thought I knew what geography was until I met Myra," he mumbled to himself. "Here I am just a banjo player. I can't be hookin' up with someone so damned smart as she is. Besides, she seems more interested in sex and her novel than anything else."

Instead of meeting Myra for lunch he walked all the way to Teton Village, thinking about what he should do. On one hand he had never met a more passionate woman than Myra Paxton. There was also the unexplainable restlessness that constantly gnawed at him.

Joe Spencer stood behind the bar at the Mangey Moose.

"You're here early, Billy," Spencer said.

"Yeah, I walked out here tryin' to figure out what to do."

Spencer uncapped a bottle of Budweiser, and put it on the bar in front of Billy.

"Have one on me. I had to lay off Julie, so I'm the afternoon bartender."

"Thanks, Joe. Too bad business takes such a dive after Labor Day."

"That's for sure, but we've learned to live with it."

"I'm thinkin' about headin' south to Arizona, and maybe hit Las Vegas on the way."

"You could do worse. I spent a winter in Tucson once. Not a bad city, and there are plenty of joints there where you can find a gig."

"What were you doin' in Tucson?"

"I bartended at a place on North Fourth Avenue where there's lots of artists and craft-people. They hold street fairs and draw big crowds. I did pretty well during the winter, but that's their tourist season. The tourists haul ass before it even begins to get hot."

"What about Vegas?"

"That's one fast town. I tried it for a month. The money was all right; the slot-machines got me. I drove out of town with a tank of gas and fifty bucks."

"Do you think I could find a gig in Vegas?"

"Vegas is loaded with entertainment, but they are all stars. There's not too many small joints where a banjo player like you could find a gig."

"I guess Tucson sounds like the place for me to spend the winter," Billy said.

"Tucson would be better for you than Vegas."

"Yeah, you're probably right. I'd sure as hell hate to land in Vegas and not find a gig."

Spencer put another beer in front of Billy.

"Here's another one. The least I can do. You were damn good for business, Billy. I wish you could stick around for the snow, but you never know when that will start."

"I'm feeling too damn restless to stay here."

"Were you in Vietnam?"

"Two tours."

"A lot of you guys seem restless when you get back. I did a stint in Germany. I guess I was lucky."

"I wish I had never seen 'Nam," Billy said. "I keep havin' crazy dreams that wake me up in the middle of the night."

After playing that night at the Mangey Moose, he caught a ride back to Jackson with Joe Spencer, who left him off at the Cowboy Bar. Myra brought him a beer.

"How did it go tonight?" she asked.

"Not much business so Joe closed down early. How has it been here?"

"Not bad, I'll be done in an hour or so."

By the time Myra checked out with the bartender, Billy had consumed four beers. Putting her gin martini on the small table, she sat next to him.

"I had a talk with Joe Spencer today," Billy said. "He thinks Tucson, Arizona is a good place to spend the winter."

"You're thinking about leaving, aren't you?"

"I guess I am gettin' restless," Billy answered. "Who knows how long I would have to wait around until the ski season gets here. I sure don't want to go back to Springfield and my father. We would get into an argument within ten minutes after I walked in the door."

"I can understand that. I'm glad I have the job I do, even though the tips go down for a while. I make enough to get by on while I write."

"I have been thinkin' about that, too," Billy said. "When it gets cold up here, where the hell would I go to practice in the mornin's and afternoons?"

"Billy, listen to me carefully," she said. "I think I know what you're leading up to. I love you a bunch. There isn't a man on earth I would rather make love with than Banjo Billy. But, I also love my writing. It has become an addiction. When it gets cold, I would hate to see you out there trying to practice with numb fingers. I would tell you to stay in the trailer where it's warm. Then, I wouldn't get any writing done. I would probably begin to resent you, and I don't ever want to feel that way about you. I've also heard that Tucson is a good place to winter."

Billy was impressed with her attitude toward him leaving. In some ways he wanted to stay, but his restlessness was a stronger pull toward his decision. "Goddammit, Myra, you are one helluva wonderful woman. I'll be back next spring."

"I'll be here for you. And, I expect I'll really be hot and bothered," she said, and smiled.

Reaching over, Billy squeezed Myra's hand. "I have two more nights at the Moose. I reckon to get on the road Monday mornin'."

"Then, we had better get home and get our clothes off, Banjo Man."

Monday morning Myra walked to the bus station with Billy. The bus for Laramie and Cheyenne, due to leave in ten minutes, stood with its door open as the passengers stepped aboard after surrendering their tickets to the driver.

"I guess this is it, Myra," Billy said, putting his duffel bag and banjo case on the sidewalk. "I love you, woman. Good luck with your writin'."

"I love you too, Banjo Man. I miss you already."

Billy took her in his arms and kissed her. "I'll think about those freckles in Arizona." Then, without another word, he reached down for his things and boarded the bus.

Watching through the window Billy saw Myra walking slowly away from the bus depot. He wished she would look back to wave, but she kept her back to him. He noticed her hand go up to her eyes as if she might be brushing tears away. The driver took his seat, started the motor, and eased the bus out to the street. Billy's thoughts shifted to wondering what Tucson would be like. It was good to be going somewhere new.

CHAPTER THREE

Stepping off the air-conditioned bus, Tucson's late afternoon one hundred degree temperature smacked Billy like a wall of fire. Just from unloading his duffel bag, beads of sweat popped up on his forehead. The trip, though uneventful, had exhausted him. Receiving directions from the man at the ticket office to an inexpensive place to stay, Billy carried his belongings a block to the Congress Hotel. By the entrance to the hotel, he stopped on the sidewalk, put down the duffel bag and banjo, and, with his shirt-sleeve, wiped the sweat from his stinging eyes. Passing through the open door to the front desk, he watched the old clerk push himself out of a scarred swivel-chair. "I'd like a room."

After adjusting his spectacles with his index finger the clerk looked at him with squinting, suspicious eyes. "You'll have to pay in advance. Twenty dollars a night."

Billy counted out the money, signed the mimeographed registration sheet, and waited for the clerk to bring the room key. "Room two-fourteen. Turn right at the top of the stairs."

With the key in his pocket, Billy carried his gear upstairs, unlocked the door, and entered the dusky smelling room. Locking the door behind him, he plunked his duffel bag on the frayed carpet and put the banjo case on top of the chipped, green painted chest of drawers. Without undressing, he stretched out on the sagging double bed, and closed his eyes.

Awakened by his recurring nightmare, he looked through the dirty window to find that dusk had settled. Leaving the duffel bag in his room, he grabbed the banjo case and left for the stairs, stopping at the desk to ask directions to North Fourth Avenue. The evening air was somewhat cooler as he stepped out of the hotel and turned right, heading for the underpass over which ran the Southern Pacific Railroad tracks. Graffiti artists had filled the walls of the underpass, and a car horn startled him when he reached the halfway point in the tunnel.

Above ground again, he passed a dilapidated looking bar called the Shack, that had two cars parked outside. Further along the street he came to a darkened Salvation Army store beside a co-op grocery just before the various shops began. He stopped in front of a small bar and grill, the Hungry Eye, to read the "special" scrawled on a small chalk board. Entering the open doorway Billy sat at the counter and leaned the banjo case against the wall. From a dark-haired girl, wearing a long blue skirt and a tie-dyed tee-shirt that showed the outlines of her nipples, he ordered the roast beef special and a Budweiser. Returning with the beer, the girl looked closely at Billy. "Are you new in town?" she asked.

"Yeah," Billy answered. "Just got in this afternoon."

"Do you play banjo?" she asked pointing to the case.

"Yeah. Do you know where I might find a gig?"

"Gosh, I really don't. Most of the times there are guys playing something out on the sidewalks. I'm Ginny, by the way."

"Hi, I go by Banjo Billy."

"Nice meeting you. Are you just passing through?"

"No, I'm figurin' to spend the winter here. It gets too cold in Wyoming."

"You from Wyoming?"

"I spent part of the summer in Jackson."

"I've never been there, but I hear it's pretty."

The bell in the serving window rang. Ginny left the conversation to bring Billy's supper. A couple came in and sat at one of the tables. Ginny brought them two tattered menus and returned to her station behind the counter.

Billy devoured the roast beef, the small salad, and the mashed potatoes. Ginny brought another beer.

"Have you lived in Tucson long?" Billy asked after taking a pull at the beer.

"No, I'm from southern California. I've been here two years going to the 'U', but I'm taking a semester off to work."

"What are you studyin'?"

"I plan to major in economics."

Billy wondered if Ginny wore tie-dyed tee-shirts to classes. Finished with the beer he paid the bill, leaving a dollar tip on the counter.

"Stop by again," Ginny said, smiling. "We always have good daily specials."

"That's good to know," he said, picking up the banjo case. *Tucson's not bad. That Ginny's nice enough, but she is no Myra.*

Ambling along the sidewalk Billy looked in shop windows and noticed the mixture of people, mostly strolling. Toward the end of the block a short, round-bellied man wearing a black cap and playing a guitar drew his attention. Stopping to listen, Billy noticed the cap was embossed with "USS Warren Black DD 73," and the crossed anchor navy symbol. Underneath the cap the man's long scraggly brown hair stuck out in disarray. His rounded face matched his belly and a pudgy nose separated his beady dark eyes.

Billy liked the way he played the guitar, and when the man began to sing, Billy thought the coarseness of his voice had a certain charm. His battered guitar case, plastered with decals, lay open on the sidewalk. Billy glanced at the handful of coins and a few dollar bills. Finished with the song he looked up at Billy and arched his eyebrows.

"Howdy," he said. "Banjo?"

"Yeah," Billy replied. "I like what you did."

"Thanks, I'm Clearance."

"Banjo Billy. Navy?" Billy asked, nodding at Clearance's cap.

"Yeah, four damn years," Clearance replied.

"I was army."

"'Nam?" Clearance asked.

"Two tours. I got out last August."

"I did a stretch on the Mekong gunboats."

"I heard that was a bitch," Billy said.

"It was all a bitch," Clearance said.

"Yeah," Billy replied. "Two years in that stinkin' jungle was too much for me."

"I got out a year ago," Clearance said. "I've been on the road ever since. Where you from?"

"Springfield, Illinois, but I am not about to go back there."

"I was from Ohio," Clearance said. "I don't go back there either. I go to New Orleans once a year for Mardi Gras. That's the most home I have now."

"The way I feel, I'm home wherever I am. Maybe in a year or so I'll find someplace. There's a girl in Jackson, Wyoming I wouldn't mind bein' at home with, but I felt like I was gettin' too tied down. I came down here for the winter. It gets too cold up there."

"I just got here myself," Clearance said. "I was messing around Seattle."

"How's the street-playin' here?" Billy asked.

"The last five days I've made beer and breakfast," Clearance said. "That's all I need."

"Where do you sleep?"

"I found an old empty garage. Nobody has run me off yet."

"I just got in on the bus. I got a room in the Congress Hotel."

"How about jamming?" Clearance asked. "Maybe together we can do better than alone."

"Let's give it a try," Billy said.

Billy flipped open the case, took out his banjo, and tuned it to Clearance's guitar.

"Do you know 'Raindrops Keep Fallin' on my Head?'" Billy asked.

"I know the tune, but not the words," Clearance answered.

"Let's go for it," Billy said, and began strumming.

After playing a few bars of the song Billy sang the words. In spite of never having played together before, the song sounded good enough so that two couples, obviously out on the town for the evening, stopped to listen. When Billy and Clearance finished the song, the people clapped their hands and both men put a dollar in each opened case. Billy and Clearance thanked them. Billy turned to Clearance. "Proud Mary?" Billy asked.

"Right on," Clearance answered.

The two couples stood watching and listening as the two troubadors played and sang. Another couple stopped, nearly blocking the sidewalk. A long-haired, bearded man with a young blond girl who had a pearl earring attached to her left nostril stood apart from the rest of the onlookers. Billy and Clearance watched each other as they ended the song with a series of chords. After the applause the first two men dropped bills in the cases again. The other man contributed, but the long-haired fellow and the blond stood where they were and smiled.

They played together for some three hours before they stopped, divided the money, put their instruments away, and crossed the street to enjoy a beer at a small bar, Ray and Red's Royal Italian Cafe. There were no empty barstools, so they leaned against the back wall with their Budweisers. After midnight, the customers began leaving. Billy and Clearance sat down at the bar and stayed drinking beer until the bartender told them it was closing time. "How about breakfast at the Hungry Eye," Clearance suggested.

"Good idea."

Clearance headed for his garage and Billy ambled back to the Congress Hotel.

Billy liked Clearance and enjoyed playing with him. Their session together reminded him of the times back in Springfield he had played with his friends. Thinking about Springfield dragged up memories of his father and made him scowl until he reached the hotel.

At breakfast, Clearance suggested that Billy bring his duffel bag to the garage to save money. "It's a roof over our heads and it will probably be cold in winter," Clearance said, "but it's better than a lot of places I've spent nights."

Finished with breakfast, Clearance took Billy to the alley where the rear entrance to the abandoned garage stood. Two bent and dented trash cans overflowed with rusted, cast-off auto parts. The corrugated siding showed patches of rust and dirty, white paint that had mostly flaked off. A large garage door, with tall weeds growing at its base appeared to have been in its closed position for a long time. On one corner a standard, wooden door, its white paint scattered on the crumbling asphalt, was closed, but there were no weeds growing in front of it.

Clearance glanced up and down the alley before yanking the stubborn door open. Billy followed. Although the sunlight was bright outside, the large cement floored room was dark because all six windows had been boarded up. "Like I said, it isn't much, but it's a roof over our heads," Clearance said.

"Is it safe to leave our stuff in here while we're out on the street?"

"I've been using this place for four days, and nobody has bothered me."

"It sure will be better than payin' out bucks for a hotel room," Billy commented. "I'll go get my things and check out of the hotel."

"How long will that take?" Clearance asked.

"I'll be back here in less than an hour."

"All right. I'll stick around here until you get back. Then we can practice a few songs together."

Billy left his banjo with Clearance, hurried to the hotel, and was back at the garage with his duffel bag in forty-five minutes. During the short trip he wondered about Clearance's invitation to play with him on the sidewalks. Depending on tips alone was not like finding a gig with steady income in a bar. *I like to play for a bigger audience than we get on the sidewalk.*

Before leaving the garage, Billy changed to another shirt. The two musicians, carrying their instruments, headed for the small park by the railroad station where they found a bench shaded by a large mulberry tree. They practiced songs together until early afternoon. "There should be some traffic back on the street soon," Clearance said. "Let's grab a beer at the Shack before we set up."

"Sounds good to me," Billy said. "I'll buy you one."

As they entered the Shack, Billy glanced around. There

were six disheveled looking customers, the men with long hair and varying lengths and styles of beards. Two women, with dark circles under their eyes, stood chatting with the men. *These people remind me of the dopers in Haight-Ashbury. This must be the sleazy side of town.* The horseshoe shaped bar showed many years of wear. On the wall a long set of shelves held a vast collection of beer bottles, each with a different label. Many were from Europe and Asia. The bartender, a muscular, stocky-built man, wearing a faded Peter, Paul and Mary tee-shirt took Billy's order for two Budweisers.

"A lot of hop-heads come in here," Clearance whispered, leaning toward Billy.

"Looks like it," Billy said, looking across at the people.

"They get their methadone in the morning and come over here to get loaded on beer," Clearance said, still in a low whisper.

"Where do they get their money?" Billy asked.

"Dealin' weed. Just wait. One of 'em will be over to check us out."

Billy and Clearance were half way through their second beer, when a tall, thin man in his twenties, with long, unkempt, black hair, and a short, patchy beard ambled around the bar, and stood between the two musicians.

"You two dudes play together?" he asked.

"Yeah," Billy answered, turning slightly to look at the visitor.

"That's cool, man. Where you playin'?"

"Down the street on the sidewalk," Clearance answered. "Across from Ray and Red's."

"I'll come down and check you dudes out."

"We ought to set up after another beer," Clearance said.

"I got some good weed, if you're interested."

"What's it go for?" Clearance asked.

"For you dudes, I'll let you have a lid for ten bucks."

"We'll see how the tips come in," Billy said.

"That's cool. You can find me here most of the time. I'm Kevin."

The marijuana dealer returned to his place at the bar with the others. Billy and Clearance finished their beers, and Clearance ordered two more.

"Lubricates my vocal chords," he said.

On their way to set up, they passed a small jewelry shop. A sign in the window advertised engraving for fifty-cents a letter. Billy remembered how the banjo he had left in Springfield had his name engraved on the underside of the neck.

"Let's go in here a minute," Billy said.

"Can I help you?" a man wearing a headpiece with magnifying lenses asked.

"How much to engrave my name on the neck of my banjo?" Billy asked.

"Let me see it."

Billy opened the case, took out the banjo, and handed it to the jeweler.

"What do you want on it?"

"Banjo Billy, on the underside of the neck, near where it joins the base."

"Wood's easier than metal. I'll do one pass for two-bits a letter."

"You've got a deal," Billy said.

"Printed letters or cursive?"

"Printed is fine."

The man took out his electric engraving tool, and had "BANJO BILLY" engraved in less than five minutes. Billy gave him two dollars and fifty cents, looked at the lettering, smiled, and put the banjo back in its case.

They set up on the sidewalk at the same spot as the previous night. Occasionally people stopped to listen and some dropped bills into the cases. Kevin, the marijuana dealer, came by and listened to two songs before inquiring if they wanted to buy some pot.

"Maybe tomorrow," Billy said, annoyed by Kevin's interruption.

"Cool music," Kevin said, and started weaving unsteadily

back to the Shack.

After the foot traffic dwindled, Billy and Clearance decided to split the money in the cases, and go to Ray and Red's for some beer. Billy asked the bartender about a gig. "Nothing here," the bartender said. "But you might try Gus and Andy's out Oracle Road. They hire musicians once in a while."

"How do we get there?" Billy asked.

"It's a mile or so. Go down to north Stone; head north to Drachman. That will take you to Oracle Road. There's a city bus that goes by there, too."

Billy thanked the bartender and ordered two more beers to go.

Just as they opened the door to enter the garage a police cruiser drove through the alley and stopped them in its spotlight. "Hey. You two. Hold it right there!" the officer yelled.

Billy and Clearance stopped and waited, the spotlight blinding them as the officer approached.

"What are you doing?" the policeman asked.

"Just goin' in here to sleep," Billy answered.

"Do you have permission to enter this building?"

"We're sorry, Officer, but we don't know who owns it," Clearance replied.

"You know you're trespassing?"

"We just sleep on the floor in there," Clearance said. "We sure aren't going to damage anything."

Billy watched the officer glance at Clearance's navy cap.

"Navy?"

"Yeah, four years. One tour on the Mekong River gunboats."

"I was navy, too," the officer said. "VS 21, air anti-submarine."

"I had two tours in the stinkin' jungles," Billy added.

The radio in the patrol car blasted forth suddenly.

"Hang on. That call's for me."

He went to the car, reached in for the hand-held microphone and talked to the dispatcher. Returning to Clearance and Billy the officer stood in front of them. "Just don't have a party in there and make a lot of noise. The neighbors will report it, and I'll have to run you off."

"Thanks, Officer," Billy and Clearance said, in unison.

The policeman returned to the cruiser to continue patrolling the neighborhood.

"There's one cool cop," Clearance said.

"For sure," Billy agreed. "For a little while, I thought we would be sleepin' in jail tonight."

"I guess I'll keep wearing this navy cap."

The next morning after breakfast they followed the directions to Gus and Andy's, arriving just after eleven o'clock. A man wearing a black vest over a pink, oxford-cloth shirt had just unlocked the front door. The two musicians sat down at the bar.

"What'll you have?"

"A couple of Buds," Clearance replied. "Is the manager around?"

"I'm the manager. The bartender's car broke down. He'll be in soon.

"We play and sing, guitar and banjo," Clearance said. "We're looking for a gig."

The manager put the beers down on the bar in front of the musicians.

"I've got a jazz piano man right now. He'll be done in a week. Let's hear how you play."

They uncased their instruments, spent a minute tuning, and began to play several songs they knew that they did especially well together, and ended with "Proud Mary."

"You guys will do fine. I have a sound system you can use."

"I don't think we need a sound system," Billy said.

"Well, come by in a week. You can play from seven until we close at one in the morning. Pay is forty bucks a night for each of you, plus any tips you get. I get a pretty generous crowd in here; this place has been here for years."

"Sounds good," Billy said. "We'll be ready in a week."

"Good," the manager said, and put two more beers on the bar. "The beer's on me today, fellers."

"Hey, thanks," Clearance said.

"Yeah, thanks," echoed Billy.

They chatted for a while, then, happily walked back to Fourth Avenue. Stopping at Ray and Red's for more beer before they began playing, they discussed expanding their repertoire of songs. Later, when the sidewalk traffic increased, they again attracted listeners, some of whom were generous. Just before they decided to play their last song Kevin approached, with a forlorn look on his face, carrying his bedroll.

"What's happenin'?" Billy asked.

"A bummer, man," Kevin said. "My old lady got pissed and ran me out."

"That's heavy," Clearance commented.

"Do you dudes have a pad I can share for a night or two? Maybe she'll cool off so I can go back."

"We don't have much, but you can hang out there," Clearance said.

"That's cool," Kevin said. "I've got a little weed we can burn."

After drinking several beers at Ray and Red's, the three headed for the garage. Kevin produced his baggie of marijuana and a package of cigarette paper, and rolled a joint. After lighting it, he passed it to Billy. Billy took a deep drag, and handed the joint to Clearance. Billy thought, I don't know what the rest of Tucson's like, but this part of town is sure weird. Two joints later they settled themselves for sleep.

As usual, Clearance used his guitar case for a pillow. Billy curled up with his head on his duffel bag. Kevin rolled out his bedroll and prepared to sleep on top of it.

Awakened by Clearance's loud, guttural snoring, Billy sat up. In spite of the sun having risen four hours before, the light in the garage was dim. Glancing over, he noticed that Kevin and his bedroll had gone. Clearance continued to snore.

Reaching for his banjo case where he had left it leaning against the wall, Billy found it missing.

"What the hell!" he exclaimed.

He reached over and tapped Clearance on the shoulder. Clearance snorted as he awakened.

"What's going on?" Clearance asked, groggily.

"That Kevin dude is gone. So is my banjo," Billy said.

"Are you sure?"

"Last night, I left it leaning against the wall right next to me. It's gone. It has to be that hop-head son-of-a-bitch."

"Did you leave any money in it last night?" Clearance asked.

"I never leave money in it."

"I guess we had better try and find Kevin," Clearance said, and yawned.

"I'll bet he won't be easy to find," Billy replied. "Why the hell did you invite him to stay here, anyway?"

"How was I to know he was a thief? After breakfast, we can ask at the Shack if anyone has seen him."

"Those hop-heads will probably cover for him."

"Well, it's as good a place as any to start looking for the son-of-a-bitch," Clearance said.

After breakfast at the Hungry Eye, Billy and Clearance began their search. The Shack was closed until eleven o'clock, but the bartender drove up as they turned to leave. "We are looking for Kevin. Have you seen him?" Billy asked.

"I just got here," the bartender replied. "He was here yesterday."

"Do you know where he lives?"

"Probably in somebody's back yard like most of the junkies."

"That doesn't help much. He stole my banjo. But, thanks, anyway," Billy said.

"No problem," the bartender replied. "Good luck finding him."

Later in the day, after looking everywhere they could think of, Billy and Clearance stopped in at Ray and Red's.

"It looks like you will be playin' alone tonight," Billy said.

"You can still sing."

"I suppose. I wish I could find that son-of-a-bitch. Here we found a gig at Gus and Andy's and I don't have my banjo."

"We might find that Kevin dude before the gig starts," Clearance said.

"We sure struck out today," Billy said, with a dismal tone to his voice. As he ran his fingers through his beard he had thoughts that he should have stayed in Jackson and waited for the skiers. He would still have his banjo and Myra next to him in bed.

Clearance played his guitar and Billy sang with him. But Billy had a difficult time concentrating on the music. Around ten o'clock when the sidewalk traffic had begun to dwindle, Billy spotted the policeman they had met at the garage. In the middle of a song Billy stepped into the street, waving at the officer to stop. The patrol car pulled in to the curb next to a fire hydrant. Billy met the policeman as he left the cruiser. "I am in a real bind," Billy said. "Do you know a dude named Kevin, with long, stringy, black hair and a patchy lookin' beard?"

"That description could fit a lot of people down here," the officer said. "Why are you looking for him?"

"He stole my banjo last night. He said his old lady had run him off and he needed a place to stay. Stupidly, we let him go with us to that garage. He's a junkie."

"Does he hang around the Shack with the others?"

"That's where we first met him trying to sell us a lid of pot."

"He might be on methadone maintenance. You might find him at Hope Center in the morning."

"What about my banjo?"

"He probably pawned the banjo to get a fix of heroin. You might look in that Congress Pawn Shop."

"If I find it then I'll have to find Kevin to get it back."

"Here, take my card. If you find your banjo in the pawn shop call the number and ask the dispatcher to contact me. What's your name?"

"Banjo Billy is what I go by."

"I think your best bet is the pawn shop."

Billy looked at the card. "Thanks, Steve. I'll give it a try tomorrow."

"Good luck. I go on duty at three in the afternoon tomorrow."

When Clearance finished the song, Billy told him what the officer had said. "Let's try the pawn shop in the mornin'," Billy suggested.

"From what you said, it seems like the only logical place to look," Clearance said.

Before retiring in the garage they looked for Kevin at the Shack. Of course, none of the customers at the bar had seen Kevin.

The following morning the two musicians peered through the glass show window of the Congress Pawn Shop. "Hey, man," Billy said. "There's my banjo hangin' on the wall. See it?"

"It sure looks like it," Clearance replied.

They entered the pawn shop and took a good look at the banjo behind the cash register. The proprietor, a short, man with thinning gray hair, ambled over behind the counter. "Can I help you with something?" he asked.

"That's my banjo on the wall," Billy said.

"I took that in yesterday. You don't look like the fellow who brought it in."

"The fellow who brought it in stole it from me night before last."

"You know the rules; you have to bring him in to pay his loan, or wait thirty days until it's dead pawn. Then you can buy it for the loan plus the interest."

"That doesn't sound right to me. It's my banjo."

"I'm sorry, but that's the way I have to operate."

Leaving the shop, Billy wrinkled his brow and flung his fist forward. "This is the shits. There's my goddam banjo on that bastard's wall, and I can't have what belongs to me."

"Maybe that cop, Steve, can help."

Billy and Clearance waited at the Shack until three o'clock that afternoon. From the public telephone outside the bar, Billy contacted the police dispatcher and asked her to tell Officer Steve Halloran that Banjo Billy had found his banjo in the pawn shop. But the man in the pawn shop had said he couldn't have it for thirty days, and then would have to pay for it. The dispatcher put Billy on hold while she radioed the officer. "Sir, he will meet you at the Congress Pawn Shop in half an hour," the dispatcher said over the telephone.

"Thanks," Billy replied, and hung up the receiver.

Returning inside he sat down next to Clearance. "Finish your beer," Billy said. "He's going to meet us at the pawn shop in half an hour."

Arriving early Billy and Clearance stood next to the pawn shop entrance. The patrol car pulled into an empty loading zone nearby. Officer Halloran got out of the car and greeted them. "Before we go in there, here's the plan. I'll do the talking. You guys just stand by until I need you. Abe will do what he can to keep the banjo in order to make money on it. But, he can't argue the fact that it's stolen property once you identify it. Let's go."

"Good afternoon, Officer Halloran," Abe said. "What can I help you with?"

"Hello, Abe. This man claims you have a banjo here that was stolen from him."

"He was in here earlier. I told him to come back when it's dead pawn and he can have it for the loan and the interest. The loan is thirty bucks."

"Billy, can you identify your banjo?"

"It has 'Banjo Billy' engraved low on the neck. It also has a case and three books of music. The banjo's over there on the wall," he said, pointing to the instrument.

"Abe, if you'll be good enough to hand me the banjo, I need to look at it."

The pawn broker pursed his lips and jutted out his chin. He took the banjo down and carried it over to the officer. Steve turned it over, saw the engraving, and placed the instrument on the counter. "It looks like you have a piece of stolen property here, Abe," the officer said. "If you will get the case and the music books, we can get this matter settled quickly."

"Who's going to pay the loan?"

"You know the rules, Abe. Stolen property is stolen property. You'll have to eat this one."

"How do I know stolen property from unstolen property?"

"Come on, Abe, get the case and the music books," Halloran said.

The pawn broker went to the back of the store, picked up the banjo case from a pile, brought it back and put it on the counter next to the banjo. Billy opened the case. "Where are my music books?"

"There were no music books," Abe replied.

Billy looked at Halloran with questioning eyes. The officer shrugged. Billy put the banjo in the case and put it on his shoulder. At least the picks are still in the case.

"Thanks for your help, Abe," Halloran said.

"Don't mention it," the pawn broker said, still scowling. "When am I going to quit lending to those goddam junkies?"

Outside on the sidewalk the three chatted by the patrol car.

"Steve, you are one okay cop," Billy said. "We have a gig at Gus and Andy's startin' next week. Stop by. I'll buy you a beer, and we'll play you a song." Billy and Clearance smiled warmly as they shook hands with Halloran.

"I'll do that, Billy. I go on days next week. If you see that Kevin character, don't try to bust him yourselves. Give me another call."

"Will do, Steve, and thanks again. If we can do anythin' for you anytime, just shout."

"I'm just glad we got your banjo back and I'll keep your offer in mind. Good luck."

The gig at Gus and Andy's lasted a month. The tips were especially good on weekends. Steve Halloran stopped by after work and enjoyed his friends' music as well as the beer Billy ordered for him. The garage continued to provide shelter for the two troubadors, and they made sure never again to invite anyone to share their roof.

Tucson's winter and a few drizzling rains kept them off the sidewalk some days. They purchased some used blankets from the Salvation Army store, two blocks south of their sidewalk stage. Christmas and New Years came and went without much fanfare. Then Ginny, the waitress at the Hungry Eye, told them about an art festival, held every year in Tubac, forty-five miles south of Tucson on the highway to Nogales.

"The festival lasts nine days," she said. "They have all sorts of arts and crafts in booths around the village. You guys could do well there, even if you just set up on one of the streets."

"Is it like the street fair they had here?" Billy asked.

"They are all about the same, except Tubac's is nine days. You might get a gig at one of the bars there."

"Maybe we'll give it a try. Is there a bus?" Clearance asked, raising his eyes.

"You take the bus that goes to Nogales. I think it runs every hour."

"What day does it start; do you know?" Billy asked.

"There's an ad in the newspaper. Let me check."

Ginny took a well-read newspaper from under the counter, opened it, and leafed through the pages. "Here it is," she said, and slapped her fingers on the advertisement. "It starts this Saturday. I was thinking about going down there myself, but I have to work. The other girl quit yesterday."

She handed the open newspaper to Billy, who shared it with Clearance. After reading it Billy handed the paper back to Ginny. She folded it and shoved it under the counter.

"What do you think, Clearance?" Billy asked, wrinkling his brow and scratching his beard.

"Might as well. We could use another gig right about now. Besides, I need to get bus fare to New Orleans for Mardi Gras."

CHAPTER FOUR

Early the next Saturday morning they were packed and ready for their trip to Tubac. After breakfast they carried their gear to the bus station. "I'm glad to get away from here," Billy said. "We could do pretty well at this festival."

"Yeah," Clearance agreed. "After Tubac, I'll be ready for New Orleans. Are you coming with me?"

"I don't know," Billy answered. "New Orleans is a long way."

They boarded the Nogales bound bus and found an empty seat. Most of the passengers conversed in Spanish. Billy looked out of the window, not wanting to listen to Clearance talk about the money they could make from the Mardi Gras. As the bus headed south through groves of pecan trees growing in rows on the floodplain, he saw the mountains and foothills in the distance forming the eastern boundary of the desert valley. Shifting in his seat, he looked across the aisle to the west recognizing the huge mountainous mine dumps from the large open-pit copper mines he had read about in a tourist magazine article.

The bus driver stopped at the entrance to the village of Tubac to let them out after the hour long trip. The two musicians stood and stretched at the side of the road, looking at the booths set up throughout the village. "So this is Tubac," Billy said, glancing at the large sign that announced, "Tubac, Where Art and History Meet." They began strolling down the street. Tucked in back of a real estate office, the Sombrero Bar's blinking neon beer signs caught their attention.

"Let's go in there and try for a gig," Clearance said.

"Maybe we should check out all the bars first," Billy suggested.

"I could use a beer right now, anyway," Clearance said.

They trudged up the rocky driveway leading to the bar, passing by a tall cedar tree with Christmas lights still hanging on its branches. Inside, a long, oak bar, in front of which green Naugahyde covered barstools stood empty of customers. At the far end, the round-faced bartender leaned against the inside of the bar with his complete attention fixed on a television screen. Occasionally he rubbed his shaved head. The high volume of the program echoed in the nearby empty pool table room.

Billy and Clearance sat down. Engrossed in the soap opera, the bartender did not notice that he had customers at the bar. To attract his attention Clearance rapped on the bar top. The man glanced over, turned down the volume on the television set, and waddled over to face the two troubadors.

"What can I get you?"

"Two Budweisers," Billy answered.

Opening the chest-type cooler he took out two bottles and brought them over.

"Is the manager here?" Billy asked.

"I'm the owner," the man replied.

"We are wonderin' if you would like us to play here during your festival."

"What do you play?"

"I play banjo. My partner here, plays guitar."

"You can play here if you want; I can't pay you. I don't get the business to warrant entertainment. Besides, all these damn artists drink is beer."

"Is there another bar in town?" Billy asked.

"There's one on Camino Otero, one block over. They call the joint Cantina De Anza. Their drinks are expensive and they serve Mexican food."

Billy paid for the two beers and he and Clearance left the Sombrero Bar. Outside, they noticed the traffic coming into the village had increased. A lot of people were ambling along, looking at the various crafts offered for sale in the booths. Food booth operators, advertising everything from Thai food to candied apples, worked busily preparing their creations to be ready in time for lunch.

There were only two empty barstools at La Cantina De Anza when Billy and Clearance arrived. They put their gear and instruments on the floor next to them and sat down. Billy watched the bartender prepare six margaritas. The man looked familiar. His thinning, blonde hair grew down to the neck of his tee-shirt. His ruddy complexion showed on his clean shaven face. When he turned to glance at his two new arrivals Billy saw the light blue eyes, separated by the thin, long nose, and recognized his comrade from Vietnam. "Pete Stanton!" Billy exclaimed. "Remember me, Bill O'Leary?"

"I'll be go to hell," Pete said, surprised. "I didn't recognize you with that beard. What are you doing in Tubac?"

"Playin' banjo. This is my partner, Clearance."

Pete dried his hand on his apron and offered it to both men.

"Jesus Keerist, Bill. What a helluva surprise to see you. What's it been, two years?"

"Yeah, Pete," Billy answered, with a serious tone in his voice. "The last I saw you was when I was helpin' you into that 'copter after that land mine blew off your left leg. We figured you had bit it for sure. Man, am I ever glad to see you made it."

"It took a while."

"You sure get around good," Billy remarked.

Pete took a long stirring spoon and soundly struck his left leg. The blow made a hollow sound. "Ain't fiberglass wonderful?"

"When that Huey took off with you on that stretcher, I got so pissed that I emptied my rifle into the jungle. I guess I was close to goin' bonkers."

Tears filled Billy's eyes as he remembered the incident. After helping lift Pete into the helicopter, a savage rage had taken over his mind.

Controlling his tears as he conversed with his war time buddy, Billy wiped the moisture from his eyes with his sleeve.

"They got me to the field hospital just in time, so they told me. Eventually they flew me back to the States. Six months later I got so I could walk pretty well with old Oscar. That's what I call this leg. The surgeon's name was Captain Oscar Sandoval."

"So, what have you been doing since?"

"I spent a year in La Paz, Baja California. Stayed drunk on Coronas, trying to forget 'Nam and all the bullshit. A couple of months ago, I decided I didn't want to die in Mexico, so I came back. I drove my VW camper up here from Nogales, stopped by for a beer, and got to like the owner. She lets me bartend for tips."

"Do you mean they don't pay you any wages?"

"That doesn't matter to me. She has been trying to make a go of this place after her husband died a year ago. I get a good disability pension and live in my camper out behind. I get tips, food and beer."

"We are lookin' for a gig during this festival. Do you think the owner would pay us?"

"I doubt it, but I'll ask," Pete said. "Why don't you start playing. I'll go back to the office and have her come out to listen."

A waitress came in from the adjoining patio before Pete could leave.

"Two Pacificos, one dry gin martini and a perfect manhattan," she said.

As Pete made the drinks, Billy and Clearance took out their instruments and tuned them. Pete placed the drink order on the waitress's tray just as Billy and Clearance began playing. Limping only slightly, Pete left the bar and returned with Katherine, owner of La Cantina de Anza.

Billy and Clearance broke into "Proud Mary." Pete took his place behind the bar, and Katherine stood by the hallway entrance, with her arms crossed in front of her, listening to the two troubadors. Halfway through "Proud Mary," Katherine beckoned to Pete. He stepped over to her side. Leaning toward him she said something, turned and went back to the office.

The people in the bar applauded after "Proud Mary," and one man ordered the pair two more beers. Billy and Clearance returned to their barstools. Setting the bottles on the bar in front of them Pete told them that Katherine would let them play for beer and tips. "She will probably feed you, too," he said.

"When should we start?" Billy asked.

"I would wait until noon, or a little after, when the people start coming in for lunch. The patio out there will be full."

"Thanks for the help, Pete," Billy said.

"No problem, Bill. You guys should do all right out there in the patio."

Billy and Clearance set up in the large open patio that was filled with white, wrought-iron tables with umbrellas in the centers and white wrought-iron chairs. They "salted" their instrument cases with a few dollar bills, and began playing when the lunch crowd began arriving.

Pete made sure they had beers during the short breaks they took during the afternoon. After dark, the supper crowd stayed in the dining room, but the bar area filled with a few locals and a good number who Pete called "booth people," the craft people who made the festival and fair circuit.

During one of their breaks Pete beckoned Billy over to the bar. "Where are you staying?" Pete asked.

"I have no idea," Billy answered.

"The man wearing that old cowboy hat, sitting over at the end of the bar, has a place he might let you two crash in."

"Sounds good to me," Billy said.

"Step over there, and I'll introduce you."

Billy approached the man as he sipped his drink, a calloused hand holding the glass.

"Brian, I'd like you to meet Bill O'Leary, a buddy of mine in 'Nam. Bill this is Brian McTavish."

The two men shook hands. Billy noticed that McTavish looked at him in an appraising manner.

"I was wondering, Brian, if Bill and Clearance could use your sleeping porch? They're here for the festival."

"Fine with me, Pete," McTavish said. Then, turning to Billy, "How long will you be playing here tonight?"

"I guess when we either get tired or the people leave," Billy said.

"I'm leaving after one more drink," McTavish said. "If one

of you wants to walk to my house with me, I'll show you how to get up to the sleeping porch."

"Sounds good," Billy said. "Give me a wave when you're ready to go, and I'll be with you."

Billy and Clearance began playing again. After the second song McTavish waved at Billy. Leaning his banjo against the wall, he followed Brian out of the door and a block south to a long, narrow, adobe house. He led Billy down an alley to the rear of the building where an outside stairway led up to an open porch built over the original roof of the old adobe dwelling. "Be careful of the handrail; you can get splinters from it easily," McTavish warned.

"Thanks," Billy said. "We sure do appreciate your hospitality, Brian."

"My pleasure. I always have a pot of coffee going. Stop by in the morning."

Billy rejoined Clearance at La Cantina de Anza. Billy liked the atmosphere of the place. The room was large enough to accommodate thirty customers, yet the Mexican decor gave it a cozy ambiance. The crowd listened while they played and sang, pleasing Billy that they were not merely background sound to loud conversations. By midnight the crowd had left, and one remaining local merchant staggered to the door. The troubadors put their tips in their pockets and packed up their instruments.

"How did it go?" Pete asked.

"Not bad for a first night," Billy replied.

"Katherine told me to give you guys twenty bucks apiece. She enjoyed your music and wants you back tomorrow," Pete said, and handed them the bills.

"Hey, that's cool," Billy said. "Tell her thanks."

"Come over in the morning and have breakfast," Pete said.

"We'll sure see you in the morning, Pete," Clearance said, and smiled at the thought of breakfast.

"It sure is great to see you again, Pete," Billy said.

"Likewise."

Stretched out on his bedding on McTavish's sleeping porch, Billy's thoughts returned to the jungles of Vietnam and the day the land mine blew off Pete's leg. Damn, I hope I don't have that dream tonight.

Startled awake early the next morning by the sharp whine of McTavish's table saw ripping a slab of mesquite lumber, the two musicians descended from the sleeping porch and watched their host saw parts for a coffee table he was making. Seeing the two through the doorway of his workshop, McTavish shut down the saw.

"How about that coffee?" McTavish said.

"We're ready," Billy replied.

"Go on into the kitchen and help yourselves. I'll be there in a minute."

McTavish turned the saw on again as Billy and Clearance went through the back door to the kitchen. They helped themselves to the strong, inky black coffee. McTavish joined them shortly, and poured some for himself.

"Let's go out front and watch the tourists," McTavish suggested.

They passed through two small, dark rooms with high, wooden ceilings and Mexican tiled floors. McTavish opened the rustic front door made from heavy, barnwood planks. The rafters of the front porch were discarded cross-arms from power poles; the floor was made of flat river rocks, grouted together. An old, iron hay rake wheel served as the entrance gate.

Balancing his coffee on an old stump and sitting in a cushioned wicker arm chair, McTavish lit his curve stemmed pipe. Billy and Clearance sat on a mesquite bench.

"Where are you guys going after the festival is over?" McTavish asked.

"I'm thinking about New Orleans," Clearance said.

"Someone was telling me about Arivaca," Billy said. "Do you know anythin' about it?"

"I lived there quite a few years ago. It was mostly a mining and cow town back in those days. Then a rancher sold out his large spread and the place was subdivided into forty acre parcels. Now the whole area is full of people looking for alternative lifestyles. They say there's a lot of drug traffic from Mexico coming through there these days. It's close to the border so the smugglers find it easy to get into the country."

"How do I get there?" Billy asked. "I heard there was a bar where I might get a gig."

"Go north to the junction and go west. It's about twenty miles up that road. There is a bar. I know a dude who bartended there for a while. There's a new owner every several years. I doubt if you could get a gig, but they would let you play for beer and tips. Don't count on many tips, though. Those hippies live mostly on food stamps."

"I think I'll go there and check it out just for the hell of it," Billy said.

"Incidentally, if you guys want a shower, you're welcome to use mine. The only thing is that the hot water heater is a wood burner. It takes about a half hour to heat the water in the tank."

"After livin' in a garage in Tucson, we could use a shower. Thanks," Billy said.

"When you're ready, the heater's in the alley. There's wood stacked next to it."

"We'll be back after breakfast over at the bar."

Breakfast with Pete included conversations about their experiences in Vietnam. Billy finished the story about the time he had helped lift Pete into the Huey helicopter. "I went crazy after the 'copter lifted off and I emptied my M-16 into the jungle. Lieutenant Jacques started chewin' me out when a loud groan came from the jungle. He assembled the squad and went to investigate. When they came back the lieutenant told me I had killed two Cong. He asked me how I saw them in the jungle. I told him I saw the vines wiggle. I had to say somethin' to get him off my back."

Clearance told how he had been sent from the gunboat to

rescue an army officer. As he had followed a path through the jungle, one Vietnamese soldier had jumped out onto the path in front of him and another to his rear. Both had automatic rifles pointed at him.

"There was a moment when I thought I would fill my dungarees, but they turned out to be friendlies and took me to where a wounded lieutenant was hiding. Between the three of us, we got him back to the river."

"Before I went to Mexico," Pete said. "I wanted to see how much work I could do getting around on this fiberglass leg. I had an old pickup truck and I bought a chain saw. I drove up to Tahoe to cut firewood for the rich guys. One evening I was drinking beer in a bar after busting ass all day cutting wood. Three burly-looking bikers swaggered in. They were big and tattooed. All three had beards that looked like there might be lice crawling around in the whiskers. It was obvious they had been drinking before they came into the bar where I was. One of them snarled at me and asked me if I was tough. Do I look like I'm tough?"

"You may not look like you're tough, Pete, but I know you're as tough as they come," Billy said.

"Anyway, this biker, they called him Big Moose, he spreads his left hand out on top of the old wooden bartop. Then he takes an ice-pick and stabs it through that web of skin between his thumb and index finger. Then, he looks at me and says, 'That's tough'."

"Sounds like a big dumb shit to me," Clearance said.

"Well, I decided to give this dude some hell, so I went out to the pickup, changed to my spare leg that didn't fit too well, grabbed the chain- saw, and went back into the bar. 'So you think you're tough,' I said to Big Moose. I started the chain-saw. The smoke shot out the exhaust, and the motor on the son-of-a-bitch whined as I pulled the trigger. Then I aimed the blade at my leg and started cutting. I hadn't got through more than an inch when Big Moose fainted and fell on the floor. One of the others puked, and the third dude ran out the door."

"Was Big Moose's hand still stuck to the bar when he fainted?" Billy asked.

"Yeah, and the ice-pick stayed stuck, ripped right through the skin when he fell to the floor."

"I'll bet he doesn't try that crap again," Clearance said.

"I wouldn't bet on it," Pete remarked.

The three laughed at Pete's story, but the conversation lapsed for a few minutes. Billy rubbed his beard, thinking about the war. "I have a restless feeling most of the time," he said. "I'm beginnin' to wonder how long it's goin' to last."

"Don't feel like the Lone Ranger, Bill," Pete said. "I have a helluva time staying in one place."

"I spent two tours in that goddam jungle, scared every minute; just plain old scared."

"I was the same damn way. I hate to think of the times out on patrol when I got so goddam fearful, I'd crap in my pants," Pete said.

"You weren't the only one. I can't count the number of times I shit my drawers just listenin' to gunfire, wonderin' when I'd buy the farm."

"The army probably issued olive drab skivvies so when we washed out the crap and hung them up to dry, they wouldn't look like surrender flags."

The three veterans laughed.

"I think I'm still scared," Billy said. "At least I haven't shit my pants since I left 'Nam."

Pete took a sip of coffee. "The trouble with 'Nam was we could never see the Congs in the jungle even though we knew they were there and probably taking aim at us."

"Then, when we get back to the States, all the peaceniks look at us as scum. Hell, I didn't find a bit of pleasure killin' Congs."

"I'll tell you what guys," Pete said, stretching. "I'm tired of thinkin' about all that bullshit."

Happy that Katherine had paid for their breakfast, Billy and Clearance promised to return and play for the lunch crowd. Returning to McTavish's house, they found the wood-burning hot water heater and built a small fire under the tank. As they waited for the water to heat they wandered around the village looking at the booths full of various crafts the booth people had brought into town to sell.

Refreshed by the showers, Billy and Clearance set up in front of one of the stores and began playing. A small crowd gathered to listen, and the dollar bills began to accumulate.

At the end of their third song a middle-aged woman, dressed in leather pants and a blouse that exposed her cleavage, strode up in front of the troubadors, and put her hands on her hips. "You bums cannot play on the streets unless you pay a booth fee and register with the festival committee," she said. "I am Millie Hazelwood, co-director of the festival."

"Now, wait a minute," Billy said. "We don't have a booth. And we have a gig at La Cantina de Anza starting in a few minutes."

"I don't care where you have a gig. I want you off the streets or I'll have the deputies arrest you."

A man with his hair braided into a ponytail and with bracelets adorning both wrists approached. "Millie, leave these guys alone. They can play on the streets as long as they want to. You may be the co-director of this festival, but you don't own the streets," he said.

"Listen to me, Bob Grinnell," Millie said. "I don't want this undesirable element in the village. Is that clear?"

Grinnell turned away from the co-director to face Billy and Clearance. "My shop is over on Tubac Road. It's called Indian Bob's Jewelry. I'll give you each forty bucks a day to play out in front."

"Thanks for the offer, but we promised Katherine we would play for her lunch crowd."

"You're an asshole, Bob Grinnell," Millie said, and turned to leave.

"Why, thank you, Millie," Grinnell said. "You're a very sweet lady."

"Man, this is quite a town," Billy said. "Does everybody here hate each other?"

"Not everybody," Grinnell said. "Millie is very rich and has nothing else to do but drink and play God. She's drunk already and it isn't even noon."

"If she's that way, how did she become co-director of the festival?" Billy asked.

"Because nobody in town wants the job. She gets drunk and tries to throw her power around, just like she tried to do with you guys."

"She is something else," Clearance added.

"I have to get back to my shop. If you get tired of playing for Katherine, my offer is good for the rest of the festival."

"Thanks, Bob, and thanks for gettin' that crazy Millie off our backs," Billy said.

"My pleasure. She's a real bitch."

On McTavish's front porch the next morning, Billy told Brian about the episode with Millie Hazelwood.

"She's a sad woman," McTavish said. "She has tons of money, but no friends in the world. I have heard that she calls two or three women, invites them for lunch at the country club, and then pays for everything. Otherwise, she would have to drink alone."

"She sounded meaner than a wounded bear," Billy remarked.

"She's a classic example that money cannot buy happiness. Look at the three of us sitting here enjoying the morning over coffee. None of us has any money to speak of. I have the house paid for, finally, and I make enough furniture to pay bills, eat and enjoy a couple of scotches in the evening. I'm happy and have no regrets about my life."

"All I need is beer and breakfast," Clearance said. "By the time this festival is over, I'll have bus fare to New Orleans. Then, I'll go back to playing for beer and breakfasts."

"I reckon I'm as happy as I can be right now," Billy said. "I don't hanker to settle down anywhere, so this wanderin' minstrel life suits me just fine. If I could stop havin' dreams about 'Nam I would be even happier."

"Happiness is nothing more than a state of mind, and that sure as hell cannot be bought," McTavish said. "I see so many of these rich folks, in this valley, who have little to do besides checking their stocks in the Wall Street Journal and playing golf at the country club. You can see them coming for their mail at the post office. Very few have smiles on their faces. Many of them scowl even when you wish them a good day."

"When I think about it I guess I'm lucky, not wantin' to get caught up in a society that demands that you make a pile of money to be looked at as successful," Billy said. "Hell's fire, I am successful just to get out of 'Nam in one piece."

"You mentioned that Bob Grinnell offered to pay you to play in front of his store," McTavish said. "I wouldn't if I were you. He is quite a bullshitter."

They continued playing during afternoons and evenings at La Cantina de Anza. The tips mounted and they drank all the free beer they wanted. Clearance took particular pleasure eating breakfasts paid for by Katherine. After nine days everyone in the village, including the booth people, were glad that the festival had ended. Many of them gathered at La Cantina de Anza for what they called "The End of the Festival Party."

Millie Hazelwood and Harriet Lang, the other festival director, joined the party. Obviously quite drunk when she arrived, Millie announced that she was buying a round for everyone. The crowd cheered. Billy and Clearance continued to play for the party goers until the tips ceased to drop in their open instrument cases. Then they put their instruments away and joined the party.

Half staggering Millie approached the musicians and apologized for her behavior on the street. Leaving Clearance to Millie, Billy moved away to chat with Brian McTavish. An hour later Clearance went over to Billy and McTavish.

"Hey, that Millie broad wants to take me home with her," Clearance said.

"Go for it," Billy said. "Just watch out. That barracuda could tear you apart."

"Shit, man," Clearance said. "Remember, I was a sailor. Any old port in a storm. Take my guitar to the sleeping porch, will you, Billy?"

"Sure, Clearance, but don't you want to serenade the lady?"

Billy and McTavish laughed as they watched Clearance steadying Millie as they left the bar.

When the guitar player reached McTavish's front porch the next morning, Billy and Brian had almost finished their coffee. "Well, lover-boy," Billy chided. "How did you make out with Miss Tubac Festival of the Arts?"

"Jesus, what a beast!" Clearance said. "All she wanted to do was have someone to drink with. When we got into her house she took off her clothes and poured out two stiff whiskeys. Her saggy tits look like summer squashes. I was glad she passed out on the couch after the second drink. I found a bedroom and crashed. She was still on the couch when I left a while ago. What a beast!"

Billy and McTavish laughed at the forlorn look on Clearance's face.

After breakfast, Pete drove Billy and Clearance to the junction. They had two rounds of beers at the Junction Bar before Pete said good-bye and returned to his bartending job at La Cantina de Anza. With his duffel bag and banjo, Billy waited for a ride to Arivaca. Clearance had boarded the bus to Tucson after promising Billy he would try to get up to Jackson for the next summer's tourist season.

Billy thought about Myra as he stood on the side of the road. In his mind he pictured her standing naked in front of him. "Too bad Jackson is so damned cold in the winter," he muttered to himself. "Illinois is cold, but Jackson's a deep freeze."

A battered pickup stopped. Billy tossed his duffel bag in the rear, and climbed in carrying his banjo. For a while the countryside passing by was a broad mesa, studded with small mesquite trees and other bushy plants. Then the road dipped down to a valley divided by a large arroyo with cottonwood trees standing like sentinels, waiting for warm spring weather to sprout their new, yellow-green leaves. The pickup passed a ranch headquarters before climbing the winding road over foothills, also covered by small mesquite. As the pickup climbed to the top of a long ridge, Billy looked out over the hilly country he had seen on the way. Then, down again and around a long curve, they arrived at the little town of Arivaca.

The driver stopped the pickup in front of the bar called El Gallo Negro. Billy jumped out with his banjo and grabbed his duffel bag. Thanking the driver for the ride, he turned and looked at the wooden, carved figure of a black rooster that needed new paint. El Gallo Negro, The Black Rooster. The bar, similar to the horseshoe-shaped one in the Shack, in Tucson had another black rooster on the wall above the cash register. The rusty barstools were chrome,edged with well-worn green padded backless seats. The bartop looked fairly new except someone had scarred it with a chisel to make it look old to fit the rest of the decor, if one could call the old beer-ad posters decor.

Two long-haired, bearded men surrounded a bland-faced woman with long stringy, black hair. The men conversed around the woman, who had a look of boredom on her face as she sipped from a bottle of Coor's.

After putting his duffel bag on the floor and leaning his banjo against the bar, Billy sat down on the opposite side of the horseshoe from the other customers. A middle-aged man with white, curly hair and ruddy complexion took his order for a Budweiser.

"Are you new in town?" the man asked.

"Just now arrived," Billy answered.

"Welcome to Arivaca and the Gallo Negro. I'm Jerry. I own

the place."

"I'm Banjo Billy. Nice to meet you. I was told in Tubac that you might use a banjo player here."

"I wish I had the business to pay a banjo player," Jerry said. "All we have here are cowboys, miners, and hippies. The cowboys show up once a month on pay day. The miners come in once in a while, and the hippies come in to sip their beers in-between smoking weed outside."

"How about playin' for beer and tips?"

"I'll slip you a beer once in a while, but I wouldn't count on tips. The cowboys don't make enough wages to leave any on the bar. The miners think it's against their principles to tip an owner of a bar, and the hippies are lucky to have money for beer. If it wasn't for food stamps they'd starve. But, you're sure welcome to play for beer and tips."

"When does the evenin' crowd generally show up?"

"No telling. It varies every night. I don't know why I ever bought this joint. I've been kicking myself in the butt for two years."

"I'll have another beer, and then I'd like to have a look around for a place to sleep," Billy said.

"There's some old abandoned adobes next door. They don't have roofs. Or, you can throw down under the cottonwoods by the crossing. They are a block west and a hundred yards south."

Standing in front of the Gallo Negro, Billy could look at the entire town of Arivaca without turning his head. After the dingy bar that smelled of stale beer, the clear air and bright sunlight outside raised his spirits. Across the dirt main street, a small general store with two gasoline pumps dominated a corner. The post office, part of the same building, was distinguished by a flagpole with an American flag fluttering in the gentle breeze and a blue mail box to one side of the door. The next building to the west, an old adobe structure, bore a single green and orange sign advertising Arizona Feeds. As Jerry had said, the old, roofless adobe ruins stood as witnesses that

Arivaca had once been more prosperous.

Ambling toward what seemed to be the end of the street, Billy noticed an antique store with myriad harness and horse-drawn vehicle parts hanging on the outer walls. Turning the corner, he looked southward and saw the small stream draining the *cienega*. Beyond, huge, stately cottonwood trees with a carpet of dead leaves at their bases made Billy decide he would sleep there, instead of in the adobe ruins next to the bar.

Glad that he had kept his army boots, Billy crossed the stream and reached the cottonwood grove. A barkless deadfall served as a bench as he played some tunes on his banjo, and thought about meeting Pete in Tubac. *Talkin' to Pete about all the death and bloody wounded in 'Nam was something he and I had to do.* People who weren't there could never understand. Then, switching his thoughts to Myra, he wondered what progress she had made on her novel. So far, Arivaca did not excite him as a place to remain for any length of time.

Hunger forced him to return to the Gallo Negro where he had noticed there was a list of sandwiches available. Jerry took his order for a cheeseburger and a bottle of Budweiser. The three people sitting at the bar nodded at him, and returned to their conversations. The space in front of the bar had several small tables and chrome chairs with worn and cracked plastic covering the padding in the seats and backs, same vintage as the barstools. Billy decided the best place for him to play would be sitting on a barstool back against the front wall next to a small table.

Finished with his meal Billy ordered another beer. Jerry agreed with Billy's idea of where he should play. Carrying a barstool across the room he was soon ready to play. Several more customers had entered the Gallo Negro. As he began picking his way through various chords, Billy noticed the people turning to look his way.

CHAPTER FIVE

In the middle of his second song Billy looked down at the neck of the banjo to make sure he fingered the chord properly. When he looked up again he saw a girl walking from the entrance to the bar. Her long honey-blonde hair rippled over a blue denim dress that came down slightly below her knees, showing her finely tapered legs. She wore beaded, buckskin moccasins. After waving at the other customers, she spoke to Jerry. He went to the cooler and brought her a bottle of Michelob. She counted out her change, left the coins on the bar, picked up the bottle, and turned to walk over to one of the small tables next to where Billy sat on the barstool playing music.

As she came toward him Billy could not take his eyes away from her. Her bright blue eyes and blonde eyebrows were enhanced by her tanned oval face. Wearing no makeup whatsoever, her finely shaped mouth below her thin nose distracted Billy from his music. Almost forgetting the words, he looked away as she sat at the table.

Finishing the song, he glanced her way and found her eyes looking into his. Small dimples, just above and to the sides of her mouth, showed as she smiled at him. Embarrassed to be caught looking at her Billy grinned, and immediately began another song.

With a Budweiser in his hand, Jerry came over, motioned to Billy by raising his eyebrows toward the table where the girl sat. Billy nodded his head as he sang and Jerry put the bottle down opposite the girl. Billy glanced at the girl, and she smiled at him again.

When he finished the song, Billy leaned his banjo against the wall behind him, got off the barstool, and sat down at the table with the girl.

"Hi, I'm Banjo Billy."

"I'm Primrose," the girl said, lowering her eyes. "I like your music, Billy."

"Thanks, I try hard at it."

"You're new in town, aren't you?"

"Yeah, I just got here today. It's kind of a sleepy little place."

"That is why I like it. I live way out in the hills. I don't even come in this bar much, but I heard the music."

"I'm glad you did. None of the others seem to care if I'm playin' or not."

"Don't take that to heart. They are probably too stoned to care. How long are you planning on staying in Arivaca?"

"That's hard to say. I reckon it depends on the tips."

"If that's the determining factor you probably won't be here long. The people around here are not known for their big tips. Where are you staying?"

"Jerry told me about the adobe ruins next door and the cottonwood grove down by the crossin'. I'll try the cottonwood grove. It has to be better than the jungles of 'Nam."

"I don't know much about the jungles except what I saw on the news before I left home. How long were you over there?"

Billy briefly told her about the two tours and how it was trying to sleep in the jungles wondering if he would see the next sunrise. During their conversation he could sense that Primrose became more relaxed than when he had first sat down at her table. There is something about this girl that makes me feel comfortable to be with her. I wonder if she feels the same about me.

With her elbows on the table and her chin in her hands, Primrose said, "this might sound strange to you, but I don't mean it the way you might think. You can stay at my place if you want. I have a cabin with a roof that doesn't leak."

"That sounds a whole lot better than the cottonwood grove."

"Good. I'll take you out there when you're done here. If it doesn't suit you, I can bring you back to town in the morning."

"I am close to finishin' since nobody has noticed my open banjo case. Jerry told me not to expect any tips, but I said I would play for beer. Meetin' you is enough payment, Primrose."

"It's really nice to meet you too, Billy."

Billy clinked his bottle against her half-full bottle of Michelob, and stood up.

"I'll play "Proud Mary" just for you; then we can go," Billy said.

"That's one of my favorites."

Billy looked directly at Primrose as he sang. She kept smiling at him even when she occasionally closed her eyes. She clapped her hands when he ended the song. As he put his banjo in its case, she stood up and softly told him she would meet him outside the bar. Billy took the two beer bottles and the barstool up to the bar.

"Guess I'll call it a night, Jerry. Thanks for the beer."

"Hey, Banjo Billy, you play a mean banjo. Thanks," Jerry said.

Billy picked up his duffel bag and banjo, and joined Primrose as she stood next to an old Chevy van with the side door open. He put the duffel bag and banjo case inside. Primrose closed the door and walked around to the driver's side. Billy climbed into the passenger's seat, glad that he had met the beautiful Primrose, but wondering why she had invited him to her home to spend the night.

She started the motor, put the four-speed transmission into low, and headed toward the antique store. Passing the cottonwood grove, Billy glanced over at Primrose, smiled and felt happy that he was heading home with her. The gravel road, rutted in places, curved up into the foothills. In the moonlight Billy could make out the landscape of small mesquite trees and bushes growing on rounded hills. When they had traveled about five miles, Billy began to wonder just how far out in the hills Primrose lived.

"We have another three miles on this road before we turn off," Primrose said as if reading his thoughts. "Then, it's three miles over a two-rutted road to my place."

"Does anyone else live way out here?"

"Just Toby Watkins, but he lives over two hills away in another part of the gulch. He doesn't come around my place anymore. Let's say I had to discourage him even though my cabin is on his land."

"How come you live on his land?" Billy asked.

"Toby's parents were killed in a car wreck four years ago. They had a bunch of money, I guess. Toby was their only child so he inherited what his folks had. He was already into smoking weed. He took the money and bought this chunk of patented mining claims. He built a cabin on one of them and has lived there ever since."

"What does he do?"

"Mostly growing or smoking weed. He let me build my cabin on his land thinking he was going to hook up with me. That never happened, but we're friends. Toby's pretty mellow."

They arrived at the turn-off to Primrose's cabin. She slowed the van to ease it over the two-rutted road.

"Where did you come from, Primrose?" Billy asked.

"Southern California. I grew up in Malibu. My father is a screenwriter and my mother is a freelance stylist. Being connected with films neither one of my parents spent much time at home. When they did they surrounded themselves with weirdos."

"Why did you come to live way out here in the boonies?"

"My parents were insisting that I go to acting school after I graduated from high school. I guess they thought I would make it in Hollywood, especially with their connections. I never wanted to be an actress. I didn't like all the greed and lies. I almost dropped out of high school, but I had a plan."

"What kind of plan?"

"I figured that if I graduated from high school, I could get a car from my father as a graduation present. That way I could get away from that whole scene. I remember one day just before graduation. My father stopped at the breakfast table in his usual big hurry to get to the studio. He took his checkbook out, wrote a check for fifteen thousand dollars, and handed it to me. He told me I should go buy a car for a graduation present."

"Fifteen grand! Wow, that's quite a present."

"Part of my plan was to cash the check, buy an older van that I could sleep in, and get the hell away from Malibu and the rest of southern California."

"Sounds like you really hated livin' there."

"It is too fast, too many people, too much stress from everything and everyone, especially from my father and mother. I rarely saw them, but when I did they kept telling me what they thought was best for me. They didn't care what I wanted. I finally determined to go somewhere peaceful, some out of the way place where I could live with myself in quiet surroundings, doing whatever I decided to do."

"Do you think you have found that place?"

"Oh, yes," she replied. "It's totally righteous living here away from everything and everybody."

"That's cool, but what do you do for a living? That check you cashed in California wasn't enough to live on forever."

"Malibu High has a large tax base, so they have all sorts of creative courses. I got into beadwork and leather. That's what I do here. Toby poaches a lot of deer and he knows how to tan hides. He sells them cheap to me. Then I make purses, moccasins and vests. I put beadwork on them and sell all the stuff to a shop in Tubac."

"That's really far out," Billy said.

The van's headlights struck the small cabin. Primrose stopped the van, put the transmission in neutral, and opened the door.

"Wait here for a minute. I'll go inside and light the lamps."

Billy watched as Primrose, followed by a tan goat, went into the cabin. A few minutes later he saw light glowing through the curtains on the two windows at either side of the door. Returning to the van, Primrose turned off the headlights and the ignition.

"Here we are, Billy. Don't mind Pamela, she's a very friendly goat."

Billy got his things from in back of the van and followed

Primrose into the cabin.

"Put your stuff down, Billy. I'll heat up some coffee," she said.

Billy looked around at the inside of the cabin as Primrose lit the Coleman stove and put a blue enameled coffee pot on a burner. The wall away from the front door had two, old wood frame windows, each with eight panes of glass. A back door went outside from the kitchen area that occupied the left wall. There was a small sink, missing its faucets, sunk into the pine counter-top. Another window had been placed above the sink. A wood-burning box heater stood to the right of the back door. To the right end a double bed dominated a corner, and under one of the windows he saw the work bench where she did her bead and leather work. *This is really far out. She sure seems like a friendly sort to be living alone way out here.*

While the coffee heated, she started a fire in the cast iron box heater to warm the inside of the cabin. The dried piñon caught quickly, and the spicy scent of it burning filled the room.

"Coffee's ready," she announced. "You can have the kitchen chair; I'll get the one from my work bench. I have some goat milk and sugar if you want any."

"Just black is fine," Billy said. "You really have a nice pad here, Primrose."

"I love this place. I love living here with Pamela and the chickens. My father and mother would have fits if they saw how I lived, but I don't care about that anymore. They have no idea where I am."

"How did you manage to leave Malibu without them knowing it?"

"That was the easiest part. After I bought the van I parked it at a friend's house. My father didn't come to my graduation because he was on location somewhere. My mother was late. The morning after, I waited until my mother drove off to wherever she was working. I drove the van over, threw in all the stuff I wanted to take with me, and left. I'll bet I was in Arizona before my mother got home. I left a letter to them in which I asked them not to try and find me. Also, that I would write sometime in the future."

"Have you written to them?"

"That was almost three years ago. I have no more to say to them now than I did then."

"You and I are a lot alike when it comes to our parents," Billy said. "My father always wanted me to work for him sellin' farm machinery. He always complained about me playin' banjo. I got sick of it like you did, so after high school graduation I joined the army. I might have been better off sellin' farm machinery."

"Why is that?" she asked.

"I never realized what two tours in Vietnam would be like. Now that I am out, I can't stay put very long. I don't know why either."

"What a stinking war," Primrose said.

"For sure."

"I heard a speech once in Malibu," Primrose continued. "The dude said that all war is economic. The military/industrial complex and the politicians get us into wars to help our economy without caring about how many people get killed. They are finding out that a lot of people are rebelling against this war."

"That sounds reasonable," Billy said. "But a lot of those people who are against the war are blaming the guys who are in the service. Hell, I didn't have any choice. The army sent me to the stinkin' jungles for damn near two years."

Primrose filled their coffee mugs.

"Where did you hear about Arivaca?" Billy inquired.

"I went to Tubac first thinking that, being an art colony, I could do my thing there. But the rent's too high. I heard about Arivaca from the gal who sells my stuff. I drove up here, stayed under the cottonwoods for a week, and then met Toby in the Gallo Negro. I decided to change my name to Primrose instead of Ingrid Wallenbach."

"I guess you can meet everyone in town at the Gallo Negro."

"There are a few who never go in there. Anyway, I followed Toby out here and fell in love with the place. Toby helped me build the cabin from the old boards from two of his mining shacks. I bought the bed, the chairs and table, the sink and the curtains at a yard sale and moved in. I got the chickens and Pamela from a dude who was moving back to New York. I had a dog for a while, but he ran off or someone stole him."

"I have to say that I am a little confused," Billy said. He was still surprised at her invitation to stay at the cabin. She seemed to live a simple life even though there was something deeper about her that he could sense. This gal is different. She is beautiful all the way.

"How so?"

"You are very beautiful. You live way out here with some chickens and a goat. I don't understand why some dude besides Toby hasn't come into your life."

"The answer is not simple, but thank you for the compliment. Growing up with a father like mine either makes a girl want go out and screw around, or not trust men in general. I suppose I could have any number of men if I chose to, but I don't. The last time I had sex with a man was just before graduation. I thought I loved him and he me. Three days after that I saw him out with another girl."

"Why did you invite me out here, Primrose?"

"I guess I like your smile. I like listening to your music. There's something about you that I trust. I can't explain it. I was asking myself the same thing on the way out here."

"I like your smile, too."

"Just because I invited you here, doesn't mean I want to hop into bed with you, Billy. I just feel good being with you. And, don't get me wrong. I am not trying to tease you. I am not a tease. You are the only man who has been in this cabin besides Toby, and he knows I will not be anything but friends with him."

"There's something about you that makes me tingle." Billy said.

"I might as well tell you something I have never told anyone before," Primrose said. "Maybe you will understand me better. When I was sixteen my mother was on location and my father came home after I had gone to bed. Suddenly I woke up after he plunked himself down on my bed and put his arms around me. After telling me how much he loved me he began feeling my breasts and then began to climb onto me. It was awful. His booze smelling breath almost made me throw up. I was terrified. I wanted my father to love me, but not that way. He started hugging me and kissing me. I tried pushing him away, but in spite of his drunkenness, he was too strong for me. Those were not fatherly kisses. I didn't know what to do. I felt his hardness on my leg. Suddenly, I panicked and screamed."

"What did your father do then?"

"I guess my scream sobered him up enough that he got off me and left the room. I got up out of bed and pushed the dresser against the door, and went back to bed crying. I was scared and couldn't stop trembling all over. I felt hatred when I stopped shaking. If he had come back to force his way into my room, I would have beaten him with my tennis racket."

"What happened after that?"

"I was afraid of my father, and angry as hell. The bastard had betrayed me. After that awful night I wouldn't stay in the house if my mother wasn't there."

"Did you tell your mother what had happened?"

"I told her, but she didn't believe me. She told me not to worry about it because he was drunk. Then I was afraid of both of them."

"Did he ever try anything again?"

"I didn't give him a chance."

"I understand you better now. That's a helluva thing to go through," Billy said, and took her hand, squeezing it gently.

They talked for another hour. In his mind, Billy could not help comparing Primrose with Myra, who greeted sex with a passion like an athlete. He wondered what making love to

Primrose would be like.

Finally, Primrose suggested that they should get some sleep. Billy dug his blankets out of the duffel bag, folded them into a bedroll, and arranged it on the floor away from her bed. Fully clothed, except for his boots, he crawled in using the duffel bag for a pillow.

Primrose turned out one of the butane lamps and lowered the flame on the one on her bedside table. Billy could not keep his eyes away from her as she took off her denim dress. He saw her firm, round breasts in the dim light and the way her slender hips matched the rest of her contours. *I have never seen such a beautiful woman.* She fluffed out her long, blond hair and rubbed her belly. He wished she would remain standing by the bed so he could drink in her beauty, but she crawled between the sheets, and extinguished the lamp.

"Goodnight, Billy," she said, sweetly.

"Goodnight, beautiful Primrose."

He kept her naked image in his mind, and felt a yearning to take her into his arms. *I wonder if she is thinking about me like I'm thinking about her.*

It seemed to Billy that he had lain awake for an hour. He listened to the sound of her tossing and turning under the sheets.

"Billy, are you awake?" she asked softly.

"Yeah."

"Me, too. I hate thinking about you sleeping on that hard floor."

"It's softer than some floors I've slept on."

"Why don't you come and sleep on the bed?"

"With or without clothes?"

"You will probably be more comfortable without."

Getting out of his blankets Billy undressed, and in the dark, stepped carefully over to the bed. As soon as he had settled in next to her she put her arms around him and began kissing him.

"I guess I have made up my mind, Billy," she said. "I don't know what there is about you that gets me all excited. I can't get to sleep with all those feelings."

He caressed her breasts, kissed her tenderly, then passionately. She sighed as he ran his fingers over her silky thighs. "Oh yes, yes," she whispered, and reached for his swollen manhood.

Exhausted in a state of bliss, Primrose continued to hold Billy next to her. "I don't have much to compare with, but all I can say is that I have never felt this way before, Billy."

"There is no comparison," Billy said. "Before, it was different. With you I feel a deep sharing. It's mind-blowin'."

Primrose sat up on the side of the bed, struck a wooden match, and lit the lamp on the bedside table. Billy reached for her, drew her tenderly to him, and kissed her. "I have never known a woman like you, Primrose. Where in the world did you learn how to make love like that?"

"I must have learned tonight. I never thought a man could affect me the way you do."

Billy got his banjo. Sitting on the edge of the bed next to her, he composed a song about finding a primrose growing wild in a valley. The words seem to have been waiting for the music. "I am going to remember that one," he said.

"It's beautiful, Billy."

"That's because you are beautiful."

He leaned the banjo against the wall and took her in his arms again.

"I don't think I will ever have enough of you, Primrose."

"I know what you mean."

The sun had long since splashed light among the oak trees along the creek when Pamela's bleating awakened them. Billy opened his eyes, looked over at the peaceful look on Primrose's face as she eased herself out of bed. The night chill in the cabin made her shudder momentarily. She slipped into a well-worn bathrobe, built a fire in the box heater, and took the coffee pot outside to toss out the old grounds. Pamela trotted over and nudged Primrose, letting her know that milking time was long overdue. "In a minute, Pamela." he heard her say as he watched her scratch the goat behind her ears.

Back inside, Primrose filled the coffee pot with fresh water from a bucket that stood next to the sink. Placing the coffee pot on the box heater she pulled on a pair of threadbare Levi's, put on and buttoned up a dark blue woolen sweater. Slipping into her moccasins she was ready to deal with the goat. Opening a five gallon garbage can, she filled a coffee can with grain. But before leaving the cabin she opened the door to the box heater and added two pieces of piñon along with a chunk of oak to the fire. "I'll be back before the coffee's ready. Pamela's an easy milker."

Billy left the bed to watch through the window.

With the ration of grain for Pamela and her milk pail Primrose proceeded with her morning chores. Pouring the grain in the feed trough at the front of the milking platform, she sat on a stool at Pamela's side, facing the rear of the platform. Placing the pail under the goat's teats Primrose stroked Pamela's bag, and began to milk.

Returning to the cabin with the full milk pail she glanced at Billy by the window. Still naked, he stood smiling at her. "You're even beautiful milkin' that goat."

"And you're handsome standing there naked as a jaybird."

Filling a measuring cup with fresh coffee grounds she took the top off the pot and dumped them into the nearly boiling water.

"The coffee will be ready in a little bit. I'm going out and get the eggs."

Billy had been watching her every move, marveling at his good fortune at meeting such a woman. Her tousled hair and the way she did everything gracefully made him feel fully content. He followed her with his eyes as she came back with the eggs. "Those old biddies are laying pretty good," she said, putting a wicker basket on the counter. "Eight eggs from twelve old hens in winter isn't bad at all."

"How did you learn all these things?" Billy asked.

"When you're out here alone, you either figure things out for yourself or find someone to ask."

The coffee began boiling and the slight overflow sizzled on the top of the box heater. Primrose took a dish towel, grabbed the handle of the pot, and put it down on the counter next to the sink. After dipping the measuring cup into the bucket of water, she removed the top of the coffee pot, tilted it, and poured some of the cold water down the inside. Returning the pot to its upright position she rinsed out the mugs they had used the night before and filled them with the fresh brew. "After our coffee and eggs, I'll show you around outside," she said.

"Why did you pour water into the pot?" Billy asked, sitting in the chair he had occupied the previous night.

"That's one way to settle the grounds. I learned that from camping with my uncle up in the Sierras."

Primrose sat down at the table and sipped her coffee, looking at Billy over the rim of her mug.

"Your uncle sounds very different than your father."

"Uncle Dave was my mother's brother. I was closer to him than to my own father. He was a commercial fisherman, but he loved camping in the Sierras. His boat capsized during a bad storm off Baja California. He and his crew drowned."

"That must have hit you hard."

"It still does when I think about it," she said, a tone of sadness in her voice.

Primrose refilled Billy's mug, and began preparing scrambled eggs in a cast iron skillet. She took a bottle of olive oil from a shelf, and poured some into the skillet. "Don't let me forget to get the ice out of the van. I forgot all about it last night."

"I forgot about everythin' last night," Billy said, and grinned.

Before breaking the eggs into a bowl Primrose stepped over to Billy, leaned down and kissed him.

Adding a little goat milk, she whisked the eggs to combine the yolks, whites and milk. Then emptying the contents into the skillet, she began stirring the eggs slowly. When they were done to her satisfaction, she spooned them onto two plates. She handed Billy a fork as she put the salt and pepper shakers on the table. Then she filled her coffee mug, and sat down.

"I never had a man to cook for," she said. "It feels good."

"It feels good to be on the receivin' end," Billy said. "I'm tryin' to figure out how I can help you, but you seem to have everythin' solved."

"Today we can haul water up from the creek and go out for firewood. But first, I want to show you around."

"That sounds good to me," he said.

"Once we get those chores done we can do whatever."

"That sounds even better," he said, and grinned.

Realizing what she had said, Primrose lowered her eyes to her plate.

"I'll show you how I take a bath without running water," she said, trying to recover from her slight embarrassment.

Finished with their breakfast Primrose put the dishes in the sink and lifted the bucket of water onto the top of the box heater. Opening the door to the firebox, she tossed in more piñon. "All right," she said, "time for the grand tour."

She began with the chicken pen. "I have a self-feeder for the old biddies. As they eat the feed from under the bin, more feed falls down into the trough. The water trough is designed the same way. I used to let them run loose because I didn't have to feed and water them, but they would get into the cabin and crap on the floor. My method now is more expensive and more work, but it keeps the chicken shit off the cabin floor and I never loose any eggs in the bushes. And, the pen keeps the coyotes away from my egg machines. I should probably get a rooster and raise some chicks to replace these old gals. But, fertile eggs spoil without refrigeration. Unfertile eggs last a long time."

Next, they came to a black bucket, hanging from a wooden framework by a rope that went through pulleys. A shower head and a valve with a small chain had been attached to the bottom of the bucket. "This is my solar shower. I fill the bucket with water, hoist it up with the block and tackle, and the sun heats the water. As I stand under it and pull the chain, the warm water comes through the shower head and I get wet. After I soap up, I use what water is left to rinse. This is a spring, summer and fall shower."

He visualized her rinsing the soap out of her hair. "I'll bet you are a beautiful sight to watch. Have you ever been caught naked out here?"

"Toby almost caught me once, but he was too stoned to notice from a distance."

She pointed to a smooth pole lashed between two oaks.

"That's the biffy, or whatever you want to call it," she said. "It's not much fun in the rain, but building an outhouse isn't fun either."

Primrose led him by the hand down to the creek, a distance of about twenty-five yards. Standing silently with their arms around each other's waists, they listened to the soft sound of the stream as it gurgled over rocks and stones on its way to a major canyon several miles below.

"In high school, we had to read some book about a pond," Billy said. "This reminds me about that even though it's a creek."

"That's weird, I have thought about that too. Thoreau's *Walden*, or something like that. We had to read that, too."

They stopped their conversation and listened to the creek.

Returning to the cabin they got buckets for carrying water. Back at the creek Primrose showed Billy where she had dug out a shallow hole and where she filled the buckets under the small waterfall she had made by piling rocks to form a dam. When full, the load was heavy. Billy marveled at the ease with which Primrose carried the water to the cabin.

Lifting the bucket of warm water from the stove to the floor, she replaced it with two others and put more wood on the fire. From outside she carried in a big, galvanized washtub and put it on the floor. From some shelves she brought a large beach towel, unfolded it half way, and spread it on the floor next to the washtub. "When the water warms up, we can have our bath. While we wait we might as well have some coffee. I'll heat it on the Coleman stove."

She lit the stove and put the coffee pot over the flame. Billy picked up his banjo and began to play chords. When he felt ready, he played the song he had composed for Primrose.

Periodically she felt the water in the buckets on the box heater and added wood to the fire. To get ready for the bath she brought out more towels, a coffee can and a bar of soap. Finally satisfied with the temperature, she poured the warm water from the three buckets into the washtub.

"I've never taken a bath with someone else before. I guess I'll get into the tub and you can pour water on me with this can. Then, I'll do the same to you. We can stand on the big towel and soap each other down. After that, it's back in the tub for the rinse off."

They took off their clothes. Primrose stepped into the washtub and sat down. Billy took the coffee can, and poured the warm water over her head until she was thoroughly wet. She raised herself up and stepped out on the towel. Billy knelt down in the tub while she poured water over his body.

They took turns soaping each other. Covered with lather, they put their arms around each other. "Wow," Primrose said. "What a way to take a bath!"

The lather making their bodies slippery, the sensations raised their desire for one another.

"I wonder if this is the way seals feel when they do it," Billy said.

"Let's lie down and find out," Primrose laughingly suggested, and unfolded the towel.

By the time they had finished their love-making, the soap had dried. After rinsing and drying themselves, Billy helped carry the washtub outside to dump out the soapy water.

"I forgot the ice again," Primrose said.

They got dressed, went to the van, and brought in another

styrofoam chest containing a block of ice. Primrose opened the chest in the kitchen area, rearranged the contents, and put in the block of ice. While making room for the ice, she had set a bowl of beans and a package of venison on the counter. "I've got some beans and there's some venison Toby brought over the other day. We'll have a feast tonight."

"You're the cook," Billy said.

She opened the chest again.

"I forgot. I have a couple of beers left."

"Now you're talkin' feast," Billy said. "Let's have the beers now."

"I've got a little weed," Primrose said. "We can do a number along with the beer."

"Helluva good idea."

"We have enough firewood to last until tomorrow," Primrose said.

"Besides, we're all clean," Billy added. "There's no sense in spoiling that great bath by chopping wood."

"I have a little mesquite firewood. The venison will taste better broiled on mesquite coals than fried. I'll get the fire started outside, then we can smoke a joint."

She started the fire in the middle of a circle of rocks. Billy sat playing chords on the banjo while she waited for the piñon to start burning well before she added four logs of mesquite.

Back in the cabin she handed Billy the two beers and dug into her beaded buckskin purse for the baggy of marijuana and cigarette papers.

"There's enough for a couple of numbers," she said. "Go ahead and roll one while I put the beans into a pot and on the grill."

Billy took a cigarette paper from the package, held one end with his thumb, index and middle fingers on his left hand, and sprinkled some pot into the valley in the paper. Then, deftly folding and rolling in one motion, he formed the joint, held it up to lick the glued edge with his tongue, and sealed it with his two index fingers. Folding one end over, he put it on the table.

Satisfied with the fire and having placed the pot of beans on the grill where they would warm but not burn, Primrose returned and sat down. Billy lit the joint and took a drag, holding it in his lungs. He passed the number to Primrose who did the same. They sipped their beers in between hits on the joint until it was too small to smoke without burning their fingers. They laughed together when Billy commented, "That's pretty good stuff."

"Home-grown. I had a few plants last year. This is all that's left. I doubt if I'll grow any this year. It is so mellow out here that I don't smoke dope much anymore."

"Me neither," Billy said. "We did a lot in 'Nam, but since I got back, I don't really care about it much. It is kind of nice to smoke a number with you, though. I don't have the same high I used to feel. It's just a mellow feeling."

"I know what you mean."

"In 'Nam we'd go into Saigon and really get stoned out of our minds to escape the bullshit." *For some reason I can talk about 'Nam with her differently than I could with Myra.*

"Vietnam must have been pretty brutal. I've heard that the guys over there did a lot of drugs."

"Some got hooked on heroin and coke. I didn't go any further than pot. A bunch of those guys on heroin didn't come home. I figured I needed my mind to be clear out in the jungle, so I only smoked dope when I got into Saigon. Since then, I have often wondered why it was so easy to get over there."

"The whole Vietnam thing makes a lot of people wonder about a lot of things," Primrose said.

She suddenly remembered the beans, jumped up, grabbed a wooden spoon from the counter, and went outside to check on them. Billy looked out of the door.

"Are they burned?" he asked.

"They're fine," she replied, looking up from her stirring. "The coals look just right for the venison, too."

"I'll bring the meat out."

"There's a long fork under the sink."

Billy unwrapped the venison steaks and took the fork from underneath the sink. At the fireplace he placed the steaks on the grill. Wisps of smoke puffed up when the meat came in contact with the hot metal.

"I'll get the plates while you do the steaks," she said.

As he watched the venison broil, Billy's thoughts were about the joy he had felt since arriving at the cabin. And the only time he had thought about 'Nam was when it came up during their conversation.

Flipping the steaks over he thought about playing and singing at the Mangey Moose, and the satisfaction he derived from his audiences showing their appreciation. At La Cantina de Anza the people had tossed dollars into the open banjo case. But, at the Gallo Negro the only appreciation shown him was a couple of beers from Jerry. However, he was discovering that the most important audience he ever had anywhere was Primrose.

She brought the plates out of the cabin and held them as he speared the steaks from the grill. Billy followed her carrying the pot of beans.

Next day with an axe and a Swiss saw they spent the morning cutting firewood. They cut up a dead oak tree that was within walking distance, but Primrose wanted some piñon for quick heat. That meant driving the van up a narrow road to a slope where piñon and juniper grew in scattered stands. She had been there before, and knew there were five dead trees, four piñon and one juniper.

After stacking the firewood Primrose, with her hands on her hips, stood back to look at what they had accomplished. "That should last a couple of weeks if a cold spell doesn't come in," she said.

"We can always go out and cut more," Billy commented. *It's fun working with her. She knows what she's doin', too.*

"It's nice to have you along."

"How is the food supply?" Billy asked.

"I have plenty of beans and lentils. I'll bake some bread tomorrow."

"Let's go into Arivaca. I have money. We can get some ice, beer and anythin' else," Billy suggested.

"Beer sounds good," she said. "Are you thinking about playing for beer at the Gallo Negro?"

"I'll bring my banjo, but I am not about to play for that bunch. I would rather play for you out here."

The store in town offered an adequate variety of meats, produce and canned goods. Besides the groceries and ice Billy insisted on putting ten dollars worth of gasoline in the van.

"Let's have a beer for the road at the Gallo Negro," Billy suggested.

"We have a whole case in here."

"That's all the more we will have at home. Besides, I'm buyin'."

CHAPTER SIX

They locked the van outside the bar. Inside there were two cowboys sitting on one side, and on the other side, a man with wavy, brown hair wearing green polyester trousers and a Raider's jacket sat chatting with Jerry.

Primrose sat down at one of the small tables while Billy went up to the bar to order their beers. Jerry reached into the cooler for the Budweisers, opened them, and handed the bottles to Billy.

"Did you bring your banjo?" Jerry asked.

Billy pursed his lips and slightly shook his head. "I'm not playing today; just came by for groceries."

Jerry brought the change, and slapped the coins on the bar. With the bottles in one hand Billy picked up the change, put it in his pocket and took the beer to the table. "Here's to the most beautiful woman in the world," Billy said.

They lifted their bottles and clicked them together, smiling as they looked into each other's eyes. Out of the corner of his eye Billy watched Jerry huddle over, talking to the man in the Raider's jacket. The man rose from his barstool and ambled over to stand by the table where Primrose and Billy sat. Reaching into his pocket he took out a business card and put it in front of Primrose. "Well, Ingrid Wallenbach, it took me a while, but I found you," he said. "Henry Jameson. I'm a private investigator from Los Angeles retained by your father and mother. You can call me Hank."

Primrose, obviously startled by the sudden appearance of the man, looked furtively at Billy, then back to the private investigator. Without being invited Hank had reached for a chair from an adjoining table, and had sat down.

Billy felt a surge of anger at Henry Jameson. Waving his index finger at the private investigator he said, with firmness in the tone of his voice, "I don't think she wants to talk to you, Mr. Jameson."

"I don't know who you are, sir, but my business is with Miss Wallenbach."

Billy glared at the man. *If he gives Primrose any shit, I'll toss his ass out into the street.*

"I really have nothing to say to you," Primrose said curtly. "You can go back and tell my parents that you found me and collect your money. Other than that I have nothing to say to you or to them."

"Ingrid, they are very concerned about you and want you to come home."

"When I lived with them they were never home," Primrose said. "Neither of my parents ever had any time for me. They are both married to their work. I left their home. Now I have a home of my own. Maybe you can tell me why it took them so long to look for me."

"I have no ideas about that, Ingrid," Jameson said.

"Look, Mr. Jameson, you really should leave her alone," Billy said.

"What is your name?" Jameson asked.

"My name is my business," Billy replied. "And the lady doesn't seem to want anything to do with you," Billy said, angry at his insistence.

"All right, Ingrid, I'll tell you what," Jameson said. "I get paid by the day, but if you return with me to Malibu, I will get a five grand bonus. I am willing to split that with you."

"Mr. Jameson, you are not going to get your bonus at all because I am not going back to Malibu."

"Come on. Let's get out of here, Primrose," Billy said, and stood up. "Mr. Jameson is a pain in the ass."

Primrose stood up and put her arm around Billy's waist.

"Have a nice trip back to Malibu, Mr. Jameson," she said, and pointing to the business card on the table, "I won't be needing your card."

Billy and Primrose left the Gallo Negro, and hurried into the van. Backing up into the street, Primrose turned west after noting the white Ford sedan with California license plates. She scowled.

"Those bastards," she said. "Why can't they leave me alone? They didn't care about me when I was home, so why are they sending a stupid ass like Jameson after me?"

"I wonder how the hell he found you," Billy said.

Primrose sighed disgustedly. "Probably from the van's registration. I had to register it in Arizona. I just hope he doesn't try to follow us out to the cabin."

"I'll keep a lookout," Billy said, turning to face the back windows in the rear door.

"That son-of-a-bitch, Jerry. I'll bet he pointed me out to that stupid private-eye."

"Yeah, I saw Jerry whisperin' to him just before he came over to our table."

"I will never go in that dump again," she said.

"That goes for both of us," Billy agreed.

The dust from the dirt road churned up by the van obscured Billy's view. When they were within a half mile of the turnoff to the cabin, Billy suggested that Primrose stop to let the dust settle, and to see if Jameson might be following. With no sign of the white Ford, they continued to the cabin, and unloaded the groceries and Billy's banjo.

Billy opened two of the beers and put them on the table. Primrose picked one up, but did not sit down. The scowl returned to her face.

"I can't figure out why they took so long to try and find me," she said.

"That does seem strange. Maybe it took this long for their guilt to build up enough."

"They are both so wrapped up in their work that I can't see why they would even miss me."

"I wouldn't worry about it. I think you have seen the last of Jameson."

"I sure as hell hope so. Here, I have found a real mellow life. I enjoy doing what I do, and now the very people I escaped from are bugging me."

Billy started a fire in the box heater. After the wood was burning strongly, he closed the damper on the galvanized chimney pipe, and took Primrose into his arms.

"There isn't a damn thing they can do to you, Beautiful."

"I suppose you are right, but knowing how screwed up my parents are there's no telling what they might try."

"I'll bet that if we get out of our clothes and under the covers, you will forget about Jameson and your parents."

"It's worth a try," she said.

Warmed by the heat radiating from the cast iron box heater, the cabin felt snug and comfortable as they lay naked next to each other after their love making.

"I think I'll get up and make that spaghetti dinner we planned on," Billy said. "You, my beautiful princess, can stay here in bed so I can look at you."

Primrose smiled and kissed him.

"I will," she said. "If you stay naked so I can look at you."

Billy kissed her and left the bed. Adding wood to the fire, he began preparing the meal. In between stages, while waiting for water to boil or sauce to heat, he sat on the edge of the bed caressing her. "This is really righteous," she said. "I never would have believed a man could make me feel so beautiful and calm and wanted."

"You do the same to me, sweet lady."

They sat naked at the table, enjoying the dinner and each other.

"You are quite a cook for a banjo player, Billy."

"I've never done a lot of cookin', but I've watched some."

"Have you ever cooked in the nude before?"

"I can't say that I have," Billy replied, and grinned.

"I like being naked around here. There are days in the summer when I don't put on any clothes."

They heard Pamela bleating by the back door.

"Good lord, I forgot all about milking," she said. "I'll have to get dressed now."

"Bummer," Billy said.

For the next two weeks they lived an idyllic life in and around the cabin. Primrose worked on her beading and buckskin purses while Billy practiced songs on his banjo. He enjoyed watching her work as he played for her. Thinking back to his days with Myra and having to leave the trailer while she wrote her book, there was no comparison with the way he felt toward Primrose.

The recurring dream about the Viet Cong coming out of the jungle snarling at him awakened him some nights. On those occasions Primrose took him into her arms and they fell back to sleep again.

One afternoon, Primrose finished the last of the beaded, buckskin purses she had been working on. "I have to go to Tubac to deliver all this stuff before the tourists leave," she said. "Do you want to go with me and visit your buddy, Pete?"

"That would be fun. You name the day."

"Let's get away early tomorrow morning."

Tubac looked different from the last time Billy had walked through the village. The festival booths were gone, but a few automobiles with out-of-state license plates crept through the streets as the occupants gawked at the shops and local craft people. Primrose parked the van in front of an adobe complex with several shops located around a central patio.

"Come in and meet Brenda, Billy. Then, I'll see you later at La Cantina de Anza."

Billy took his banjo out of the van, and followed Primrose to a small gallery called Serendipity. She introduced him to Brenda, a thirtyish looking woman with streaks of premature gray in her black hair. Brenda's smile and arched eyebrows looked like she was thinking about Primrose sleeping with the banjo player. The women began looking at the things Primrose had brought, so Billy left to visit Pete.

"Hey, Bill, where have you been hanging out?" Pete asked from behind the bar.

"Arivaca," Billy replied.

"Did Clearance get to New Orleans?"

"I expect he did. He said he had the bus fare."

Pete opened a Budweiser, and put it on the bar in front of Billy. "Thanks, Pete."

"Are you playing in Arivaca?"

"Hell, no. I played one afternoon and didn't make a dime."

"Then what have you been doing?"

"Hangin' out with a beautiful chick," Billy replied. "She will be over here in a while. We came down here to deliver the stuff she makes."

"Sounds like you're having fun."

"Most fun I ever had."

"We had some good times in Saigon, remember?"

"Yeah," Billy replied. "But those times can't compare with the fun I'm having now."

"Damn, this sounds serious," Pete said.

"I think it might get that way if I stick around much longer."

The two ex-soldiers reminisced for a half an hour before an older couple came into the bar. The man wore a cap with "Retired" embroidered on it, and a tee-shirt stretched over his large stomach, stating he was an Ohio State football fan. The flower-patterned shorts didn't cover his knobby knees and nearly hairless, bony legs. The woman dressed in the same patterned shorts, wore a blouse that revealed the contours of her large sagging breasts and the rolls of fat going down past her waist. The fat rolls, like foothills below a mountain range, continued past the bottom of her shorts.

They sat at a table. Pete, still behind the bar, asked for their order.

"Give us a couple of margaritas," the man said. "Do you serve food?"

"The kitchen opens for lunch at eleven," Pete said, and began preparing the drinks.

The man turned his fat wrist to glance at his watch. Billy

took out the banjo and after leaving the case open in front of him with a dollar in it, began tuning the instrument. "I'll entertain you while you're waitin' for lunch," he said, and began "Camptown Races."

Primrose came in before he had finished the song. She sat on the barstool next to him, smiling. Finishing the last verse, he turned toward Pete. "Pete, this is Primrose."

Pete stepped over and took her hand.

"Sweetheart, this is my buddy, Pete."

"Goddam, Bill," Pete said, with his eyes on Primrose. "You always had a good eye for a pretty girl, but this one is beautiful."

"That's what I thought when I saw her," Billy said.

Primrose blushed slightly at the compliments. "You guys probably say that to all the girls you see," she said.

The fat man called for another round, then glanced at his wrist watch again. "Lemme see your menu," he called out to Pete.

"Primrose, what'll it be?" Pete asked. "It's on me."

"The same as Billy."

Billy began playing again. Primrose thanked Pete for the beer, and turned to watch with adoring eyes as Billy sang and played his banjo.

Pete glanced at the clock on the wall, stepped up to the order window going through to the kitchen and tapped the bell to summon a waitress. A nice looking Hispanic girl, wearing a white peasant blouse and large, red, oval earrings appeared. Pete directed her to the table with the fat couple. The lunch crowd began to come into the bar and patio. Pete stayed behind the bar making drink orders. Billy continued with the entertainment.

The waitress brought heaping combination plates of Mexican food to the fat couple. They began gorging themselves. The patio soon became crowded. Two more waitresses began handing out menus and taking orders. Pete made drinks, uncapped beer bottles, and handled the cash register.

The Ohio couple cleaned every morsel from their plates. The man, with surgical scars on both knees, waddled up to the bar with his check and a fistful of bills. Pete rang it up and handed the man his change. He took a five dollar bill from the change, leaned over with a grunt, and dropped it into the open banjo case.

"Thanks young feller. That was mighty nice music," he said.

Billy stopped singing long enough to thank the man. Finished with the song, he suggested to Primrose that they go out on the patio where most of the people had gathered for lunch. Billy set up where he had played before, and as people finished their lunches and left, they put money in the open case. By two o'clock in the afternoon the lunch crowd had thinned.

Katherine came out to the patio just as Billy finished his last song.

"Wow, you were singing them right off the street, Billy," she said. "You should be here every day. Have you had lunch?"

"Not yet," he said, and turned toward Primrose. "Katherine, this is my friend, Primrose."

"It's nice to meet you, Primrose. Let me get both of you our green chile luncheon plate. It is really delicious."

"That would be great," Billy said.

He gathered up the bills from the case, counted them quickly, and put the banjo away. "Hey, Beautiful," he said. "I made sixty-four bucks."

"That's wonderful, my man," she said. "You earned every nickel. You were great up there. I have good news, too. Brenda paid me six hundred for the stuff she sold of mine during the festival. I was pleasantly surprised."

"That is super good," Billy said. "Don't tell anyone here, or we might have to pay for our lunch."

Pete joined them at their table in the bar. Katherine stopped by and asked Billy to come in regularly to play for the lunch crowd. "It will only be another month before all the tourists go back east," she said.

"I appreciate the chance, Katherine, but it is quite a drive from Arivaca."

"Come by whenever you can. You can always count on lunch."

They were in great spirits driving back to the cabin. Primrose milked Pamela while Billy started the fire in the box heater. After a light supper of warmed up beans, they sat at the table sipping their beers.

"You really like entertaining people, don't you, Billy?"

"I have to admit that it makes me feel good."

"You were on a terrific high today. I was watching the people out there. Most of them stopped talking while you played."

"That sure is a different crowd than at the Gallo Negro," he said, "Too bad Tubac is so long a drive."

"Maybe you should go down there for the month," Primrose suggested. "You could make good money and have fun making it."

"The money isn't worth it right now. Bein' with you is worth more than any money I could make playin' banjo in Tubac."

"That is nice of you to say, Billy. How about I drive down there once or twice a week so you can play. I got that big bunch of money from Brenda, so I don't have to work too hard. Besides, I left her enough stuff to sell until the season's over."

"I guess we can think about it," Billy said. "I would want to pay for the gas."

"Okay," she replied. "What days do you want to be there?"

"There is only one thing I am thinkin' about right now."

"And, what might that be, Banjo Billy?"

"Don't tell me I have to talk you into making love."

They laughed together, and playfully removed each other's clothes.

They decided that Saturdays would be best for playing at La Cantina de Anza. For the next month they drove to Tubac, arriving before the lunch crowd began coming in. Primrose dropped in for short visits with Brenda before joining Billy at the cantina. The first three Saturdays brought good crowds and good tips, and Billy had established a small following from the wealthy locals living in the country club estates. On the fourth

Saturday, it was almost as if someone had shut off a valve.

Billy asked Katherine if the season had come to a screeching halt.

"It happens every March," she replied. "Now, we have to tough it out over the rest of spring and summer. I may close the restaurant and just keep the bar open this year."

"I guess I might as well stay home," Billy suggested.

"I wish I could tell you to keep coming here to play. I like your music and you have been very good for business. Wait here a minute. I have something for you."

Billy and Primrose continued to chat with Pete. Katherine returned a few minutes later and gave Billy a small white envelope. "I hope you will be back in the fall," she said. "Have a good summer, you two."

"Thanks, Katherine. You, too," Billy said.

"We will probably see you from time to time, Pete. Will you be here for the summer?"

"I doubt it. Since I work for tips here, there's not much point in staying. I'm thinking about trying San Diego, or even going to Mexico to buy silver jewelry for import. But, for sure, I'll be here for the next festival."

"That's good," Billy said. "I don't want to lose track of you again. If something comes up, write me at General Delivery, Arivaca."

"I'll do that, Bill, but I'll probably be here. It's good food; the beer's free, and I like the winter weather."

As Primrose drove back to the cabin, Billy was silent most of the way, thinking about all the fire fights and other crap Pete and he had gone through in the jungles of Vietnam. Primrose suspected what was going on in Billy's mind, and left him with his thoughts.

After supper Billy asked her if there were any old outhouses at the claims where she got the lumber. "I remember one. Why?"

"I've been thinkin' about you sittin' naked on that damn pole out there. It is unpleasant in the rain. And it does rain here sometimes."

"When it rains I use the old chamber pot that's under the bed."

"Anyhow, Toby or somebody might come in here before you were able to get off the pole. I just wouldn't want that to happen."

"It hasn't happened yet," she said.

"That doesn't mean it won't."

"Billy, I think you're too worried about me."

"I just love you, Primrose, and I don't want anybody else lookin' at you naked."

"I love you, too, Banjo Billy. When do you want to start on moving that outhouse?"

"Tomorrow will be fine," Billy said, and grinned.

Billy felt a little scared after his declaration of love, but it did not prevent him from taking Primrose into his arms, and carrying her over to the bed.

The next morning, they drove to one of the claims to dismantle its old outhouse. With a wrecking bar and hammer they had it in pieces before noon. Billy had been careful not to split the old gray lumber, and removed the rusty nails as he had proceeded. After their lunch Primrose decided where she wanted the structure, and Billy began digging the hole.

Using nails that Primrose had kept after building the cabin, Billy had the outhouse ready for use by early afternoon the following day. Primrose had been working at her workbench. When he called, she went to see his handiwork. Running her hand over the "one-holer," she giggled.

"What's funny?" Billy asked.

"I was just wondering how many asses have sat on that hole over the years."

"Yours will be the prettiest."

"Guaranteed no splinters?"

"I already went over it with the sandpaper you had with the nails and screws."

She put her arms around him.

"I love you too much. You are so nice to me."

"Build a girl an outhouse, and no tellin' what it'll get you."

The next of Billy's projects was more demanding. He told her about his plan one morning after she had milked the goat. "I'm thinkin' that I could fix things so you would have runnin' water to the sink."

"Good lord, first an outhouse, then running water. Next you'll have me using electricity."

"I could do that too."

"Forget the electricity. Let me hear about this running water scheme."

"Back in Springfield, the old man used to sell sump pumps to farmers who had basements. They get a lot more rain there than here, and sometimes the basements got flooded. So, to get the water out of the basements the farmers used sump pumps to pump the water out. Other people besides farmers used them too."

"What does that have to do with running water in my sink?" Primrose asked.

"I can put a sump pump down by the creek, run a pipeline to a storage tank up the hill from the cabin, then another pipeline from the tank to the cabin. The water in the tank will flow by gravity right to the sink. All you have to do is turn it on."

"This sump pump; how does it work?"

"I can rig it with a gasoline engine, and it will suck water from the creek and pump it into the storage tank."

"I don't know a thing about gasoline engines," Primrose said.

"I can show you how to start it and that's about all you need to know, except how to change the oil once in a while. That's easy, too. With this system you won't have to carry water to the cabin from the creek in buckets."

"Hauling buckets from the creek is good exercise."

"Are you being stubborn?"

"Not really," she said, and gave him an impish smile. "But, I'll bet carrying those buckets of water keeps my boobs firm."

"If that's true, maybe I had better forget about the water

system," Billy said, and grinned.

They laughed at the banter between them.

"What will all this cost?" Primrose asked.

"That depends on how much a used sump pump is worth around here. But, you don't have to worry about that because I want to pay for it."

"It sounds like a lot of work, too."

"There will be work with a pick and shovel to dig a trench for the pipeline. You can keep your boobs firm helpin' with that."

"You are really bad."

"We can check in Arivaca for an old sump pump, but it's probably easier to find one in Tucson. Besides, we need to get the pipe there."

"When do you want to go?"

"Tomorrow. I might as well get started."

Early next morning, while Primrose milked Pamela, Billy paced the distance from the creek to the spot on the hill where he wanted to install the storage tank, then back to the cabin.

After breakfast they drove into Arivaca. Checking the bulletin board where people posted messages, they saw nothing that might lead them to a pump, so they continued driving into Tucson. Remembering a store that he had passed while walking to Gus and Andy's to play his banjo, he gave Primrose the directions.

By noon Billy had bought everything he needed. The store had a re-built sump pump already equipped with a small gasoline engine, and the PVC plastic pipe and glue.

Out in the yard behind the store Billy found a small, used, galvanized storage tank that would fit in the back of the van. There were several bullet holes in it so the man sold it for five dollars. Billy bought enough bolts, nuts and steel and rubber washers to patch the holes, two cheap adjustable wrenches, and a hack-saw with which to cut the plastic pipe.

"Here, you are a musician and you know all this other stuff," Primrose said, as they drove out of the city. "Where did you learn how to put in a water system?"

"I worked for the old man before I joined the army. I never did put in a water system before, but it's easy enough to figure out."

"Is it going to work?"

"Damn right, it will work, but it will take a lot of diggin'."

Back at the cabin, they unloaded the storage tank at the spot Billy had chosen to install it. Billy carried the pump down to the creek, and left it on the bank near the rock dam where Primrose filled her buckets.

He found a rounded, smooth rock to use in planishing the bullet holes in the tank. Holding the rock on the outside, he hammered all the jagged flanges flat where the slugs had entered. Then he placed a steel washer on the cap end of each of the bolts, then a rubber washer that would seal against the outside of the tank. After inserting a bolt through a hole, he put two more washers on the bolt in reverse order before threading the nut onto the bolt. After they were hand tight, he used the adjustable wrenches to tighten, and thereby seal the holes.

Concentrating on the project helped Billy to diminish his desire to return to performing. During the previous week he had been thinking a lot about Jackson and the Mangey Moose Saloon, wondering if he could find a gig in Tucson.

The pick and shovel work began the following morning. They worked together, alternating between swinging the pick and shoveling the loose dirt from the trench. Loosening the rocks imbedded in the ground became the most difficult part of the project. Working steadily through the morning, they were a third of the way to the storage tank from the creek by noon.

After taking a break for lunch they went back to digging. Several large rocks required a lot of effort and time to dislodge. By early evening, they quit for the day, with about a third of the distance yet to finish. Billy leveled off the spot where he planned to install the storage tank while Primrose milked the goat. They welcomed the stew that had been simmering all afternoon.

Finished with the trench by mid-morning the following day, Billy made a base for the sump pump, started it to make sure everything worked properly, and began gluing the pipe together. When he had the line to the storage tank in place, he started on the line to the cabin, placing it in the same trench where it came close to the building. After chiseling out a hole in the floor, he installed the pipe and valve so that all Primrose would have to do to have water in the sink would be to turn the handle.

They started the engine on the pump, trotted up to the storage tank, and watched as the water gurgled in. The flow was slow, just what Billy had wanted so that the pump wouldn't exceed the streamflow in the little creek. "Tell me when it's full," he said. "I'm goin' down so I can shut off the pump."

He trotted back down to the creek and was happy to see that the creek's flow was sufficient. When Primrose waved, he shut off the engine.

"Let's go see if this system works," he called.

They stood in front of the sink. "Go ahead, turn on the valve," he said.

Primrose turned the handle and the hissing sound of air came out of the valve. Soon, splashes and spurts of water exploded into the sink. Then, a steady flow came out of the valve. She turned the valve off. Looking at his accomplishment, Billy grinned broadly.

"That is really far out," Primrose said, and kissed him.

Billy covered the pipeline in the trench, packing the dirt down by stomping on it with his feet. The last task was to chain the pump to one of the trees away from the stream in case of a flash flood. He felt proud of the water system and the outhouse and glad that he could add to Primrose's comfort.

Aside from driving into Arivaca for ice, beer and a pork roast, Billy spent the next week working on his songs while Primrose fashioned buckskin and beads into purses and headbands. A winter storm had rolled in from the west coast. The slow drizzle lasted intermittently for four days. The storm chilled the air, so that the fire in the box heater felt good. Billy enjoyed watching Primrose work, and she commented on his playing and singing many times during the days. One morning Billy noticed that Primrose had something on her mind. "Is somethin' buggin' you?" he asked.

"I've been thinking about that private-eye and my parents hiring him to find me. I wonder if I should write them a letter. After all, they know where I am now."

"I have thought about writin' to my folks, too," Billy said. "My mother is probably worried, even though she always took my father's side when he would tell me I should make somethin' of myself instead of playin' banjo."

"Maybe we should write them," Primrose said. "I have a pad of paper we can use."

"Yeah, maybe my mother thinks I am still in 'Nam."

Billy felt sorry for his mother being so dominated by his father. He wanted to let her know he was happy and living the life he had chosen without his father's influence.

Primrose took out her pad of paper, tore a sheet off, and handed it to Billy. They sat together at the table writing to their parents. For a while Billy sat with the blank sheet in front of him. Without any hesitation, however, Primrose began writing. When she looked up to see Billy gazing off into space, she put her ball-point pen down. "What's the matter?" she asked.

"I just don't know how to start the damn thing."

"Just tell them 'Hi' and that you hope they are well and happy. That's how I started mine. You can always rip it up. There's more paper."

He started writing. After the first sentence the words came more easily to him, and soon he had said what he wanted to say. Primrose finished her letter soon after Billy finished his. "What did you tell your folks?" Billy asked.

"I just told them that I didn't appreciate the private detective invading my space and to please not send any more. I also told them that I was happier than I ever was before. The one thing I emphasized was that I had no plans whatsoever to return to Malibu."

"Did you tell them not to try and visit you here?"

"I made that as clear as I could. What did you say?"

"I told them I was out of the army and making a good livin' playin' my banjo. I asked them to send my old banjo and my music to me. I also said that I was too busy to go visit them."

"Our letters are almost the same," she said. "The next time we go into town, we can mail the letters. I don't have any envelopes, but we can get the kind that are already stamped at the post office."

"We are going to need ice in a day or so," Billy said.

Billy received a reply from his parents in two weeks. His mother wrote most of it, saying she had worried about him and included news about some of his friends from high school. The message from his father preached that he should come back to Springfield, go to college under the GI Bill, and eventually take over the farm machinery business. Billy was not surprised that there was no mention of the old banjo being sent to him. "My father will never understand that I don't want to sell farm machinery," Billy said, and handed the letter to Primrose to read. "And, I'll bet he never sends my banjo."

"Your mother sounds quite different than your father," Primrose said.

"She is, but my father rules the roost. My mother has no interests of her own."

A week after Billy's letter arrived, Primrose received a letter from her mother. The brief message said that the private investigator was her father's idea and that they were both very busy with their respective work. "Things don't seem to have changed in good old Malibu," Primrose said. "My letter was a waste of time and effort."

"Our parents just don't seem to get it," Billy said. "At least, my mother knows I got back from 'Nam."

They bought what they needed at the store, and returned to the cabin to continue working on getting the garden planted. Primrose had put up a fence of chicken wire to keep most garden pests out of the twenty by twenty foot area near the creek. She had explained to Billy that during May and June, before the summer rains began, she had to irrigate the plants by carrying water from the creek.

"I can rig the water system so you won't have to carry any buckets," he suggested.

"The garden is too far from the water line," she said. "That's a lot of digging and a lot of pipe to buy. Besides, I only plant the corn early. I wait for the rains before I plant beans, squash and the other stuff."

"What do you do with what you can't use yourself?"

"Sometimes I sell it, or trade with Alex at the store."

When they had finished making neat rows about thirty inches apart at one end of the garden, they planted the corn.

"The soil seems moist enough," she said. "We can wait a while to see if it germinates without irrigating."

"I remember the huge cornfields back in Illinois," Billy said. "It's so flat there that it seemed there was nothin' in the world but corn with some trees around the houses."

"If your parents were different, would you want to go back there?"

"No way do I want to live there again. I'm stayin' in the West where there are mountains." He also thought about his happiness with Primrose and the joy he had found playing his banjo for people to listen to and applaud. Returning to Springfield did not occupy any of his thoughts or plans. I guess I've changed just like everything else.

For several years, the hippy population of Arivaca had been celebrating May Day with a party. Very loosely organized, there were no invitations and people just came straggling in to a grove of large ash trees that grew along the creek that drained the cienega. Everyone brought their own beer and marijuana.

It was understood by everyone that Toby Watkins would provide food. Living so far away from everyone, he always managed to have a deer or javelina to roast. How Toby avoided being caught by the game rangers amazed the participants.

The day before the May Day party, Toby and four of his pot-smoking buddies assembled in the ash grove, cleaned out the pit, and built a big fire in it. After dark, when the wood had burned down to a big bed of coals, they wrapped a deer carcass in wet gunny-sacks, lowered it onto the coals, and then shoveled dirt on top to keep the heat in the pit.

People began to arrive by mid-morning. Billy and Primrose drove in just before noon. She had described the party of the previous year and suggested he bring his banjo.

After parking the van so that they could leave easily, they strolled over to the gathering carrying a six-pack of Budweiser. Billy left his banjo locked in the van. Primrose spotted Brenda and waved. The Tubac gallery owner and the man she was with seemed to be in an important conversation, so Primrose took Billy over to the pit and introduced him to Toby. She could tell that Toby was already stoned.

As he looked around at all the people, Billy felt out of place. He recognized a couple of people he had seen around the town. Everyone was gathered in small groups talking, drinking beer, or smoking. He sensed that Primrose was ill at ease, too. He opened two bottles of Bud and handed one to her. "This is sort of a weird party," Billy said.

"I told you it might be strange. These are weird people."

"I'll bet I could do 'Proud Mary', and nobody would know I was playin'."

"Maybe we should have stayed home," she said.

"Some of these people take one quick look at us and turn away. Others don't even look. I don't think it is us they are snubbin', because I've seen them do the same to others." Billy felt uneasy in the situation.

"They are definitely weird. Either that, or we are weird and don't know it," Primrose remarked. "When I first moved here, these May Day deals were kind of interesting, but these people don't seem the same. Maybe I am the one who has changed."

"I see Toby is startin' to uncover the meat," Billy said. "I would just as soon boogie out of here if you don't mind."

"I'm with you a hundred percent. Let's vanish from this spot."

Strolling slowly away from the grove they reached the van, climbed in, and drove back to the cabin.

"I didn't realize so many people lived around here," Billy remarked.

"Some of those people there are ex-residents, but return every year for the party and free food."

"What does Toby get out of all that?"

"Toby is a strange human being," Primrose said. "For all his insistence on isolation, he thrives on get-togethers in the community. One thing he enjoys is providing illegal meat. It's his way of rebelling against society."

"The game rangers must know about his poachin'."

"They are either afraid to try and arrest him, or they are stupider than we think."

The next time they went to town for ice and groceries they stopped at the post office in case they had any mail. Surprised when the lady postmistress handed him a long package through the window, Billy immediately looked at the return address. "Look," he said, excitedly. "It's from my mother. She must have sent my old banjo."

Back inside the van Billy opened his pocket-knife and began to slit the tape that held the long box together. Opened, the box revealed the banjo case Billy remembered well; also some familiar music books. He unsnapped the latches, opened the case, and stared at his old banjo for a moment before taking it into his hands. "Wow," he said. "It has been four years since I played this baby. See here on the neck. I had this one engraved soon after I got it."

"That was really nice of your mother to send it," Primrose commented.

"It's my guess that she probably did it without tellin' my father."

He strummed on the dead, out-of-tune strings, and began to tune the instrument. Accomplishing that, he strummed chords and picked out songs all the way back to the cabin.

They continued their usual routine, but two weeks after the May Day party Billy began to feel restless. He thought about his promised meeting with Clearance in Jackson. He remembered Joe Spencer's promise of plenty of work at the Mangey Moose. He wondered if Myra had finished writing her book, but that was all he pondered about Myra. He also found it difficult to think about leaving Primrose for the summer. But the pull of performing again grappled with his emotions.

One morning he took his old banjo down by the creek and picked out songs. Primrose watched him from the window over her workbench. Two hours later when he came back inside the cabin, she stopped working, went over, and put her arms around him, leaning her head against his chest. "You're getting antsy as hell aren't you?"

"I guess I must be," he replied, crinkling his brow and rubbing his hands up and down her back. "I can't seem to sit still for very long, and I keep thinkin' about playin' music for people again."

She pushed away and looked up at him. "I've been watching something eating at you," she said tilting her head. "I figured you must be feeling weird. I love you, Billy. I love you with all my heart and soul. I understand your need to play for people and will never stand in your way. There has been nothing finer than living here with you and loving you and feeling you loving me. But, if it's time to go, then go."

Billy felt his eyes trying to cry. "My sweet, beautiful lady. You understand me better than I understand myself. I am uneasy, but I hate the thought of leavin'. I love you with all my heart and soul, too. I reckon, though, that I need to go back to Wyomin'. You can count on me comin' back as soon as the tourists leave Jackson." Tears began flowing from his eyes as he looked at her. "Come here," he said, pulling her into his arms.

Wrapped in his embrace, she put her head against his chest again. "I know I can count on that. I'll miss you every minute you're away. Will you write once in a while?"

He released her, left one hand on her shoulder and gently touched the tip of her nose with his finger. "The first thing I'll do in Jackson is buy a pad of paper and a ball-point pen. I want to leave my old banjo here with you. That way you'll know I'll be back."

"When do you want to leave?"

Putting his hands on her hips, he looked down at the ground. "I don't want to leave, but I think I might as well get goin' in the mornin'. Maybe it will cure me."

"I'll drive you to the bus station in Tucson."

"Just drive me to the junction. I'll catch the bus from there. But, right now, I want to take off your clothes."

CHAPTER SEVEN

She saved her tears for the drive back from the junction. Billy watched the back of the van until it disappeared over the hill. He could still feel the sensation on his chest made by her breasts as he kissed her good-bye. Suddenly his eyes filled with tears. *I must be crazy to leave her.*

Once aboard the bus he began to feel better. He felt lucky that the bus for Las Cruces would leave shortly after he arrived in Tucson. "Soon," he thought. "I'll be in Jackson."

Three days later as he looked at the Wind River Range from the bus window, he pondered how Myra would react to him being so in love with someone else. And, would Clearance have arrived yet? *I wonder if I should look in on Myra. She'll probably be pissed when I tell her about Primrose. I reckon it would be better to get that over with as soon as possible.*

The bus pulled in to the Jackson depot shortly after noon. Billy put the strap of his duffel bag over his shoulder. Carrying the banjo he headed for Myra's trailer. His knock on the door was answered by a large woman wearing a faded, pink housecoat that had seen better days. "Yes? What is it?" she asked.

"I'm looking for Myra," Billy replied.

"I don't know any Myra. Are you sure you have the right address?"

"This is the right address. Myra lived here last summer. Well, thanks. Sorry to disturb you."

"That's perfectly all right," the woman said, and closed the door.

Billy was taken by surprise that Myra did not live in the trailer anymore. He started for the Cowboy Bar to see if she might be on a different work schedule and be there. As he passed the square with all the old elk antlers, he looked over at the bench where he had once played and handed out Mort's handbills. There sat Clearance playing an instrumental tune on his guitar. Billy crossed the street and headed toward his friend.

"It looks like you beat me here," Billy said, his eyes sparkling with happiness at finding his friend.

"Hey, dude, it's sure good to see you," Clearance replied, his face breaking into a broad grin. "I've been here two weeks, wondering if you'd ever show up."

"I told you I would. I see you got a gig with Mort at the Spur."

"Any old port in a storm," the round-bellied guitar player said, arching his eyebrows. "You were talking about coming here in late April when we left Tubac," Clearance continued. "How did the bar in Arivaca turn out?"

"I played it once for two beers."

"Where did you spend the winter?"

"Arivaca," Billy said.

"Where did you play?"

"I went back to Tubac a few times, but the tourist season ended."

"I think there is something you're not telling me, Billy."

"I spent the winter with a beautiful woman in a cabin outside Arivaca."

"All right!" Clearance said. "Is it serious?"

"I know I love her."

"Better watch out. If I know women, you'll end up getting married."

Billy scratched his chin whiskers and changed the subject. He didn't want to get sucked in to talking about his private thoughts of Primrose. "How was New Orleans?"

"Breakfast, beer and bus fare," Clearance replied.

"So how are you doing with Mort?"

"So far, so good. I don't make much from handing out these free margarita handbills, but he pays me and I have that storeroom to crash in. The tips are not so hot, but Mort says after Memorial Day the business will pick up."

"I might have to crash with you. It's either that or the Bison Hotel's ten dollar cot. Right now, I think I'll have a beer at the Cowboy Bar, and say hello to Myra."

"I thought you said you were in love with a girl in Arivaca," Clearance quizzed.

"I just need to tell Myra that I won't be staying with her this summer."

"Wish I could join you instead of handing out these flyers."

"I probably won't be too long over there."

"I'll be here for a couple more hours," Clearance said. "Leave your stuff if you want to."

"Just keep an eye on my duffel bag, I don't let the banjo out of my sight after that lesson in Tucson."

Billy crossed the street and made his way through the sidewalk traffic to the Cowboy Bar. There were a few afternoon customers. He found a place at the bar and ordered a beer from the bartender he recognized.

"Back in town for the summer?" the man asked.

"Yeah, just got in," Billy replied.

The bartender took a Budweiser from the cooler, uncapped it and put it on the bar in front of Billy.

"Does Myra work nights or days right now?"

"Myra doesn't work here anymore."

"Do you know where she works?"

"She quit two months ago. One night she came in with some dude and announced that she was done with cocktail waitressing. I think he's a lawyer."

"I'll be damned," Billy said.

"I remember you and Myra were pretty thick last summer."

The bartender left to wait on his other customers. Billy finished his beer and left. "That solves one problem," he mumbled, walking to the corner to cross the street.

"Did you find Myra?" Clearance asked, cutting short the song he was playing.

"She hooked up with some lawyer, and quit working there."

"Win some, lose some."

"Actually, that solves one problem for me."

"What do you mean?"

"I am going to be faithful to Primrose. I thought I should tell Myra."

"How about jamming a couple songs?"

"Let's do it," Billy said, and opened the banjo case.

He tuned the banjo to Clearance's guitar, and they began playing together for the first time since they had played in Tubac at La Cantina de Anza. Several people stopped to listen, and when they had finished four songs there was money in the open cases. Clearance handed out several handbills. Then they packed up and headed for the Golden Spur.

Mort stood behind the bar when the two musicians came through the door.

"Well, Banjo Billy," Mort said, and smiled. "You finally got back. Good to see you."

"Hello, Mort," Billy said. "It's good to see you too. I see you and my partner, Clearance, are doing fine."

"Thanks for sending him."

"Mort, is it all right if Billy crashes in the storeroom tonight?" Clearance asked.

"No problem, but there's only one cot."

"There's room on the floor," Clearance said.

Billy stashed his duffel bag in the storeroom, then joined Clearance for a beer at the bar. Mort brought the beer, waved his right hand, and told them the beer was on the house. "Billy, did you know Myra's got a boyfriend?" Mort asked.

"Yeah," Billy answered. "The bartender at the Cowboy said she hooked up with some lawyer."

"He's supposed to be quite wealthy. They live on his ranch downriver."

"That should be good for Myra to be away from things so she can write her book."

"I dunno. They don't come in here."

Finished with their beers, Billy and Clearance set up two barstools, and began playing songs together. Two couples arrived with their handbills for free margaritas. Recognizing them,

Clearance waved. As the evening wore on, Mort kept busy behind the bar until eleven o'clock, when the last customer left. "You guys play well together," Mort said, putting two Budweisers in front of them. "I wish I could afford to pay both of you."

"Don't worry about it, Mort," Billy said. "I have a gig waitin' at the Mangey Moose. I'll go out there in the mornin'."

Billy left his duffel bag in Mort's storeroom and had breakfast with Clearance. Then he caught the bus to Teton Village, arriving at the Mangey Moose Saloon just as Joe Spencer opened the front door.

"Billy, you made it," Spencer said, raising his arms with the palms of his hands stretched. "How did your winter go in Arizona?"

"Hello, Joe. Arizona's a great place to spend the winter."

"Did you get some good gigs?"

"I did a couple,"

"I hope you are ready to come to work here again. I have been holding your spot because you are the best banjo man I know of."

"That's why I'm here, Joe. When do you want me to start?"

"If you want to, you can start tonight. Want a beer?"

"Might as well. I need a place to stay. Do you know anywhere I can crash cheap?"

"What happened between you and Myra?"

"She's livin' with some lawyer on a ranch."

"I reckon that takes care of Myra. Let me think about a place for you to stay. Anything out here in the village is out of sight. All the working people here in the village live in Jackson."

"I don't mind living in Jackson. All I need is a place to sleep."

"I just had an idea. My brother has started a river running deal. He has some rubber river boats, and takes tourists down the Snake. He mentioned the other day that he wanted to do something extra so his clients would send their friends to him."

"What's that got to do with a place for me to sleep?"

"I'll talk to him. He has a big house rented for his boatmen and cook. I'm thinking you could play your banjo at the lunch stop in trade for a place to sleep in the house. You would get a meal and probably tips from the tourists. How does that sound to you?"

"That would solve a big problem," Billy replied.

"I'll give him a call right now."

Joe picked up the telephone and dialed. Joe tossed his idea to his brother and hung up the phone. "Max will be over in half an hour. He sounded interested."

"That's great, Joe. I sure appreciate your help."

Twenty minutes later Max Spencer drove up. Joe introduced him to Billy and the three talked about the idea of Billy playing at the lunch stop. Max enjoyed Billy's rendition of "Proud Mary" and told him about the river running operation.

"I'll drive you over to the house and introduce you to the crew," Max said. "Our first trip is the day after tomorrow, so everyone is just kicking back."

"Billy," Joe said. "You have a lot to do today, so why don't you start here tomorrow night."

"If I get everything squared away, I'll start tonight. I'm lookin' forward to playin' for people again."

On the way to the house Billy asked Max to stop at the Golden Spur so he could pick up his duffel bag. The house, located five blocks from the center of town, had two stories. After Max introduced Billy to the boatmen and Toad, the cook, he took him upstairs to show him a room with a cot. "This is all that's left in the place. At least you won't have to sleep on the floor."

"This looks fine to me," Billy said. "Thanks."

Max shut the door to the room and ambled over to the window. "Before I go, I want to explain a little about Toad. He used to be a ranch roundup cook and really knows his business, but he can get a bit cantankerous at times. See what you can do to give him a hand setting up and breaking down. He'll be your friend for life, once he decides you're okay."

Billy crossed his arms over his chest. "He seems nice

enough. Sure, I'll give him a hand. I won't be playin' until the boats arrive and they will be gone once the lunch is over."

"Billy, I think you'll enjoy working with us, and those tourists are usually pretty good tippers and nice people. When we get outside, I'll show you Toad's pickup truck he made into a chuckwagon.

Max led Billy out to the rear of the house where Toad kept the pickup close to the kitchen door. After showing Billy the way everything worked, Max left to take care of some other business.

Billy found the crew easy to talk with. Toad kept to himself in his room, but the others, all about Billy's age, lounged around in the living room. Billy chatted with them for a while, and then walked the five blocks back to the square to find Clearance and tell him the good news. "I can't believe how this all worked out," Billy said. "I really lucked out with a place to stay just for playin' to tourists durin' their lunch, and a chance to make a few tips and a meal thrown in."

"That manager at the Mangey Moose must like you," Clearance said. "I might get sick of playing out here and handing out these handbills."

"You probably will, but it's about the only other show in town that I know of."

"Breakfast, beer and bus fare," Clearance repeated. "I guess I'd better not get sick of handing out these damned handbills, because I haven't made bus fare out of here yet."

They played a few songs together in the square before Billy left for the Mangey Moose, stopping at a stationery store to buy a pad of paper and a ball-point pen. Joe Spencer smiled when Billy told him about working with his brother Max playing during the lunch breaks. "I am changing our advertisement in the newspaper, and I need a photograph of you," Joe said.

"What for?"

"I have an idea."

"Well, your last idea worked out fine," Billy said. "What now?"

"I am going to put your picture in the ad with the caption,

'Banjo Billy is back from Arizona, and playing again at the Mangey Moose Saloon.' I talked to the ad man at the newspaper, and he thinks it's a good idea."

"Who knows Banjo Billy? I'm not Eddie Peabody, The Banjo King."

"You were here part of last summer, and lots of people heard you here at the Moose."

"I don't have a photograph."

"I have my camera. I'll take it. Take out your banjo and come outside where the light is better."

Billy took his banjo out of the case, and followed Joe Spencer out of the bar. "Let's take the first one with you sitting on this bench, playing the banjo," Spencer said.

Billy sat down on the concrete bench that was near the front wall of the building. He began playing chords. Joe snapped a couple of shots. "OK, let's get one standing up, and playing 'Proud Mary'," Joe instructed.

Billy stood up and sang the song as Joe took several photographs at different angles and distances. "There should be some good shots in here somewhere. I'll get this roll developed tomorrow morning over in Jackson at the new one-hour developing place."

"I came over early to write a letter," Billy said. "I might as well have a beer while I'm doing it."

Billy had never written a letter to a woman, so half the beer was gone before he was able to think of a good opening sentence. He told Primrose about having a place to stay with the river boatmen just for playing during their lunch breaks. The tender parts about loving and missing her came at the end.

Since there were several couples in the bar, Billy started playing a half an hour early. Gradually more people came in, but it was obvious that the usual crowds of tourists had not yet arrived. Those who were there tipped well, but Billy wondered if the newspaper ad would really increase his earnings along with the bar handle. After closing, Joe drove Billy back to the house.

Billy visited Clearance in the square the next afternoon and then went to the post office and mailed his letter to Primrose. That evening when he showed up for work, Joe Spencer showed him the prints from the roll of film. "Which one do you like the best?" Spencer asked.

"I think this one," he replied, pointing to one that showed the banjo well.

"I kind of agree, but this one of you holding the banjo above your head might attract attention better."

"It's your call, Joe."

"You may be right. It has to show up in newsprint. It will be a better shot for the handbills, too."

"Wait a minute, Joe. Handing out handbills in the square wasn't part of our deal."

"Hey, we'll leave the square to Mort. I'll have a bunch printed and pass out stacks of them to all the motels."

"That's cool. Can I buy a couple of those prints you aren't going to use?"

"Help yourself. You don't have to buy them."

"Thanks, Joe."

The crowd at the Mangey Moose stayed later than usual. The tips were good and by the time Joe drove Billy back to the house it was almost two o'clock in the morning.

The loud knocking on his door awakened Billy at eight o'clock. "Young feller," Toad said. "Time to get rollin'."

"I'll be right with you," Billy answered.

Billy swung himself out of the cot and dressed quickly. Then picking up the banjo, he made a detour to the bathroom down the hallway. Toad was sitting in the cab of the pickup truck with the engine running. "All set?" Toad asked as Billy took his place in the passenger's seat.

"Yeah," Billy replied. "I had a late night at the Mangey Moose."

"There's coffee in that thermos on the seat," Toad said. "Go ahead and use the top, I've got my own mug."

"Thanks, can I pour you some?"

"I've already had a belly full."

Billy took off the top of the thermos, and filled it with the steaming coffee. With both hands on the wheel and his old, sweat-stained Stetson hat pulled down to keep the sun out of his eyes, Toad drove through the Jackson morning traffic and onto Route 191, heading for Hoback Junction. "How long have you been cookin' for Max?" Billy asked.

"Three years," Toad replied. "When I started with him I was cooking for a dude outfit over in DuBois and heard about this job. Same money, less hours, and I only have to cook when Max has a river trip booked."

Billy liked the way Toad moved his head from side to side as he talked.

"How long have you been cookin'?"

"Aw hell, I reckon it's been twenty years. I was breakin' horses for the Gray Ranch down in New Mexico. This goddam blue-roan outlaw sonofabitch went over backwards on me an' broke my right hip all to hell. Took a helluva spell to heal up, and when I finally got to walkin' without crutches, I couldn't ride no more. Goddam blue-roan bastard! No one ever got the sonofabitch broke either. They made me the roundup cook at the Gray."

"Had you ever cooked before?"

"Hell no, I was just a young'un when I commenced breakin' horses. But, I'll tell ya, young feller, I learned cooking real quick. I quick found out that I liked it. No more broken bones, no more bruises, and the pay was better. Them ranches pay cooks more cause they think it's not as much fun as breakin' horses or punchin' cows."

"Where did you start breakin' horses?"

"I growed up over east in Sheridan County. My old man was straw boss for the E4 outfit in Big Horn. That outfit raised some mighty fine cowhorses and a bunch of polo ponies. I broke my first horse when I was sixteen, still just a button. The

E4 sold out most of their cow country and didn't need anyone to break colts, so I went to work for the OW out on Hangin' Woman creek. I heard about the Gray Ranch from an old boy who had drifted north. I hankered to get out of the cold winters, so I tossed my saddle and war bag in that old boy's pickup and headed south with him when he went that fall."

Toad slowed the pickup as they reached Hoback Junction. Driving down a narrow two-rut road, they came to a spot on a big bend in the Snake River where a small sandy beach offered a landing for the rubber river boats. A gradual slope on the bank gave Toad plenty of room to set up the lunch. Toad limped around to the back of the pickup. "I reckon you can do as you please until it's time for you to pick that banjo," Toad said. "I gotta get this crap set up, get the stew and beans heated up and the biscuits made."

"Tell me what to do, and I'll give you a hand," Billy said. "When I see the boats coming, I can tune my banjo in a minute."

"I'm not used to help, but you can start by buildin' a fire in that circle over yonder. It'll burn down pretty good by the time they git here. Then I put the coffee pot on the coals so's it looks like a cow-camp. They don't know the difference."

Billy took some of the firewood from the back of the pickup and built a fire in the middle of the circle of rocks. Then Toad showed him where to set up the folding serving table and how to arrange the heavy duty paper plates with rocks on them to keep them from blowing away and the plastic utensils. In the meantime, Toad had mixed the batter for the biscuits, put the dollops of it on greased trays and into the portable butane fired oven.

With the kettles of beef stew and boiled pinto beans heating on two small, butane fueled stoves, Toad paused to roll a cigarette from a package of smoking tobacco. He passed the tobacco and papers to Billy who was sipping a cup of coffee. "No thanks," Billy said.

Toad put the tobacco back in his shirt pocket. He struck a wooden stove match with his thumbnail, and lit the end of his home-made cigarette. "With you a helpin' out, we're early. Let's grab a plate and have a bite of stew and beans. Thataway we won't have to eat after the boats have gone."

"That sounds good to me," Billy said.

"I gotta check the biscuits first. I git to talkin' and they're liable to burn."

Billy took a plate from the stack on the table, ladled on some stew and beans. Sitting cross-legged on the ground, he began eating. Toad joined him after handing him a hot biscuit. "If you're as good on that there banjo as you are at helpin', you'll have them river runners a dancin'."

"I just hope they like what I play."

"Hell, they will, don't you go to worryin' 'bout that."

Finished with their meal, they tossed their used plates into the plastic lined garbage can.

"By damn, I almost forgot," Toad said, going to the pickup and bringing back an enamel johnny-pot inscribed *Tipping is not a city in China*. "I always set this by the garbage can. A feller can't come right out an' ask for tips, but this here piss-pot does the trick."

Billy laughed at the inscription just as the first boat rounded the bend.

"I keep a couple dollars to salt my banjo case," he said. "Do you salt that piss-pot?"

"By gollies, that's a good idee," Toad replied, an took two dollar bills from his roll to put in the pot.

After putting the coffee-pot on the coals, Billy set up near the fire, and waited for the people to emerge from the boats. Tuning the banjo, he waited until they all had full plates before starting to play.

The river runners consisted of both men and women. The way they went after the food proved that the trip, so far, had made them hungry. Billy started playing. After thinking about what songs to play, he was planning on a few slow ones to begin with, and ending with "Proud Mary." He felt that the part about rolling on the river would be appropriate for the river runners.

Surprised that a number of the people turned around from their meals to look at him, Billy began strolling around among the people as he played. After each song they applauded with enthusiasm. When they had all dumped their plates into the garbage can, Billy began "Proud Mary." All conversations stopped and the people, now standing, watched and listened intently as he sang and picked out the song on his banjo. He took care that he ended the last few bars standing in back of his open banjo case.

Everyone present gave him a great ovation when he ended the song. Most approached him to shake his hand and thank him for the music. Not un-noticed, the banjo case collected a substantial pile of bills. The lunch break over, the boatmen called out to load the boats for the afternoon's run.

After the boatmen had shoved off into the channel, Billy stacked the bills as he counted his earnings. From the twenty river-running clients he had made forty-eight dollars. Putting the banjo back in its case, Billy started helping Toad break down the camp. When they had packed everything back into the pickup they started back to the highway. "By damn," Toad said. "I got fifty two bucks outa that there piss-pot. I generally feel lucky as a Las Vegas gambler if I get thirty. That music of yours damn sure primed 'em and loosened 'em up. How'd you make out?"

"I counted forty-eight, and that's more than I expected," Billy replied.

"Looks like I can thank you for helpin' out and bringin' in more tips."

"When do we go out again?"

"I think in a couple days. I know Max ain't booked for tomorrow."

"Once the season starts, how often does he make a run?"

"It'll be every day."

Toad stopped before getting back on the highway. Taking

advantage of a lull in the traffic, he pulled out, gunned the pick-up into the near lane, and headed back to Jackson. "I was a tellin' you on the way down about breakin' colts an' all. Well, back on the Gray there was plenty of work bustin' broncs, but all that's changed. Even cookin' for roundups is pretty much a long gone thing. These days I'll bet there ain't but two, mebbe three outfits runnin' chuck wagons."

"Why the change?" Billy asked.

"A lot of the outfits are broke up into smaller ranches what don't need chuck wagons cause they ain't brandin' the calves the big outfits did. Some of the outfits sold out to them real estate developers 'cause the environmentalists has got the guvment agin the cowmen and have cut the grazin' permits down to nothin'. Then these real estate yahoos build subdivisions. With all them houses and roads there ain't no grass left to absorb the rain. Even a overgrazed ranch is better for the land than a bunch a houses an' roads. Godamighty, I can't figure the sense to it all."

"What do you mean?"

"Well, it seems to me that a cow pasture is easier on country than a bunch a goddam houses an' roads what concentrates the rainfall an' it all runs off. But, there's a helluva lot more environmentalists than there is cowmen anymore. Damn shame what's happenin'. A young feller like you won't be able to get ranch work pretty soon, 'cause there won't be no ranches to work for."

"What are the cowboys going to do?"

"There won't be no more cowboys as we know 'em. Some will get into the rodeo game, I reckon. I never did, an' never would. Hell's fire, I rode broncs every day tryin' ta keep 'em from buckin'. Why would a feller like me want to go into one of those circuses an' try to make a horse buck."

"I've never been to a rodeo. All they had back in Springfield, Illinois was county and state fairs."

"What was you doin' back there?"

"My old man has a farm machinery business. He wanted me to go to work for him after high school, but I joined the army."

"Farm machinery," Toad said, and paused. "Ya know, young feller, I remember when I was breakin' colts for the E4. We all had to go to work in the fields once hayin' started, and we stayed with it until the hay was all put up. We used teams on the machinery back then. I skinned a team of Missouri mules, ol' Tip and Ada. Goddam fine a pair of mules as you'd want. They always put me on a buck-rake with those mules 'cause I knew how to run one better than most."

"When I worked summers for my father, he would send me out to demonstrate tractors to farmers," Billy said. "I didn't know much about drivin' tractors, so I would take the tractor out to some farm and let the farmer drive it. Some of those machines had air-conditionin' and tape-decks. And, some of those farmers would go so far into debt with the banks that they couldn't pay their loans. Then, some big agribusiness would come along and buy the farm and all the machinery."

"That sounds opposite of what happened to the cow business. It started out with big outfits, and now, most of those are busted up into small ranches what can't be paid off runnin' cows."

"I don't know why the old man wanted me to do what he was doin'. He told me all about how the agribusiness people were buyin' their machinery straight from the factory. Selling farm machinery to small farmers who are goin' out of business doesn't sound to me like too good a deal. Besides, I would rather play my banjo."

"You do that real good, young feller, and you're a doin' what you want to do."

Arriving back at the house, Billy helped Toad unload the pickup, and put things away in the kitchen. Then, at the post office, he bought a stamped envelope for the photographs Joe Spencer had given him, and mailed them to Primrose. Stopping at the square to see Clearance, Billy told him about playing for the river runners and about the stories Toad had told him. "I really admire that old cowboy," Billy said. "When that outlaw horse reared over backwards and broke Toad's hip, he went to work as a roundup cook. The old devil is still working instead of gettin' the government to pay him for disability."

"I would like to meet this Toad," Clearance said.

"When you figure to take an afternoon off from passin' out Mort's handbills, come over to the house."

"If he's there right now I'll take the rest of the afternoon off. I want to see your digs anyway."

Clearance put his guitar in its case, and the two musicians left the square for the house where Billy now stayed with the boatmen and Toad.

Toad welcomed Billy and Clearance into his room. Glancing around, Billy saw, in one corner, an old saddle with a pair of time and work-worn chaps draped over it. Other than one wooden chair and a cot there were no other furnishings. A few shirts and two pairs of faded Levi's hung in an open closet.

"We thought you might join us for a beer, Toad," Billy said.

"I expect I'd like that. I don't go out catawallerin' much like I used to, but I'd sure enough like to take ya up on that. Where do you young fellers hang out?"

"How about the Cowboy Bar?" Billy asked.

"Sounds good to me," Toad replied. "I'll drive us all over."

"You drive, I'll buy," Billy said, and grinned.

"Helluva deal," Toad replied.

After getting comfortable at a table, the three men began conversing. A waitress came by to take their order. Billy and Clearance asked for their usual Budweisers. Toad ordered a shot of tequila and a glass of draft beer. When the waitress returned with the drinks, she looked at Billy quizzically. "Are you Banjo Billy?" she asked.

"Yeah, why?"

"Oh, no particular reason, I saw your picture in the newspaper. You're playing at the Mangey Moose, aren't you?"

"Yeah," Billy replied. "I haven't seen the newspaper."

"I have it over behind the bar. I'll get it for you," she said.

As she returned to the table, she opened the newspaper to the page carrying the Mangey Moose advertisement. "See," she said, handing it to Billy. "Here it is. 'Banjo Billy is back from Arizona,' and your picture. You can keep the paper if you want to."

"Thanks, I appreciate it," Billy said.

He passed the newspaper to Toad, who looked at it and gave it to Clearance. Toad picked up the shot of tequila with his thumb and index finger and raised it for a toast. "Here's to our famous Banjo Billy," he said, and downed the shot in one gulp.

Billy and Clearance raised their beer bottles to join.

"Where in Arizona ya from, Billy?" I thought ya said ya was from Springfield, Illinois."

"I just spent the winter in Arivaca, a little minin' town southwest of Tucson."

"Hell's fire," Toad said. "I wintered at Rockin' Y Ranch, north of Tubac, cookin' for the dudes. I drove up to Arivaca several times to see an old compadre of mine, Leroy Parsons. He took over the Gray Ranch colts after I got busted up."

"What does Leroy do in Arivaca?" Billy asked.

"He's still a breakin' colts. Works for the old Zopilote outfit. The owner sold out to one of them real estate fellers and now the ranch is all broke into forty-acre parcels. But, the old boy who sold out leases the graze. There ain't many colts to break, so Leroy does a lot of cow work."

"I heard about the Zopilote Ranch, but never met your friend Leroy," Billy said.

"Leroy's quite a feller. When he gets a bit too much Jim Beam under his belt he carries on about what it's like ta cowboy. He starts out by sayin', 'Ya roll outa bed at four in the mornin', put a pot of coffee on to boil, and go out an' feed your horses. Ya come back in an' drink your coffee while the horses are eatin' their grain an' hay. Then you go out an' saddle up your day horse an' climb on. The cold-backed sonofabitch farts ya off into a pile of horseshit. Ya climb back on an' ride him out. Then ya ride out checkin' cows and calves, doin' whatever has to be done and get back to the barn in the afternoon. Ya unsaddle and feed the horses agin afore you go eat supper. Ya do this for a month for three hundred dollars. Then, on pay day, ya go to town and get a little drunk, an' they call ya an alcoholic.' Leroy is a character."

Billy and Clearance laughed at Toad's story about Leroy Parsons. Billy ordered another round. Toad told more stories. It seemed to Billy that cowboys were as restless as he was. He and Clearance sat spellbound, listening about a way of life that was fast becoming history. I guess nothin' is like it used to be, Billy thought to himself.

"I've sure had a good time with you young fellers, but I best get back. Can I take ya anywhere?"

"It's too early for the Mangey Moose," Billy said. "Clearance and I will stick around for another beer before we have to go to work. I'm glad you had a good time, because we sure as hell enjoyed every minute."

Toad stood up, showing no effect from the two shots of tequila, and limped out of the Cowboy Bar.

"There is one fine old man," Billy said. "I'm goin' to enjoy workin' with him this summer."

"Man, you really lucked out," Clearance said. "A damn good gig, and a side job working with such a helluva story-teller. I have to put up with Mort and his goddam handbills."

"Yeah, I sure remember those handbills," Billy said. "Why don't you take the night off from the Golden Spur, and come out to the Moose with me. We can play together, and maybe Joe Spencer will like what he hears."

"Sounds like a winner," Clearance said. "I'd better go over and tell Mort I'm taking the night off."

"Knowin' Mort, that would probably be a good idea," Billy said.

Billy waited with another beer as Clearance took the left-over handbills back to the Golden Spur. Opening the newspaper again, he looked at the advertisement and wondered how many people would show up to hear him play.

CHAPTER EIGHT

Having eaten their hamburgers at the Totem Cafe, they took the bus to Teton Village. Approaching the Mangey Moose they saw a sign in front with a poster of Billy and the same picture that was in the newspaper advertisement. "Wow, man, they are really giving you a big play," Clearance said.

Billy stood looking at the poster and running his fingers through his hair. "Yeah, it's kind of scary. I just hope all that stuff will draw customers."

Max Spencer sat at the bar talking to his brother when Billy and Clearance came in the door. "How did it go today, Billy?"

"Just great."

"How did you get along with old Toad?"

"Toad is one fine man. He has some really fabulous stories."

"I'm glad you two hit it off," Max said. "Last year I hired a helper for him and the kid lasted one day. He just couldn't follow Toad's instructions. Toad had to watch him so close that the biscuits burned. That evening, Toad told me he would much rather work alone than having to babysit to boot."

"I liked every minute."

"The boatmen told me that the clients really enjoyed your music."

"I'm glad to hear that. I had fun playin' for them. Uh, I'd like you two to meet my buddy Clearance. Clearance, meet Max and Joe Spencer, my two bosses."

The brothers shook hands with Clearance.

"Have you got time for a beer?" Max asked. "I'll buy."

"Thanks," Billy and Clearance said in unison.

"Joe, if it's all right with you, I'd like to play a few numbers with Clearance. It won't cost you. We just like to play together."

"Go right ahead, but do mostly singles," Joe said. "Did you see the poster out front?"

"Yeah, that's cool," Billy said.

"The newspaper ad came out great, too."

"I saw it. I hope it draws the crowd."

"That's why I think it's better to play mostly singles," Joe remarked, "because people will be coming out here to listen to Banjo Billy."

"That's cool," Billy said. "I'll bring in Clearance once in a while."

"By the way, I had a bunch of those posters printed, and took them around to the motels," Joe said.

In spite of being a half an hour early, Billy set up and began playing his first set. By the time he had finished four songs the Mangey Moose Saloon had no more barstools unoccupied, and there were only two empty tables. Joe and another bartender had to hurry to keep the orders filled.

After taking a short break to sip on a beer, Billy began playing again. But, this time he introduced Clearance, and they played a song together. After each song the crowd applauded loudly. The two friends played several songs, and to the delight of the crowd, did their rendition of "Dueling Banjos." During that song all conversations stopped.

The music making continued; the cocktail waitress rushed around filling orders and bringing tips to toss into Billy's open banjo case. Some of the customers came up on their own with their tips. Finally, Billy and Clearance thought they had ended the evening with "Proud Mary," but the people remained, clapping rhythmically and asking for another "Dueling Banjos." Billy and Clearance continued to play until Joe had to yell, "last call."

The cocktail waitress brought Budweisers to Billy and Clearance, and told them the beers came from a couple sitting at one of the tables. The musicians waved their thanks. The man came over and put a ten dollar bill into the banjo case.

"You guys are great," he said. "Will you be playing together regularly?"

"Clearance is just here for tonight," Billy said. "You might mention that you liked listenin' to us together to the bartender over there in the blue shirt."

"I'll do that, and thanks for a very entertaining evening."

"Thank you," Billy said.

The people filtered out the door. Billy and Clearance finished their beer, and packed away their instruments. Billy counted the tips. "Goddam, Clearance, we made a hundred and forty-four dollars tonight."

"You mean, *you* made a hundred and forty-four dollars. It's your gig."

"Bullshit. We're splittin' it," Billy said, counting out seventy-two dollars, and handing it to his friend.

"This is your money, Billy," Clearance objected.

"We're partners, Clearance. I won't have it any other way."

They stuffed the bills into their pockets and leaned their instruments against the bar. Joe had locked the door behind the last of the customers. He put two more Budweisers in front of the musicians.

"Hey, you guys are really good together. I had a couple comments and questions from people wondering if you play together all the time. Here's your pay, Billy, and here's fifty for you, Clearance. You both earned it. Where do you usually play, Clearance?"

"The Golden Spur," Clearance replied.

"Shit, you got hooked into Mort's handbills in the square trip, eh?"

"I guess so," Clearance answered.

"After tonight, I would like to hire you on with Billy. Fifty bucks a night and tips. And, I always manage to slip in a beer or two."

"You just hired a guy named Clearance and his guitar."

"Fine, when can you start?"

"Tomorrow night, but I'll have to find another place to sleep."

"Ask Max, my brother. He won't mind you staying with Billy."

Joe drove them back to Jackson, leaving Clearance at the

Golden Spur and Billy at the river running company's house.

The next morning, Billy and Toad sat in the kitchen having coffee when Max arrived needing two of the boatmen to help him with some repairs. Billy asked if it was all right if Clearance stayed with him since he would no longer be able to sleep in Mort's storeroom.

"That's fine with me, but there's only one cot."

"We'll figure out somethin'," Billy said.

An hour later, Clearance came in carrying his bundle of belongings and his guitar.

"Mort wasn't too happy with me quitting," Clearance said. "He pissed and moaned about the handbills he had and couldn't use."

"He said the same thing to me last summer when I quit," Billy said, waving his hand to tell his friend it didn't matter. "Max said it was fine with him if you stay in my room. Put your stuff up there, and we can go look for another cot."

They found a used cot and mattress for ten dollars at the thrift store. The cot folded into an easily carried size. After setting it up in the room, they practiced some new songs for their gig together. After supper at the Totem Cafe, they rode the bus to Teton Village. Although arriving an hour early, they headed for the Mangey Moose, nevertheless, agreeing that with the money Joe was paying them they could afford to start early. Before setting up for the evening Billy and Clearance sat at the bar for a beer.

A tap on his shoulder startled Billy. He turned around to see who it might be. Myra stood smiling at him.

"Myra, goddam," he said. "How are you?"

"It's so good to see you, Banjo Billy," she said. "I don't know if you've heard about my boyfriend."

"I heard that as soon as I got to town."

"Look, he is sitting over at that table," she said, pointing to a good looking man in a tweed sport jacket. "Come over; I would like you to meet him."

"This is my friend Clearance, Myra."

"Hi, Clearance."

Myra took Billy's arm and led him to the table. The man rose as Myra introduced Billy to him.

"Billy this is my friend, Jeffrey Woolcott. Jeff's an attorney in town, but we live on his ranch south of Wilson."

She turned toward Jeff, whose impassive face stared blankly at Billy as if he was bored with everyone except himself.

"Jeff, Billy used to go over to the Cowboy to relax over a beer after playing here last summer."

"You mentioned that when you showed me the ad with his picture in the newspaper," Jeff said.

"When do you start playing?" Myra asked.

"As soon as we finish our beers. Clearance and I play together a lot."

"Don't let us keep you," Myra said. "After all, we came into town just to hear you play."

"How's the book comin' along, Myra?"

"Still writing. I have a couple of chapters to go, I think."

Billy was tempted to say that he remembered her writing while he was in the trailer, because it was obvious to him that she had not told her new boy friend about them living together. He returned to his beer wondering if the stuffed-shirt lawyer appreciated Myra's freckled tits and the way she was capable of making passionate love. Billy thought that Jeffrey Woolcott could be very dull for a woman like Myra, and wondered if it might be his money that Myra enjoyed. By the time Clearance and he had set up for the evening, he had stopped contemplating Myra's motives, and his thoughts turned to Primrose back in Arivaca. As they finished the first set, Billy saw Myra and her boyfriend get up from their table and leave.

A week later Primrose's letter arrived. Billy almost cut his finger on the envelope as he hurriedly opened it. In it she thanked him for the pictures and was glad that he had found good gigs in Jackson. The corn was doing well and the other vegetables had sprouted. Above all, Primrose missed Billy's presence. As he returned to the house, Billy pictured himself back in the cabin, singing the song he had composed for Primrose, as she danced naked in front of him. He wished he could suddenly appear at the cabin and take her into his arms.

Before leaving for the Mangey Moose with Clearance, Billy wrote a letter in which he told Primrose about his daydream of her dancing in the cabin. On the way to the bus stop, he mailed it.

They had just finished their second set, playing to a crowded Mangey Moose Saloon, when Myra came in alone, and sat at the one remaining vacant table. As Billy and Clearance left their instruments leaning against the wall, and turned to go to the bar, Myra caught Billy's eye. She beckoned him to join her. "Billy, I need to talk to you," she said.

He sat down, and noticed her blouse was opened enough to obviously display her freckled cleavage. "Hi, Myra, where's Jeffrey tonight?"

Myra spoke in a voice just above a whisper. "Jeffrey is in Denver on business. He won't be back for three more days. Billy, I need you desperately."

"You're hooked up with your lawyer, Myra."

"I am miserable, Billy, just plain miserable. Ever since I was here the other night, I haven't been able to think of anything but you. I can't write. I can't stop wanting it to be the way we were last summer."

"We had a good time last summer, but things have changed. You are livin' with your lawyer, and I have found someone I love completely."

"Why did you come back to Jackson if you're so in love?"

"I came back to play and sing. That's how I live. It has nothin' to do with lovin' Primrose."

"That's an odd name, Primrose. What is she like?"

"She is very dear to me. That's all I can say."

"God, Billy, don't you remember the joy we had last summer?"

The cocktail waitress came over to the table with a Budweiser for Billy. "Can I get you something, Miss?" she asked Myra.

"I'll have a double gin and tonic, please," Myra replied.

"Sure I remember last summer," Billy said. "But, like I said, that was last summer. I hope you understand. It wouldn't be the same."

"Billy, I want to make love to you in the worst way. I am truly sorry I moved in with Jeffrey."

"What's wrong?"

"When I met him, Jeffrey seemed like just the man for me. A month after I moved in with him, he lost interest in me. He told me he was working on an important case and could think about nothing else. I discovered that Jeffrey is a totally boring person, even in bed. His lawyer buddies are boring too."

The waitress brought Myra's gin and tonic. She took a long drink before setting the glass back down on the table.

"Why did you hook up with him?"

"I'll be honest with you, Billy. I thought I loved him and moving in with him gave me the chance to quit working at the Cowboy Bar. I would finally be able to write full-time."

"So, now you found out you made a mistake," Billy said.

"I'm afraid I made a huge mistake. After seeing you the other night, I can't even write. Please let me take you to the ranch tonight?"

"Myra, I can't do that. If we made love now, I would have that on my conscience, and I don't want anythin' to spoil the love I have with Primrose."

"She is not in Jackson, is she?"

"No, but that doesn't matter. Let's you and me just be friends."

"You sound like you're married to this woman."

"I don't need to be married to be faithful to her."

"Billy, do you realize that I am getting wet just sitting here at this table with you?"

Clearance left the bar to get ready for the second set of songs.

"I have to get back to my banjo, Myra," Billy said. "It was good to see you." *Married. I don't need that to tie me down.*

Myra stayed for one song, finished her drink, and left. Billy sighed with relief when he saw her go out the door.

That summer the tourists brought prosperity to the business community in Jackson. The hotels and motels had "No Vacancy" signs lit almost every evening. The restaurants and bars made more profits than anyone could remember. Stores and shops had to refill their inventories half way through the summer. Billy and Clearance continued to count more tips from their instrument cases than they earned in wages.

The letters from Primrose came with regularity, and Billy savored each one. He held a piece of paper that she had touched, had poured her thoughts into, had sealed in the envelope with her own warm, pink tongue. The paper even smelled like her cabin, the wood smoke and drying herbs. Each letter he tucked in a growing bundle that he kept in his duffel bag.

Primrose filled his thoughts and every pretty woman he saw in the Mangey Moose only reminded him of Primrose's gentle curves and beautiful face. He felt proud about not being lured into bed by Myra, and felt no regrets that she had not returned after stalking out of the bar.

Billy's friendship with Toad became an enriching experience for both men. Billy thought Toad was the answer to his desire for a different kind of father. For Toad, Billy became someone who not only listened to his stories, but also one who appreciated them.

Max had done well with his river running business, and spoke to Toad about going to Arizona to run the Verde and Salt Rivers during the winter. Toad told Billy that he thought Max might be getting too spread out, and didn't realize that there were times when Arizona rivers didn't come close to the streamflow in the Snake.

One day, Toad invited Billy and Clearance to ride with him to Arizona when the season ended in Jackson. "I'm headin' back to The Rockin' Y and winter there, cookin'," Toad said. "I figure to go visit Leroy before I start, so I'll take ya plumb ta Arivaca, Billy."

"That would be great, and we will all split the gas," Billy said.

"I'll get off in Tucson," Clearance said. "How long are you

planning to stay in Arivaca, Billy?"

"I have no idea, but I'll meet you in Tucson sometime."

Two weeks after Labor Day weekend, the tourist season in Jackson waned. Jubilant after an excellent summer business at the Mangey Moose Saloon, Joe Spencer threw a bash for all the employees and their guests. Billy invited Toad to join him, and the old cowboy had the time of his life listening to and watching Billy and Clearance play and sing. He also enjoyed sipping the unlimited supply of Jack Daniels.

Max gave Toad, Billy and the river boatmen bonuses for their efforts that made the river running enterprise successful. He promised employment for the next summer's season to everyone, and if he decided to set up in Arizona for the winter, he would contact each employee.

Billy wrote Primrose a letter saying that he would be back to the cabin as soon as possible. Two days after the party at the Mangey Moose, Toad, Billy and Clearance packed their belongings into the chuckwagon pickup, and headed out of Jackson. Toad explained the reasons for the route he planned to take. "I don't cotton ta them Interstates. They drive too damned fast and I like ta stop now and then ta stretch. So we're a keepin' ta the back roads."

"We're in no hurry," Billy said. "Just so we get to Arivaca yesterday."

Toad and Clearance laughed.

"You wouldn't be anxious ta see that gal of yours, would ya?" Toad asked.

"More anxious than you are to see your old partner, Leroy."

"We'll get there when we get there."

Toad drove the old pickup five miles-per-hour slower than the speed limits, sometimes even slower. But, Billy and Clearance enjoyed looking at the countryside as Toad told his stories and theories about why the cattle business had ended up in the hands of wealthy easterners.

Just before sunset, the first day out, Toad turned the pickup onto a dirt road that led to a small creek, out of sight from the highway near Rifle, Colorado. "Three hundred miles is plenty for one day," Toad said. "I've camped here before."

The next day they reached Ouray, Colorado in mid-morning. From there they began the long climb over the eleven thousand foot Red Mountain Pass and down into Silverton. Billy and Clearance were awestruck at the beauty of the rugged mountain landscape. In Silverton, Toad explained about the narrow gauge railway that carried tourists from Durango to Silverton along the Animas River. *I sure wish he'd drive a little faster*, Billy thought to himself.

They stayed in Silverton to watch the train pull into the station and the tourists swarm off to visit the old silver mining town, whose old buildings echoed a booming past. Billy thought that playing for the tourists in Silverton might be a good way to spend a summer.

Back on "The Million Dollar Highway," they climbed out of the valley and reached Durango. With plenty of daylight left, Toad drove to a place he knew outside Cortéz where they camped for the night. Billy thought about Primrose as he watched the stars from his bedroll. At the rate Toad drove his beloved pickup truck, it would be two more days before he could take the woman he loved into his arms.

Arriving in Tucson at noon, Toad and Billy said their good-byes to Clearance at the corner of North Fourth Avenue and Sixth Street. After stopping at a nursery called "Plant World" long enough for Billy to buy two small peach trees, Toad headed the pickup south. Two hours later, they were in Arivaca. Billy pointed out the road to Primrose's cabin. He felt a rush of anticipation as the pickup bounced occasionally over shallow gullies where the summer rains had caused the road to erode.

When the cabin came into view, Billy looked around to see if Primrose might be outside, and spotted her in the garden. "There she is," he blurted out.

"Ya ain't too excited are ya, Billy?" Toad asked.

Billy was out of the door before the pickup stopped. Seeing Billy trotting toward her, Primrose left the garden and walked quickly to meet him. They grinned as they approached each other, and as they met, their arms encircled one another. They kissed fervently, and felt each other's bodies tremble. Billy felt his entire body tingle with joy to feel Primrose next to him.

"Is it ever good to have you in my arms again," Billy said.

"I really missed you, Billy. I am so glad you are back."

They kissed again and their passions rose.

"We should go have you meet Toad and I'll unload my stuff. I brought you a present."

"What?"

"You'll see."

Walking with their arms around each other's waists, they reached the pickup just as Toad opened the door and stood waiting. "Toad, this is Primrose," Billy said.

"I'm right pleased to meet you. Billy's told me all about ya and I must say, you're more beautiful than he could describe."

"Thank you, Toad. He wrote a lot about you in his letters. Would you like a cup of coffee?"

"No thanks," Toad replied. "Gotta get down the road to see an old *compadre* of mine."

"Well, you know where to find me," Billy said. "Come by any time you're up this way."

"Thanks, Billy. Need any help with your gear?"

"No problem," Billy said, reaching into the back of the pickup for his banjo and duffel bag. "Primrose, here's your present."

"What are they?"

"Peach trees."

"They are wonderful. Thank you," she said, her face breaking into a smile filled with delight.

She took the trees from the pickup.

"Nice meeting you, Toad."

"The same."

"Toad, don't be a stranger," Billy said. "Come by and tell us some stories. And, my friend, thanks for the ride."

"Was my pleasure, Billy. That woulda be'n a lonesome ride without you young fellers ta talk at."

"Hope to see you soon, Toad."

Billy and Primrose waited until Toad had backed the pickup around and started back to the main road. They waved to him and he waved back. "Toad is a good old man," Billy said. "I had a lot of fun workin' with him."

Billy picked up his banjo and duffel bag and Primrose carried the two potted peach trees, leaving them outside the cabin. Once inside, they were in each other's arms again, their passion flowing rapidly.

Suddenly, Primrose broke the embrace, and stood facing Billy in the middle of the room. "I have something to tell you and I can't wait any longer," she said.

"I love you too, beautiful lady," Billy said

"I love you, Billy. I hope what I am going to tell you will make you happy, because I am happy." After pausing a moment she continued. "I'm pregnant."

"Wow!" Billy exclaimed, dropping his lower jaw.

"I thought I might be before you left for Wyoming. How do you feel about becoming a father?"

"Right off, I'm just surprised. I guess I am happy, too. When will this all happen? A father. I don't know anything about bein' a father."

"I figure I am a little over four months pregnant. The baby should be born sometime in January, maybe February. I have been seeing Francine in Arivaca. She's a mid-wife. She thinks I am doing fine."

"Wow, a baby," Billy said, both hands in a yoke over his cheeks, still in a mild state of shock. "That will really be great to have our own baby."

"I'm glad you are happy, Billy. I had to wait to tell you in person. That's why I didn't write to you about it."

Primrose unbuttoned her Levi's, pushed them down, and pulled her blouse over her head. Putting her palms over her belly, she smiled up at Billy.

"See, I am just beginning to show. Another month and my Levi's won't fit. Already they are tight."

"You are beautiful," Billy said, and took her into his arms again.

Primrose began unbuttoning his shirt.

"I have been dreaming about this since you left," she said.

"I've done my share of dreamin', too, Sweetheart."

After their supper, Billy and Primrose planted the peach trees inside the garden fence. "Does the water system still work all right?" Billy asked.

"So far, so good," Primrose replied. "I was worried toward the end of June. The streamflow went down, but the rains began before I had to start hauling water from town."

"McTavish has a wood-burning hot water heater at his house in Tubac," Billy said. "I think it would be nice to open a faucet and have hot water run out."

"How do you make a wood-burning hot water heater?" She asked quizzically, tilting her head and scowling slightly.

"Build a fire box underneath the tank from an old hot water heater. Plumb in a line from the storage tank, and plumb out a line to wherever you want hot water."

"It sounds simple when you explain it."

"It looked simple enough. Next time we go to Tucson we can get the tank, some fire-bricks, mortar and the pipe stuff."

"Another thing we need to do is go get firewood," Primrose said. "I have a permit from the Forest Service to cut dead oaks."

"Let's go to Tucson and I'll buy a chain-saw. I can cut enough wood in a couple of days to last all winter. I can get the stuff for the water heater at the same time."

"I have a few pieces of bead-work to finish so I can take a bunch to Tubac for the tourist season. We can combine that trip with the one to Tucson."

"That sounds like a good plan," Billy said.

Primrose finished the beaded purses four days later. Early the next morning they went to Tucson, bought what Billy needed for the wood-burning hot water heater and a re-conditioned chain-saw. At Tubac, Primrose dropped off the purses and joined Billy at the de Anza Cantina where they drank a couple of beers while chatting with Pete. They arrived home at the cabin at supper time. "Maybe we should get the wood cut before somebody gets it first," Primrose said. "I was over at the permit area two weeks ago. There are a bunch of dead oaks, but some had been cut down already."

"Let's go tomorrow mornin'. We can try out the chain-saw."

"It was fun talking to Pete. You two sure have a bunch of war stories."

"We were over there long enough to write a book about that stinkin' mess. Sometimes I wonder if we will ever get over it all. You will never hear some of the stories, because they will never get told. All the death and bloody bodies we saw are too awful to talk about. It was almost constant terror, horror and agony. I guess we are all trying to put that stuff behind. But, that's tougher than hell to do."

"You seem to have gotten over 'Nam pretty well," Primrose said.

"Like I said, I wonder if I'll ever get over it. I keep havin' those scary nightmares. I reckon the war is one reason I can't seem to settle down anywhere. From what Pete says, he has become resigned to wandering."

"Maybe you will settle down when the baby is born."

"I hope so, but I wouldn't count on it," Billy said. *I sure hope she doesn't talk about gettin' married. Bein' pregnant, she probably wants to build her a nest.* He changed the subject of their conversation. "How far away are the dead oaks?"

The wood cutting work went well. The oak was so hard that

Billy had to sharpen the chain on the saw with regularity. By noon they had a full load of firewood in the van. There were some logs over a foot in diameter that Billy planned to split, but they had a lot of small branches that would be just right for heating water. They hauled the wood back to the cabin, and the next day cut another load. "We might as well get another load tomorrow," Billy said. "It might be a colder winter than last year."

"You might be right. As long as there are dead oaks, we might as well use them."

The next morning they had loaded half the firewood into the van when a new green pickup truck stopped on the road. The pickup had the Forest Service logo and underneath were the words "For Official Use Only" on the doors. They watched as the uniformed ranger put on his "Smokey Bear" hat, got out of the truck and walked toward them. "Good morning," the ranger said. "May I see your permit?" The ranger folded his arms over his chest trying to look important.

Primrose scowled at the ranger, dug into the back pocket of her Levi's and withdrew the folded permit she had been issued at the Forest Service headquarters in Tucson. Squinting her eyes with a look of disdain, she handed it to the ranger. He unfolded and inspected it.

"This is a domestic firewood cutting permit. Are you selling this wood?"

"No," Primrose said, her arms akimbo.

"Are you Ingrid Wallenbach?"

"Yes."

"May I see some identification?"

Primrose pulled out her driver's license.

"Who are you, Sir?" he asked handing back the license.

"I'm Banjo Billy." *This sonofabitch acts like he owns the forest.*

"Your name is not on this permit. Did you cut any of this firewood?"

"I'm just helpin' Ingrid load it." *What I'm doin' is none of this bastard's business.*

"It looks like more than you'd need for a fireplace. Your tire tracks show you've been here more than a couple of times. Are you sure you are not cutting this wood to sell?"

"Why don't you come to my cabin and you will see that this is for domestic use," Primrose said, an edge to her voice and color blooming on her cheeks.

"That won't be necessary." He handed back her permit. "Besides, I am very busy."

Billy snapped at the pompous ranger. "Are you busy harrassin' people?"

The ranger squared his shoulders. "Sir, I could arrest you for cutting firewood without a permit."

"Go ahead and try," Billy threw at him and took a step backward. "I'll stick that Smokey Bear hat up your stinkin' bureaucratic ass."

Surprise flashed across the ranger's face. "I'll make believe I didn't hear that, Sir."

"Then make believe you have somethin' else to do, and get the hell out of here, Smokey."

The ranger turned on his heel and strode back to the green pickup, climbed behind the wheel, and spun off toward Arivaca.

"Wow, Billy," Primrose said. "You didn't give that dude any slack."

He stood watching the pickup disappear over a hill, clenching and opening his fists. "It bugs hell out of me when some asshole like that tries to get in my space. I reckon it's another example of how well I'm gettin' over 'Nam," he said sarcastically.

Primrose slipped her arm around his waist. "I have to admit, I enjoyed watching you back him down."

"Give some people a badge, and they think they own the world. I was kind of hopin' the bastard would have tried to arrest me for somethin' he had no proof of. I spent too long a time over in 'Nam to take any crap from some chickenshit like that ranger. What's it matter to them whether I cut it or you did? We're together."

They took their last load of oak firewood back to the cabin, and unloaded it with the other two. After breakfast the next day Billy began splitting the large logs to sizes that would fit into the box heater. He put the smaller pieces in a separate stack to burn in the water heater once he had it built.

After finishing splitting the logs, he and Primrose gathered a pile of flat rocks to mortar together for the outside of the water heater's fire box. Billy built a frame for a small foundation. He then mixed some cement and filled the form. By the time the sun rose the following morning, the cement had set up enough to hold the flat rocks for the outside wall of the fire-box.

Measuring the diameter of the inside tank of the old, gas-fueled hot water heater, Billy began by placing the fire bricks in a vertical position so the tank would rest on them when he installed it. Next he began laying the flat rocks around the bricks to hold them in place. Between each layer of rock he troweled on an inch of mortar. At the front of the fire box, he left an opening for building the fire and for draft while the fire burned. In the mortar joints he placed two strands of heavy wire for reinforcing the structure. Between the top two layers of rocks which would eventually extend several inches above the tank, he laid the wire in a full circle to tie the top together more securely. Finished with the rock masonry, he and Primrose carefully put the tank on the tops of the fire bricks. For the finishing touch, Billy troweled in mortar around the tank to act as grout.

Leaving the plumbing for the next day to give the mortar a chance to dry, he went into the cabin, opened two beers, and played his banjo for Primrose. Later, she went out to milk Pamela and shut up the hens for the night. Billy went with her to grab and butcher one of the young roosters for supper.

Around the first of August, two of the hens had hatched two dozen eggs. Seven were pullets that Primrose wanted to keep to replace some old hens. She planned to cook the young roosters, or trade some to Toby for sausage. Among other livestock, Toby raised a few hogs, and had a tasty recipe for making pork sausage.

Billy made quick work of dressing the young rooster. Primrose cut the carcass into manageable parts, and cooked them over the coals in the box heater. She also opened a Mason jar of green beans she had put up early during the summer.

The cloud bank that had been moving in since morning began sprinkling rain drops on the cabin's corrugated tin roof. They retired to bed shortly after finishing their supper. "I love hearing raindrops hitting the roof at night," Primrose said.

Naked, they began caressing each other. "If I were alone, the sound of raindrops on the roof would put me to sleep," Billy said.

"But, we are together, and, I am not sleepy. I am so glad you are back with me, Billy."

"I also dig that we're goin' to be parents."

"That makes me happy. I like being pregnant. Some women have morning sickness, but I feel fine."

Billy took her into his arms, and rolled her on top of him. Looking into her eyes, he paused a moment, then said, "You are beautiful. I love you, Primrose."

"I love you, too, Banjo Billy."

Plumbing the hot water heater with copper tubing into the cabin took most of the morning. When all the connections satisfied him, Billy opened the valves to fill the thirty-gallon tank, and started a fire in the fire-box. After twenty minutes he called Primrose from the garden. Inside the cabin, he turned on the hot water faucet over the sink. "Feel that water after only twenty minutes," he said.

"Nice and warm," Primrose replied, holding her hand in the water. "This will make life a lot easier. Pretty soon you will have the cabin wired for electricity."

"We can live without that. We might get spoiled."

Billy put more wood on the fire, and after another twenty minutes he could not hold his hand under the water coming from the faucet.

CHAPTER NINE

A month later, they drove into Tucson. Primrose needed some beads and supplies. Billy bought a used baby crib from a store on Fourth Avenue and found Clearance at Ray and Red's drinking a noontime beer before leaving for his gig at Gus and Andy's.

Clearance greeted Billy's news of impending fatherhood with surprise. "Will you be heading north for the summer, or sticking around Arivaca changing diapers?"

"I'll have to go north to make any decent money," Billy replied. "Southern Arizona melts durin' the summer."

"Have you seen Toad?"

"Not since he left me off at the cabin."

"If you see him, ask about getting a ride north with him."

"I will," Billy said. "I'm sure he'll take us if he's goin'."

"If you want to make some bucks, come over to Gus and Andy's," Clearance suggested. "I've been doing pretty damn good."

"I figure to hang around Arivaca. I will be going to Tubac in February for that nine day festival."

"I'll be there with you. I sure like Pete, that buddy of yours."

"Pete's a good one, for sure."

Billy left Clearance at Ray and Red's, and found Primrose sitting in the van. "We have to stop by that used furniture store next to the grocery," he said.

"What for?" Primrose asked.

"I bought somethin'."

"For me?"

"Not really. You'll see soon enough."

Primrose parked the van in the "loading zone" in front of the furniture store. Billy got out, went into the place and came out carrying the crib. Primrose jumped out of the van, and opened the back doors. "Wow, that's really neat."

Seeing the pleasant surprise on her face, Billy grinned broadly, and loaded the crib into the back of the van. "The mattress is new, but the frame needs sandin' and varnishin'," he said.

"Where can we get some sheets and stuff?"

"I'm only six months along."

"That's all right. We need to get things for the baby."

Primrose dropped her lower jaw at Billy's seriousness. "There's a store where we can get baby things on the south end of town."

Primrose drove the van to the place, and they bought sheets, blankets and assorted clothes. As they headed south to the crossroads, Primrose began to sob. Billy glanced toward her, wondering whether to pull over. "What's wrong, Primrose?" Billy asked. *I'll bet she wants me to marry her.*

"I don't know. I guess I am just happy. All this stuff you are doing for the baby makes me feel very happy. I sure do love you, Billy."

"I love you, too."

As Primrose's pregnancy advanced, Billy enjoyed feeling the movement in her belly. He told her many times that she was beautiful. They made regular visits to Francine in Arivaca. On these occasions, Francine included Billy in the conversations so that he felt a full partnership in the coming event in their lives.

Billy began to perform most of the chores around the cabin, although Primrose insisted on milking Pamela. Early morning and evening walks became a routine for them. After her seventh month, walking became more like waddling, but Francine insisted that she continue the exercise.

The winter remained mild. The rains rolled in on long frontal systems with the gentle storms lasting three to four days. They had little need for the fire except early mornings and late evenings.

Francine explained her plan. As soon as Primrose felt her first labor pains, Billy would drive to Francine's house in Arivaca. Francine would then follow Billy back to the cabin in her Volkswagen "Beetle." She thought it would be better for Primrose to give birth to the baby at home rather than in a strange place.

Primrose awakened early on the second Monday in

February. After the second labor pain, she told Billy that he had better get dressed. "How close are the pains?" he asked.

"I didn't look at the watch, but it may have been twenty minutes."

"Will you need anything while I am getting Francine?"

"I don't think so. I don't think it will come until later, but, of course, I really don't know. I never had a baby before."

Billy dressed quickly, and tossed some wood onto the coals in the box heater. Back next to the bed, he leaned over, gave Primrose a tender kiss, and left the cabin. The van started easily, in spite of the chill that had blown in. Once on the road to town, he drove as fast as he dared over the graded gravel. All the way he hoped Francine would be home. *I sure hope I'll be a better father than mine was. I want to be warm and loving, not a cold fish.*

Rapping hard on the old wooden front door of the adobe dwelling, Billy heard Francine's beagle hound barking. Dressed in a robe, Francine came to the door. "Primrose has started labor," Billy said excitedly

"How far apart are the pains?" Francine asked.

"She thinks about twenty minutes."

"There's no hurry, but I'll be with you as soon as I get dressed."

Ten minutes later, the midwife followed the van toward the cabin. As soon as she entered, Francine took charge. Going to Primrose, she asked first about the intervals of the labor pains.

"The last one came at eight minutes," Primrose said.

"Everything will be fine," Francine said.

Billy stood a short distance away, watching Primrose, and wishing he could be doing something. Going over to the box heater, he added wood. Outside he started a fire in the wood-burning hot water heater. He was glad that Pamela had dried up her milk. A month before, Primrose had taken the goat over to a male Alpine and had her bred.

Looking east, he saw the first hint of the sun rising from

behind the mountains in the distance. Back inside the cabin, he stood watching again. As another contraction started, Primrose groaned. Billy returned to the hot water heater, and stuffed more wood into the firebox. Going back inside, he heard Francine telling Primrose to push harder.

He glanced at Primrose and saw her grimace, and noticed her hair matted with sweat. Francine bent over as Primrose groaned.

"One more big push, Primrose," Francine said. "There we are."

Francine moved quickly. Billy couldn't see what was going on from his position near the box heater.

"You did a great job, Primrose," Francine said. "You have a baby boy!"

She placed the infant between Primrose's swollen breasts. Billy edged closer to the bed to see the baby. "There's hot water when you need it," he said.

"I'll get that fellow cleaned up in a little bit," Francine said. "Right now we have to wait for the placenta."

Shortly, Primrose expelled the sack that had held her baby all those months. Francine inspected the membrane to make sure all had left the womb before putting it into a plastic bag. "All right, Billy, you can bring me one of these towels soaked in warm water," Francine said.

Billy hurried to the sink to soak the towel, and returned it to the mid-wife. She cleaned the baby gently and wrapped him in a small cotton blanket. Then she tended to Primrose. Billy grinned broadly as he looked down on his new son. "Wow, Sweetheart, we have a boy!" he said.

Primrose turned her head and smiled at Billy. Taking the bundled baby into her arms, Francine handed him to Billy. "All right Dad, it's time you got acquainted. He won't break. Just take him into your arms like I am."

Billy put his arms out, and received the baby. "He is so little," Billy said. "Are they all this little?"

"He looks perfectly normal to me," Francine said. "If you had a scale here, I'll bet he would weigh at least seven pounds."

Suddenly the baby began to whimper. Billy began moving him with a rocking motion. "I think it might be time for Primrose to take over," Francine said.

She took the baby from Billy and gave him to Primrose.

"He's probably not hungry enough for much, but it won't hurt to see if he'll nurse," Francine said. "I'll rinse out these towels while you two enjoy your new baby boy."

When she finished rinsing the towels, Francine sat down at the table to fill out the birth certificate application.

"What's your real name, Billy?

"William O'Leary," Billy replied, hesitantly.

"And yours, Primrose?"

"Ingrid Wallenbach."

"Have you two decided on a name for the baby?"

"Not yet," Primrose said.

"You can fill it in before you send this to the Bureau of Vital Statistics," Francine explained. "That takes care of all the paper work."

After staying around for a while to make sure all was well with Primrose and the baby, Francine announced that she would go back to Arivaca. Billy followed her out to the Volkswagen. "How much do I owe you, Francine?"

"I've already made those arrangements with Primrose. We agreed to trade beads for baby. She's going to make me a beaded buckskin blouse and skirt."

"Then, all I can say is thanks a lot, Francine. You did great."

"Primrose is the one who did great. She paid attention to what I told her all along and had an easy birthing compared to a lot of women I have mid-wifed."

"Well, thank you again. Don't be a stranger," Billy said, and went back inside the cabin.

Primrose watched the baby as he slept in her arms. "He is just beautiful, isn't he Billy?"

"He sure is. What's all this about a birth certificate? I think he would be better off if the government didn't know he existed."

"He'll need a birth certificate for a lot of things like school, a driver's license and all kinds of stuff," Primrose said.

"Yeah, but if the government doesn't have a record on him he won't get drafted and the I.R.S. can't rip off any of his money."

"We'll have to take the chance that there won't be any more wars for him to get drafted into," Primrose said.

"There will always be wars. Right now, Vietnam seems to have convinced the people that war is bad shit. But, as long as there are politicians and industrial companies that depend on war for profits, there will be wars. Damnit, I don't want my son to go through the same shit I did."

"I understand your point of view, Billy, but he will need a birth certificate to enter school when he's old enough."

"We can teach him all he needs to know right here."

"I don't think I trust myself to do that," Primrose said.

"We can talk about all this later. There's no big rush to send in this application, is there?"

"I don't know. Francine told me it's the best thing to do. She knows two couples who didn't register their children and are home-schooling them. The kids need more of a social life and they are only exposed to what the parents are teaching them. According to Francine, they will have very limited choices when they grow up. Besides, just because I live a certain way, doesn't mean I should force that on our son. He can make his own choices when the times comes."

"I know one thing," Billy said, pointing to the Gibson Banjo hanging on the wall. "This little guy will be able to play a banjo."

"I can just see you two playing your banjos together. That will be nice."

Until Primrose regained her strength, Billy did all the chores around the cabin, including washing diapers, blankets and wash cloths. He learned how to change the baby and often put him on his shoulder to burp after Primrose finished nursing him.

After further discussion of the birth certificate application situation, Billy relented to Primrose's wishes. They named the boy,

William Cougar O'Leary, because Primrose considered cougars one of the most graceful and strongest animals in the wild.

When Cougar awakened hungry at intervals during the night, Billy watched him nurse. Billy thought that Primrose giving her breasts to their son was the most beautiful sight he had ever witnessed.

One evening, after Cougar had finished nursing and was sleeping in his crib, Billy opened two beers and sat down at the table with Primrose. "I'm thinkin' I should write to my parents to tell them they have a grandson," he said.

"I have thought about writing mine, but I wonder if knowing they were grandparents would just make them feel old," Primrose said.

"I don't want mine comin' out here. I couldn't stand havin' them around tellin' us what we should be doin'."

"They don't know how to get here, and you don't have to tell them."

"I suppose you're right," Billy said. "I think I'll write them a short letter, just so they will know about Cougar."

"I am not done thinking about writing my parents. I guess I could write a sort of announcement and see what happens."

"That festival in Tubac is comin' up in a week, but, in spite of the money I could earn, I don't feel like doin' that this year," Billy said.

"Why don't you take the van for a couple of days. I can handle everything here," Primrose said.

"I'll think about it."

After he had finished with the morning chores, Billy wrote a short letter, telling his parents about Cougar. Primrose took the pad when he had finished, and penned a short note to her parents in Malibu. When they went to Arivaca for ice, beer and flour, they mailed their letters.

Returning to the cabin, Billy had just carried in the ice chest when a vehicle drove in and parked behind the van. Billy stepped out of the doorway, and saw that the visitor was Toad.

"Hey you old cowboy, how are you?" Billy asked.

"Fine as frog's hair," Toad replied. "How's it goin' with ya?"

"Never better," Billy said. "I'm a father."

"Well, I be go ta hell," Toad said.

"Come on in and see our baby boy."

Toad limped his way over to the crib where Primrose had put Cougar down for a nap. "Now there's quite a boy," Toad remarked. "Got your red hair, eh Billy?"

"When he wakes up, you'll see he got his eyes from Primrose."

They sat down at the table after Billy opened the beers and handed one to Toad and one to Primrose.

"Well, I thought I'd drop by and see what you're a figurin' 'bout this summer. Max telephoned me at the ranch, and wanted to know when I'd be back up in Jackson. He also told me to say hello to you and hopes you'll come back to work again."

"I'm planning on it. When do you figure to leave?"

"Max wants us up there for Memorial Day weekend. He's got last year's boatmen back, 'ceptin' one, that skinny black-haired feller they called 'Tent-pole.' I figure ta start up thataway four days afore the weekend."

"Sounds good to me. Now that I'm a father, I need to go make some good bucks this summer."

Billy and Primrose sat around listening to Toad's stories. When Cougar awakened, Primrose carried him over so that Toad could get a good look at him. "He shore 'nuf has your eyes Primrose. Looks like he'll grow ta be quite a man."

Primrose sat down on the bed, opened her blouse and began feeding the child. Toad fidgeted with embarrassment, and said his good-byes. Billy followed him out to the old pickup. "I'll be ready when you come by," he said.

"If'n ya get down my way afore, stop by."

"Will do, Toad."

Still nursing Cougar, Primrose looked up at Billy when he came in.

"Billy, I've been thinking about what you and Toad were talking about."

"What do you mean? We talked about a lot of things."

"About leaving for Wyoming. I have been hoping you would stay here with me and the baby."

"Now, Primrose, you know I have to go up there to make decent money during their tourist season in Jackson."

"I understand all that, but you could make money around here."

"Southern Arizona dries up in summer. All the 'snow-birds' go back to Michigan or Illinois. I doubt if I could get a gig even in Tucson."

"I'm not thinking about playing your banjo to make money," she said. "Look at all the things you've made around here. You have all kinds of talents which you can make money from."

"I'm a banjo player," Billy said, looking straight into her eyes. "Besides, come May I'll have the itchiest feet in the country. I'm already startin' to feel a bit fenced in."

"Are you sure you love me and Cougar?"

"Dammit, woman, of course I love both of you. I adore you. That has nothin' to do with me needin' to go north to play banjo."

Primrose's question bothered him, not only because she expressed doubt about his love, but also it made him feel more restless. Both remained silent for a few minutes until Primrose eased Cougar away from her breast and held him over her shoulder. *She'll probably ask about gettin' married.*

"I'm sorry I said that, Billy. I know you love us. It's just that I don't want to see you going away for the whole summer. When you gave me the peach trees I thought you might be here to stay."

"I wish I could explain how I am, but I don't know why I'm the way I am. All I know is I have to do what I have to do. And, like last summer, I'll miss you all the time."

"I think you should go to the Tubac festival next week," Primrose said. "You would probably have a good time talking to Pete."

"Yeah, I think you're right," Billy replied. "I'll go down there for a couple of days. Clearance will probably be there too."

The following Friday, Billy loaded the van with his bedroll and banjo, and drove to Tubac. Entering the town from the frontage road, he saw more than a hundred people busily erecting their booths for the coming art and craft fair. Driving toward Cantina de Anza, he noticed that there were many more booths than last year. The town had already taken on a carnival-like atmosphere.

Parking the van next to Pete's VW bus in the lot behind the bar, he took his banjo with him around to the front entrance. There were two couples sitting at the bar with margaritas. Pete stood, leaning on the serving window talking to them. When Billy came in, Pete looked up. "Hey, Bill, I've been wondering when you would show."

"It's good to see you, Pete."

Billy propped the banjo case against the wall, and sat down on the barstool next to the doorway into the patio. Pete came over with an opened Budweiser, and put it on the bar.

"Where the hell have you been?" Pete inquired.

"Up in Arivaca. Primrose had a baby boy. We named him Cougar."

"I'll be damned. That's great news. So now you're a daddy."

"Yeah, and I really enjoy all this. He's got Primrose's eyes, but my hair."

"As long as he looks more like her than you," Pete said, and laughed. "Are you and Primrose married yet?"

"No. We haven't talked about marriage," Billy said. "Marriage is pretty scary."

"I know what you mean."

Billy took a pull on his beer. "I parked out back next to your VW, is that all right?"

"Sure, are you here for the full nine day swap-meet?"

"No, just a couple of days. I just came down to see you and Clearance, if he shows up."

"I haven't seen him yet. This place is going to be like a friggin' zoo," Pete said, disgust in the tone of his voice.

"It looks like there's a lot more booths than last year."

"Some arrogant bastard came in and bought the big vacant lot on the west end. He decided to do his own festival because he got off to a bad start with the Chamber of Commerce. He has craft gypsies coming in from all over because he is selling booth space at a big discount with no jurying. The chamber people are really pissed at him."

"I reckon that will mean more people for you to make drinks for, and me to play banjo to."

"That's the way I figure too," Pete said. "The chamber people say it will cheapen the town's image, but as long as the tips roll in, I suppose I should care less."

Pete nodded his head toward the margarita drinkers.

"Play a song, Billy. I'll bet these dudes are good for a couple of bucks."

Billy took out his banjo, tuned it as quickly as he could without looking like he was in a hurry, and started with "Night Train to Memphis." He heard Pete talk to the margarita drinkers.

"Banjo Billy is a Vietnam buddy of mine. He came down to the festival to play for tips."

"One of the women had tinted red hair and wore green eye shadow. She leaned her ample breasts on the top of the bar.

"He is really good," she said. "Do you two travel together?"

"No," Pete said. "We ran into each other here last year. It was the first time I had seen him since we were in 'Nam."

The redhead's companion, a dark-complected man, with immaculate razor cut black hair, ordered another round. Pete grabbed four fresh margarita glasses from the overhead rack, and began preparing the drinks.

When Billy finished his song, the four people applauded. Billy reached down, remembering he had not left the case opened at his feet. The applause made him feel good. It was something he had not heard since he had left Jackson. He continued playing using the "claw-hammer" way of picking for a couple of songs and frailing for others.

Their glasses empty, the margarita drinkers left a five dollar bill for Pete on the bar, and the two men each dropped fives into Billy's case. When they had left, Pete brought Billy another Budweiser. "I knew damn well they would be easy," Pete said. "This might be a good festival."

"It was sure a good beginnin'," Billy said.

"Are you going back to Wyoming this summer?"

"Yeah," Billy said. "Now that I'm a father, I need to make good money, and that's the best place I have found yet. Primrose would rather I stay with her and the baby."

"Women are like that," Pete said. "They like the idea of marriage for some reason. Seems like every time I get going with a woman, they want me to settle down and 'amount to something.' When I hear that, I get a real strong urge to split for somewhere else."

"I'm havin' a tough time explainin' to Primrose that I have to wander. I have to play the damn banjo. It's a real part of me. I love to make music and watch people enjoy what I do."

"I think a lot of us who were in 'Nam have a tough time settling in anywhere," Pete remarked. "There's a chick here in Tubac, who owns a big house. She wants me to live with her. She said she would pay for everything. That spooked hell out of me, so I won't go up to her house anymore. She'll be by after a while, and tonight you'll probably hear my VW jouncing around if you're awake."

"All this stuff is hangin' heavy," Billy said. "I love Primrose and our son completely. But I know damn well I have to go north this summer and play banjo."

"It will probably all work out as long as you both love each other enough. The trouble with all the women I've met since 'Nam is that I don't love them enough, or they don't love me enough. Maybe some day I'll run into the one. As they say in Mexico, *¿Quién sabe?*"

"I just can't stay in one place too long. It bothers me sometimes," Billy said, scratching his head.

"Yeah, I know that feeling," Pete replied. "I was reading an article in the paper the other day. It said that most of the homeless in the country are Vietnam vets and that the suicide rate for them is way above the national average. I don't know where they get all those figures but it sounded to me like you and I are doing better than most."

"I've got a home if I'll just stay there and there's no way I will ever think about committing suicide. That's just not in my mind at all. I've got Primrose and Cougar."

"I have the van to live in. That's my home so I am damn sure not homeless. I thought about suicide once when I was getting rehabilitated with this damn fiberglass leg, but it hasn't been bad enough to make me think about that for a long time."

More customers arrived. Pete took their orders and made their drinks. Billy began playing again, mostly instrumentals, because he was buried in the thoughts about why he felt like leaving. When he sang "Greensleeves," the thoughts eased out of his mind. The next song he played and sang was one he had composed earlier that winter. He called it "Peach Trees." The lyrics told about two peach trees whose branches touched as they grew together but once in a while the wind came up and there was space between the branches.

Arriving in Tubac in mid-afternoon, Clearance sought out Billy at La Cantina de Anza. Billy greeted his friend and Pete brought Clearance an opened Budweiser. "How are things in Tucson?" Billy asked.

"Same as always. I've had a good gig at Gus and Andy's."

"Are you still crashin' at the old garage?"

"I was until the owner showed up one day and ran me off. He was nice enough though. He said his insurance wouldn't cover anyone staying there."

"Where are you stayin' now?"

"Remember Ginny, the waitress at the Hungry Eye?"

"Yeah, cute gal," Billy replied.

"I'm snuggling with her."

"Goddam, Clearance, I never thought you were a lover-boy."

"I'll put it this way, Billy. We sure have a great time together. How's your love life, by the way?"

"Primrose had a baby boy. We named him Cougar."

"Hey, man, congratulations."

"Thanks," Billy said. "Toad came by the other day wanting to know if we wanted a ride back to Jackson. He said he was leaving four days before Memorial Day."

"Are you going?" Clearance asked.

"Yeah, he's goin' to pick me up."

"I've been doing a bunch of thinking. Ginny and I are really hitting it off together. She likes her job at the Hungry Eye, and I like my gig at Gus and Andy's. They slow down in the summer, but they said they would keep me on as long as they have customers."

"That sounds to me like you aren't goin' to Jackson," Billy said.

"Ginny and I have even talked about going back to New Orleans."

"Wow, old buddy, you're really hunkered in," Billy said.

"I'd say you were, too," Clearance remarked. "Banjo Billy is a daddy."

"Let's do a tune together," Billy suggested, changing the subject.

Clearance took his guitar from the battered case. After getting the instruments tuned together, they began playing and singing. The local happy hour crowd came in to mix with the festival-goers and craft people.

One of the local merchants, a former Californian who had started a shop featuring Mexican crafts, made his usual happy hour entrance, standing inside the doorway surveying the customers with his beady, brown eyes. Hatless, to reveal his wavy, salt and pepper hair that he periodically ran his comb through, he wore Levi's and a bright, Hawaiian-style, short-sleeved shirt, unbuttoned almost to his navel. His forearms exhibited tattoos of matching dragons. A heavy gold chain around his neck glistened over his curly gray chest-hair. Pete poured him a scotch-on-the-rocks, putting it on the bar when the man finally walked over. "Thanks, Pete, how goes everything?"

"Fine, Freddy, how was your day?"

"Helluva day. Did a grand before noon," Freddy said, loud enough so that some of the customers at the bar looked up at him.

"That's great, Freddy, and the festival doesn't really start until tomorrow."

Pete left to make a round of drinks for four people sitting at one of the tables. Freddy looked over toward Billy and Clearance, scowled, and turned back to try to get Pete back into a conversation. Pete had to keep moving to keep the orders filled so Freddy tossed down his scotch. Drawing a thick roll of bills from his pocket, he held it up in view of everyone as he peeled off a five dollar bill, and put it on the bar next to his empty glass.

"See ya, everybody," Freddy said. He waved, turned and left La Cantina de Anza. Nobody said goodbye.

Soon the crowd in the bar kept Pete in constant movement as he made their drinks. The large brandy snifter he used for tips came close to overflowing. The instrument cases showed a profitable evening for Billy and Clearance. The crowd thinned after eleven, and Pete closed the bar at midnight.

Clearance accepted Brian McTavish's invitation to stay on his sleeping porch again. Billy crawled into his bedroll in the van. He heard Pete and his girl friend Julie talking in the VW bus next to him, but sleep robbed him of anything more.

Katherine, the owner, stopped by the bar as Billy, Pete, and Clearance sat around a table drinking morning coffee. "It's good to see you boys again," she said. "Sorry I didn't get around to saying hello last night, but things got too hectic."

"It was busy at the bar," Pete said. "Tonight should be even better."

"I sure hope so," Katherine said. "I've got a mortgage payment due."

She turned to Billy.

"Are you here for the whole nine days?"

"I wish I could be, Katherine," Billy answered. "But, I am now a father and I need to get back to Arivaca, Sunday."

"Congratulations. As long as you want to play, it's the same deal as last year. I wish you could stick around the entire time. How about you, Clearance. Can you do the nine days?"

"I'd like to Katherine, but I have a gig in Tucson. I'll be leaving Sunday, too."

"Well, it's good to see you two, and Pete, make sure they get breakfast."

"Will do, Katherine."

She left through the door to the kitchen area. Pete signaled one of the waitresses. She came over to the table and took their breakfast orders.

"I hope tonight isn't any busier than last night," Pete remarked. "I had a helluva time keeping up."

"Just out of curiosity, who is that dude who wears the gold chain with his shirt unbuttoned?" Billy asked.

"That's Freddy Ingersoll. He sells Mexican trinkets. He came here from California claiming he was a 'narc.' Somebody came through here a while back who knew him over there. It turned out that Freddy spent most of his life in California repossessing cars. He's an asshole."

"He seemed to like you, Pete," Clearance said.

"The only reason I talk to him is that he leaves a lot of money on the bar."

"He only had one drink," Billy said.

"But, he left a five for a two dollar well-drink," Pete said. "He didn't show it, but he came in pretty well blasted. Someone said he drinks scotch and milk all day in his store. That way, his customers think he's only having a glass of milk. Some afternoons he gets here and stays too long. When he is really bombed he is a real pain in the ass."

After finishing breakfast, Billy and Clearance helped Pete restock the beer coolers before taking a stroll around the village. They told Pete they would get back for the lunch crowd.

Tent-like booths lined most of the village streets. The vendors offered everything from attractive, lathe-turned wooden bowls to refrigerator magnets. Jewelry of various designs seemed to dominate even though the festival director had attempted to scatter those booths around.

"I hope that Freddy dude stays home tonight," Billy said. "I didn't like the strange way he looked at us last night. He wasn't there long, but he impressed me that he could mean trouble."

"I picked up on that too," Clearance said. "He struts around like he owns the place."

"Like Pete said, he looks like an asshole."

"I wonder which store is his," Clearance said.

"I don't care," Billy answered.

The tourist traffic, looking for parking, crowded the streets until off-duty deputies began directing the cars to various parking lots that had been designated for the festival. Billy and Clearance returned to La Cantina de Anza at ten-thirty to get ready to play.

By noon, a line of customers waiting for tables formed outside the door. Katherine had anticipated the situation, and had set up an additional bar in the patio to help relieve Pete from having to make all the drinks. Billy and Clearance rotated between the patio and the bar for over an hour without taking a break. Business slacked off somewhat around two-thirty. Pete made sure the two musicians had Budweisers.

Freddy Ingersoll arrived just before happy hour began. Pete glanced up at him as he stood in front of the door with his usual grand entrance pose. The bar patrons were too busy talking among themselves to notice Freddy, so he swaggered up to the bar. Pete put a scotch-on-the-rocks in front of him.

"Thanks, Pete, how goes everything?"

"Fine, Freddy. How was your day?

"About two-grand. Helluva festival," Freddy said, speaking loudly and slurring his words. "Before the nine days are over, I'll have damn sure cut a fat hog in the ass."

The patrons at the bar glanced at Freddy, then went back to their own conversations. Billy and Clearance played "Proud Mary," after which a number of customers put bills in the open cases. Freddy remained on his bar stool. "Gimme another, Pete," Freddy said.

"You got it," Pete replied, taking Freddy's glass, filling it with ice and topping it with scotch.

Billy and Clearance continued playing. Some booth people ambled in for beer. Although Pete kept constantly busy making drinks or opening bottles of beer, Freddy continued to talk to him, raising his voice as the din of other conversations increased. Every so often he turned toward Billy and Clearance to stare at them.

After the fourth scotch-on-the-rocks, Freddy Ingersoll pushed out his chest, pointed his right index finger at the musicians and bellowed, "How long do we have to listen to that goddam racket?"

In the middle of "Yesterday," Billy and Clearance ignored the rudeness of the drunken question.

"Goddam hippies," Freddy roared. "Probably a couple of goddam draft dodgers."

Billy snapped. The instant rage he felt showed in the fierce look in his eyes. He quickly raised the banjo strap over his head, leaned the instrument against the wall, and strode over to Freddy Ingersoll. First grabbing the heavy gold chain in his left hand, Billy pulled Freddy off the bar stool, and threw a solid punch with his right fist to Freddy's mouth. His fist felt teeth give way and pain shot up his arm. Freddy slipped to the floor.

Pete had yelled "Cool it!" but Billy, beyond hearing anything, lifted his right leg to smash his foot down on his opponent. Pete had rushed out from behind the bar and grabbed

Billy, "Come on, Bill. Leave the son-of-a-bitch be," Pete said. "Cool it, man."

Billy put his foot down on the floor, sparing Freddy a face that would have been close to looking like hamburger. "He's a goddam loud-mouthed drunk, Pete. Nobody calls me a draft dodger."

The bar patrons had moved quickly out of the way of the fracas. Some stood against the walls while others rushed outside to the patio.

Pete looked down at Freddy's unconscious form. "The funny thing about that asshole, is he told me he had been classified 4-F. Go back to playing, Bill. I'll take care of this idiot."

Billy put the strap over his head, and started playing again, but his hand hurt too much. Pete reached over the bar and filled a glass full of water. Standing over Freddy, he tossed the water onto the man's face. Freddy struggled to regain consciousness. When he finally came up to a sitting position on the floor, Pete grabbed him by one arm, and yanked him to his feet. "Freddy," Pete said, firmly. "You are eighty-sixed. You're out of here, and right now. Let's go!"

Freddy didn't say a word as Pete escorted him firmly to the door. As the bartender opened the door to shove him outside, Freddy put his left hand up to his mouth and staggered away. Pete returned to his station behind the bar. "Sorry about that, folks," Pete said. "That character didn't realize that you don't call a Vietnam veteran a 'draft dodger.' Bill and I were there together."

The patrons murmured their approval of the way Pete had handled the situation. Several raised hands in the air to congratulate Billy. Katherine trotted into the bar. "What's going on here, Pete? Amelia said there was a fight."

"It was just Freddy Ingersoll. He got bombed and started shooting off that big mouth of his. It's all over. I eighty-sixed him."

"All right, we can talk about it later."

Billy's hand hurt so bad he couldn't frail the banjo, so he sang to Clearance's accompaniment until the crowd left. He and

Clearance divided the money from the cases. It had been a hundred dollar day for each musician.

"I really lost it big time," Billy said as the three sat at a table with their beers.

"I don't blame you one damn bit," Pete remarked. "That asshole had it coming."

Katherine came back as Billy, Clearance and Pete were finishing the beers that Pete had set up as he shut down the bar. "Tell me about the fight, Pete," Katherine said.

"Like I told you, Freddy was half in the bag when he arrived. He kept throwing down the scotch until he was loud and obnoxious. Suddenly he yelled out about having to 'listen to that racket', pointing at Bill and Clearance. Then he referred to them as hippies. The boys kept playing. Then he called them 'draft dodgers.' Billy took off his banjo, went up to Freddy, grabbed his gold chain, and punched him a good one. Freddy ended up on the floor. It happened so fast that I didn't have a chance to stop it. Actually, I was glad to see Bill wallop that asshole."

"Pete, I can't have fights going on in this bar," Katherine said sternly. "Fights are bad for business. You're the bartender and should have stopped it before it started."

"Katherine, be reasonable. It happened too fast."

"Now you have eighty-sixed Freddy Ingersoll. He's a year-round local who drops a lot of money on this bar. Don't forget I've got a mortgage to pay off."

Billy could see that Pete had had enough from Katherine.

"Katherine," Pete said, waving an index finger at her. "I don't give a rat's ass if Freddy Ingersoll drops a hundred bucks a night on this bar and another hundred in my jar. He shouldn't be calling Vietnam vets draft dodgers."

"Just let that slide, Pete," Katherine said. "You go over to his place in the morning and tell him he is welcome back as long as he behaves himself."

Pete stared at Katherine for a moment, taking in a deep breath and letting it out, his patience gone. "Katherine, I won't be here in the morning. I won't be here tomorrow night either. I am quitting as of right this stinking assed minute."

"That goes for me too," Billy said.

Clearance joined the others.

Pete reached over next to the cash register, took a key from a small shelf and handed it to Katherine. "Here's your key to the front door, Katherine. Good luck. Maybe you can get Freddy Ingersoll to bartend for tips and scotch."

"You're a bastard, Pete," Katherine said. "Right in the middle of the festival, you're quitting me?"

CHAPTER TEN

Pete didn't answer. He followed Billy and Clearance out of La Cantina de Anza. They assembled in the parking lot behind the bar. "That Katherine sure surprised me," Billy said. "She was always so damn nice to us, makin' sure we got fed and all."

"She's sweet as hell when you're making her money," Pete said. "Money is about all she has on her mind."

"She'll have a helluva time findin' another guy to bartend for tips and food," Billy said.

"Don't forget the beer. She won't. I guess I'll drive to the rest stop off the highway and stay there tonight. Julie got all pissed off at me again last night, so she won't be looking for me here."

"Where are you goin' from here, Pete?" Billy asked

"I haven't given that a single thought."

"I think I'll head back to McTavish's," Clearance said, interrupting.

"Let me know about coming with Toad to Wyoming," Billy said.

"I was thinking about that this morning, Billy. Ginny and I have enough for bus fare to New Orleans. I guess I won't be going to Wyoming this summer."

"Well, good luck, partner. I hope we cross paths again soon."

"I expect we will," Clearance said. "Sooner or later."

After shaking hands with his friends, Clearance left Billy and Pete next to their vehicles. "Why don't you follow me up to the cabin tonight, Pete. You can hang out until you figure out where you want to go."

"You know, I think I'll do just that. I want to see that son of yours anyway."

Pete followed the van in his VW camper. When they arrived at the cabin, Pete said he would just as soon get to sleep, and see everyone in the morning. Primrose had awakened when they drove up to the cabin. "You didn't stay in Tubac very long," she said, after returning Billy's kiss.

"I got into a fight with an asshole who called me a draft dodger," Billy explained. "Pete quit. So did Clearance and I. My right hand hurts too much to play the banjo anyway. How's Cougar?"

"He's just fine. I took him out to meet Pamela yesterday. He squealed with delight when she licked his little hand. Tell me more about this fight."

"I'll tell you the whole story in the morning. Right now, the only thing I want to do is go to sleep with you next to me."

The next morning, Billy took Pete around the area and showed him the water system, and the garden. "These little peach trees seem to be doing all right after the winter," Billy said as they ambled along near the garden fence.

"Are these the trees you sang about in that song you wrote?"

"I guess I imagined what they would look like in a few years when I composed that song."

They returned to the cabin and sat at the table drinking coffee while Primrose nursed Cougar on the bed.

"This is one righteous place," Pete said. "It is so peaceful out here, a guy could really get his thoughts together just listening to the birds."

"Sometimes at night, I hear noises from animals, and wonder what they are doing," Billy remarked.

"That water system you installed is outrageous. Where in hell did you learn that stuff? I know damn well it wasn't in 'Nam."

"I grew up in farm country near Springfield, Illinois. I learned some then, but I saw the wood burning hot water heater McTavish has in Tubac."

"Too bad you can't make one for my VW."

"That would be quite a challenge," Billy said.

They spent the day talking about their days in the army as they enjoyed the few beers that had been in the ice chest. About mid-afternoon, Pete drove in to Arivaca for more beer and ice to fill the chest.

"How is your hand?" Primrose asked.

"It's still sore, but it seems better than it was this mornin'. I'm glad I didn't break anythin'. I guess I hit that bastard pretty hard. He went out with one punch."

"I'm just glad he didn't get a chance to hit you."

"Me, too."

"Pete is really nice," Primrose said.

"Pete's a great friend. I'm sure glad we met up with each other again."

"After listening to you two talk, I think I understand you better, Billy."

"What do you mean?"

"About why you have a difficult time staying in one place. That sort of thing."

"I've thought a lot about that, and I don't even understand it all myself."

"That's the way it is sometimes."

"I wonder if we got married you might be able to settle down," Primrose said.

"I think about that at times, but that marrying stuff spooks hell out of me. Besides, we are all right the way we are."

"I know that, Billy. Don't get me wrong. I am not pushing you."

"I know. I'm glad you don't."

Pete returned with a case of Budweiser and the chest full of ice. He also put a package of steaks on the counter. "I even picked up some dead mesquite wood along the road," Pete said. "Let's have a beer. Then I'll start a fire for the steaks."

"You're soundin' like the old Pete again," Billy said.

"I've thought about that goddam bar a time or two today. I am really glad to get away from there, and not have to put up with assholes like Freddy Ingersoll and that greedy bitch, Katherine."

"Have you thought about what you're going to do next?" Primrose asked.

"I've been messing around with going to Taxco, down south of Mexico City. A friend of mine told me that I can buy silver jewelry cheap there. If that proves true, I can sell wholesale to the shops up and down the California Coast and make a bundle."

"That sounds like a long way to drive and a lot of work," Primrose commented.

"I'm not afraid of the work. The interesting part is going to Taxco. Who knows, it might take me a year to buy enough jewelry to make the trip worthwhile."

"If you find any pieces that are real cheap and would go with my beaded purses, I'll buy them. Wholesale, of course."

"Primrose, if I find any jewelry that will do what you want it to do, you won't have to buy it."

Pete cooked the steaks when the mesquite wood had burned down to red-hot coals. After supper, they talked a while longer. "I'll tell you two something," Pete said. "You are lucky to have each other and Cougar. I have often wished for something like this."

"You'll probably find it when you least expect it," Primrose said.

"Maybe," Pete replied, scratching the back of his neck. "I don't know if I will recognize it in myself. I think I have a bunch of wandering to do yet."

Two days later, Pete left for Mexico. Billy felt sad to see the VW camper heading out to the road to Arivaca. "I wonder when we'll see Pete again," Billy said.

"He'll be back. I can tell he is close to you," Primrose said, and patted Billy on the shoulder.

"He's sure a good one, that Pete. Damned if we didn't go through hell together in that goddam jungle."

"You both made it back. That's the important thing to consider."

"And, then some asshole calls me a draft dodger. Ingersoll's the draft dodger. He claims to have been 4-F. He probably paid some doctor to write his draft board some fake letter. Then he went out and got those stupid dragons tattooed on his forearms."

"Forget about that man. He isn't worth your energy."

"I reckon you're right, beautiful woman."

Cougar started to whimper. Billy stepped over to the crib, and bent over. "I haven't any milk for you, big guy, but I'll get you out of those soggy pants."

Father and son smiled at each other as Billy removed the wet diaper and pinned a clean one on. "I sure hope they don't get into another war when you're grown, Cougar."

Primrose received a letter from her mother. The short note contained a message of congratulations on the birth of Cougar. She had enclosed a check for one hundred dollars with her request, "Buy something nice for my grandson." A week later, Billy's father's letter arrived.

Dear Bill,

Your mother and I were surprised at the news that we are grandparents. Since we cannot reach you except by General Delivery, we assume that you will be coming to Springfield with your family sometime.

We do not understand why you did not come home when you got out of the army. I always planned that you would eventually take over the machinery business, and cannot understand why you won't come home to take advantage of a situation where you can make something of yourself.

Your mother is having a few health problems. Her doctor put her on a low-cholesterol diet, but she is having trouble sticking to it.

We have both found Christ and are active in our church. You might consider this in your life, especially with a child to rear. When you come to Springfield, we will introduce you to our congregation.

Yours in Christ,

Dad

"The old man still doesn't get it," Billy said, looking up from reading the letter. "He's now a 'born again' and thinks I'll go to Springfield." He handed the letter to Primrose.

Finished reading, she looked at Billy. "I'm glad you don't want to go to Springfield. Yours in Christ. Somebody sure has him snowed."

Just as he promised, Toad drove up to the cabin early on the fourth day before Memorial Day. Billy had packed his bedroll and the clothes he thought he would need. He put everything in the back of Toad's pickup, gave Primrose and Cougar kisses, and climbed into the pickup next to Toad. The old cowboy began telling stories before they reached the road to Arivaca.

North of Tucson, Toad headed toward Oracle Junction, driving under the majestic Catalina Mountains. At the junction he turned east to Oracle, a small mining and ranching community. He shifted his stories to the experiences he had enjoyed as a young cowboy on the ranch in the Big Horn Mountains. "My first day at the E4, after dinner, all of us went back to the bunkhouse to settle a bit before goin' back to work. Old Roy was semi-retired. The boss paid him eighty dollars a month instead of the hundred I was gettin'. But, old Roy still put in a day. Not like the rest of us, but he was determined to damn sure earn his retirement money."

Toad continued about how times had changed with the government social security system, and that old cowboys either went to town or kept working until they couldn't get out of bed in the morning. Then, he returned to his yarn.

"That first day, I was a sittin' on my bunk an' Roy was in his favorite chair. I rolled me a Bull Durham smoke and handed the sack and papers to Roy. He lifted his right hand an' said, 'No thanks, I've been awful hot at times, but never did smoke.' That was old Roy. He took care of the team of mules, Tip and Ada. He taught me how ta skin that team an' all about mules. He said a mule will live a lifetime ta git a chance ta kill ya once."

"I thought you were a cowboy on that ranch," Billy said.

"I was a cowboy on the E4, but in that country, a feller had to help with the hayin' besides lookin' after the cows."

"How long were you there?" Billy asked.

"Long enough to where Old Roy became a close friend. I look back an' figure I looked at that old man like a father since my daddy died afore I ever got to know him. When we'd git a day off, Roy and me went all over. One time we went fishin' up in the mountains, another we went down to the town of Buffalo to a rodeo. When I left to go down to New Mexico, I missed hearin' him describe somethin' as 'long as a whore's dream' or harder than a whore's heart.' He had one of them descriptions for most everythin'. Helluva good man, Old Roy."

They traveled past Globe through the Salt River Canyon and up through pine country near Showlow. By the time they reached Gallup, New Mexico, Toad pulled off on a narrow dirt road, leading to a small grove of trees next to an arroyo. "I slept here last year," Toad said. "In the mornin' I had coffee with an old Navajo. He spoke passin' English and we had a good time jawin'."

The next day, by the time they had gone over Red Mountain Pass in Colorado, Billy realized that he felt about Toad much like Toad had felt about Old Roy. Many people might have tired of Toad's constant story-telling, but Billy listened intently to everything the old cowboy had to say. When they stopped for the night, Billy took his banjo out of the case and began composing songs based on Toad's stories.

Relieved that Billy and Toad had arrived in time for the Memorial Day Weekend, Max told them that supper would be his treat. After unloading the pickup, Toad drove Billy to the Mangey Moose where Joe Spencer bought Billy a welcoming beer and Toad a shot of Jack Daniels. Joe wanted Billy to start playing the following afternoon.

Since his advertising had been effective the previous summer, Joe telephoned the newspaper to arrange for space during the summer, promoting Banjo Billy as the "Banjo King of Wyoming."

During the third night of his gig at the Mangey Moose Saloon, Billy had finished "Greensleeves" when he saw Myra sit down at a small table in the lounge. He had planned to take a break after "Greensleeves," but continued with two more songs. "I reckon she'll stay all night if I don't take a break now," he thought. As he leaned the banjo against the wall, the crowd applauded which he acknowledged with a slight bow and a big grin.

As he passed by Myra, he told her that he would be back with a beer. He saw that she was dressed to attract with a low cut emerald-colored blouse that revealed the familiar cleavage. When he returned with his Budweiser, Billy forced himself not to look lower than her eyes. "How was your winter, Myra?"

"Lots of changes, Billy. It's really great to see you."

"I've had a few changes, too."

"My biggest change is that I am no longer living with that stodgy lawyer. I just couldn't stand him, and I think he had a girlfriend in Denver."

"Are you sure?"

"Not completely, but he spent a lot of time there, and when he got back he didn't seem interested in me."

"So, what are you doin'?" Billy asked. "Did you go back to work at the Cowboy Bar? Have you finished your book?"

"I haven't written a word for months," she replied. "I may have to go back to cocktail waitressing."

"What do you do all day if you don't write?"

"Nothing, really. I am not very happy. At least Jeffrey gave me a little money to live on when I left. I think he was glad. I rented a small house in Wilson.

"I don't know what to tell you, Myra."

"Will you come to the house with me tonight? That would make me very happy."

"I can't do that Myra. I am now a father." *Dammit, I wish she would leave me alone.*

"What difference does that make?"

"It makes a lot of difference to me. I love my son and I love my son's mother."

"Where are they? They are not here, so they will never know."

Poor Myra doesn't have a clue about love. "I have to get back to playin', Myra. Why don't you go home?"

Billy went back to his place, lifted the strap over his head, and began to play "John Henry." Myra finished her drink and waved as she left the Mangey Moose. Billy did not see her again.

Later that summer, toward the end of August, he had just walked in the door of the Mangey Moose when Joe handed him the local newspaper. "Have you heard about your old girlfriend, Myra?"

"What about her?" Billy began reading the front page article. "Holy shit! It says here she was trying to shoot the Snake River rapids in a canoe. She overturned and, according to some by-standers on the canyon overlook, smashed her head against a boulder in the river."

"I know, I already read it," Joe said.

"I can't believe she's dead. I wonder if she did it on purpose. She seemed pretty miserable the last time she was here." Billy handed the newspaper back to Joe.

"Keep it, I've finished reading it."

That evening, Billy dedicated his rendition of "Proud Mary" to Myra Paxton. It was his last song of the evening. There were tears in his eyes as he packed up his banjo.

Bothered by Myra's death, Billy talked to Toad, telling him all about his relationship with Myra, and her moving in with her lawyer boyfriend. He also told Toad how she had come to the Mangey Moose, pleading for him to go home with her. "I get to wonderin' if I had agreed to go home with her, would it have made any difference? Would she still be alive?" Billy asked.

"Don't go to puttin' that crap onto yourself, Billy," Toad replied. "Sounds ta me like she made her bed and didn't like the lumps in it. A feller never knows 'bout some people. As ya said, she mighta been all lively on the outside, but somethin' was eatin' her up inside her head. Besides, yer only guessin' she did that canoe ride on purpose."

"I reckon you're right, Toad. I feel that way sometimes myself about the war. It eats on me every once in a while."

Billy and Primrose exchanged weekly letters. Primrose wrote all about Cougar's changes from infancy to babyhood. In one of her letters she enclosed a photograph that Francine had taken that showed Cougar standing up by holding the crib railing. He was laughing. Billy showed the photograph to Toad and Joe Spencer.

In one of her first letters, Primrose described how Cougar seemed to look for Billy when she changed his diaper.

Financially, Billy considered the summer a great success. He sent weekly money orders to Primrose in his letters. After the Labor Day weekend and the party at the Mangey Moose Saloon, Toad and Billy loaded the old pickup and drove to Arizona.

That winter, Billy spent most of his time at the cabin, enjoying Primrose and Cougar. He went to Tucson to play a gig at Gus and Andy's because Clearance had not shown up. He wondered if he would ever see Clearance again, and thought about going to New Orleans some day to look for him. The guitar man had given him an address of a friend who would know where to find him.

One day in March, Pete drove in from Mexico. His jewelry importing business seemed to be thriving. He stayed at the cabin for five days. He gave Primrose some pieces of Taxco jewelry to use on her leather goods. Pete offered to take Billy to California with him, but Billy wanted to stay with his family until it came time to go north again with Toad.

Cougar began saying Dada and Mama in January. By February he struggled to his feet one afternoon, and took his first two steps on his own before collapsing to the floor again. By the time Toad drove in to pick up Billy, the youngster walked everywhere. With some reluctance, Billy put his things into Toad's pickup for the drive to Jackson.

The summer passed quickly for Billy. He enjoyed all the letters from Primrose, especially the photographs of Cougar which he showed to Toad and Joe Spencer. When, in the middle of September, Toad parked the pickup in back of the van at the cabin, Cougar came bouncing out to meet them. Billy grabbed his son, and lifted him up for a long hug. Primrose came right behind Cougar. Billy hugged and kissed her with Cougar still in his arms. Toad got out of the pickup and joined them. Primrose surprised him with a hug.

"Come on in and have some coffee, Toad," Primrose said.

"Nothin' I'd like better."

They sat around the table with their coffee as Toad began a story meant for Cougar. The boy sat on Billy's lap, listening. Then, slipping to the floor, he headed for Toad. Putting both hands on Toad's leg, Cougar looked up at the old cowboy.

"You Toad," he said, and smiled.

"That's right, Cougar, me Toad."

The old cowboy reached down with his heavily calloused hand, and tousled the boy's long hair. Cougar returned his smile, and put his head on Toad's leg. "Ya know, I always wondered what it'd be like ta have a kid ta grow up," Toad said.

"We'll let you know in twenty years," Primrose said, and laughed.

Billy enjoyed the winter with his family. Now and then, he went to Tucson to play gigs. While there, he looked for Clearance, but there was no sign of his guitar-playing partner. By the time Toad picked him up for the trip back to Jackson, Billy had become resigned to the fact that Clearance had stayed in New Orleans.

CHAPTER ELEVEN

During the trip to Jackson, Billy noticed that Toad winced occasionally as if he felt pain. "Hey Toad," Billy asked when they were in New Mexico. "You feelin' bad?"

"I've been gettin' pains down in my gut once in a while. They started 'bout half way through the winter. I reckon a feller gets stuff like this when he gits as goddam old as I am."

"Have you seen a doctor?" Billy asked, wrinkling his brow.

"Hell no," Toad replied. "I ain't about to go to some saw-bones. All they want to do is start carvin' on a feller. Last time I went to one was when that outlaw bronc busted my leg. Been limpin' ever since."

Billy didn't say anything else, but he kept watching his friend out of the corner of his eye. Deep inside he worried about the old cowboy.

They arrived, as usual, the day before Memorial Day Weekend, ready for the tourist season. Billy started his gig at the Mangey Moose Saloon during the evenings, and playing for the river runners during their lunch breaks. Just as he had done before, he helped Toad with the cooking and cleanup. As the summer progressed, Billy noticed that Toad spent more and more time resting and holding his hand against his stomach as he winced with pain. Billy tried to convince the old cowboy that he should see a doctor, but Toad remained as stubborn as always.

One day, after the noon meal was finished and they headed back to the house, Toad stopped at the bank. Before getting out of the pickup to go into the building he began telling Billy what he wanted to do. "You and I know thet there's somethin' goin' wrong inside my gut. I may be wearin' out, just like an old horse what's been rode too many years over too many mountains."

"If you would see a doctor, maybe you could get fixed up," Billy said.

"We've been through all that. I don't want ta talk 'bout saw-bones. I have decided to make things easier for ya if somethin' should happen to me. I've got a little bunch of money in a savin's account. I wanna put your name on it just in case. I'm damn sure gonna die sometime, so when I do, I'd like you ta do a couple of things that I need doin'."

"Just name them, Toad."

"First of all, get me cremated. I don't wanna take up any more space than absolutely necessary. Then take my ashes to the Sheridan cemetery and sprinkle them next to old Roy's grave. I've got a map up in the room that I'll give ya. I've already signed the paper transferrin' this old pickup into your name 'cause I don't want you ta have ta walk plumb ta Sheridan."

Billy listened closely, looking at Toad all the time. His sadness came close to bringing tears to his eyes.

"There's plenty of money ta get all that done. I'd like you ta put what's left into a savin's account for that Cougar of yours. He might want ta go ta college some day or start some kinda business."

"Damn, I don't know what to say, Toad."

"Ya don't hafta say a goddam thing. I've got nobody else I'd trust with all this stuff."

They went into the bank and Toad had the customer service manager put Billy's name on his savings account in joint tenancy. When they returned to the house, Toad gave Billy the map of the Sheridan cemetery, showing where Roy Neal's grave was located.

"Here's the papers for the pickup," Toad said. "Now, you'd better get ready to play at the Mangey Moose."

Billy left Toad's room, and, with his banjo, wandered around the streets of Jackson, brooding over what Toad had said and done. During his first break that evening, Joe Spencer scowled as he handed Billy a Budweiser.

"Is something wrong, Billy?"

"I reckon I've got too much on my mind."

"Let me know if there's something I can do," Joe offered.

"Thanks, Joe. There's nothing anyone can do. I think old Toad is dyin'."

"That's not good news. Why don't you take the rest of the night off?"

"Thanks, Joe, but I'd just as soon keep playin'."

Every day, Billy did more and more to help Toad get the lunches ready for the river runners. Every morning, he was glad to hear Toad's knock on the door to get him out of bed after an evening playing at the saloon.

On Wednesday morning, during the last week in July, Billy awakened with the sun streaming through his window. He rubbed his eyes, then realized it was late. Quickly getting into his clothes, he walked down the hall and knocked on the door to Toad's room. No answer. He turned the knob, and opened the door. Seeing Toad lying in his bed, Billy paused.

"Hey, old cowboy, it's time to get goin'."

Toad remained motionless. Billy stepped over to the bed, and took the old cowboy's shoulder in his hand. It was then Billy knew that his friend had died. Tears welled into his eyes as he looked down on Toad's face, relaxed and peaceful, no longer wincing with pain. As he stood there, a deep sense of loss surged through Billy.

"If there's a heaven somewhere, old cowboy, I'm sure you are there," he said, and stood there weeping.

Drying his eyes on the sleeve of his shirt, Billy left the room to telephone the police. A patrol car arrived shortly, and Billy showed the officer into Toad's room. Satisfied that the body had not been a victim of any foul play, the officer asked Billy if he had a choice of funeral homes.

"I don't know about any of this," Billy said.

"There are two here in Jackson. I'll have the coroner call one if you want," the officer said.

"I would appreciate that. I do know he wanted to be cremated."

"You can make all those arrangements with the funeral home."

The officer telephoned and an ambulance arrived within a

half hour. Billy watched as they lifted Toad's body onto a stretcher, covered it with a sheet, and carried it out of the house. The coroner told him he could stop by the funeral parlor anytime to make the arrangements, and gave Billy his business card after scribbling the undertaker's address on the back.

Suddenly Billy realized that the river runners would be beaching their rafts in an hour, and would be hungry for lunch. He hurried into the kitchen, gathered up several loaves of bread and a large canned ham. The rest of what he would need was already in the chuck-box.

Arriving at the usual spot on the river bank, Billy saw the rafts twenty yards away. As soon as the boatmen beached the rafts, Billy went over to Max. "Max, I need to talk to you."

"What is it Billy? Where's Toad?"

"Toad died last night."

"Oh my God!" Max said, with a look of astonishment on his face. "How did it happen?"

"He just died, Max. I don't know what was wrong. He was too stubborn to see a doctor."

"I didn't even know he was sick," Max said.

"He didn't want anyone to know. Toad was that way. I'm going to miss that old cowboy."

Max patted Billy on the shoulder.

"We'll all miss him."

"I was too busy to do much for lunch, but I brought a ham and some bread. I'll get some coffee made on the Coleman Stove. I just got here, so there's no campfire."

"Go ahead and do the best you can, Billy. I'll give you a hand as soon as I explain what happened to the clients. They'll understand."

Between the two of them, they managed to get the makeshift lunch together. Before Max continued the rafting trip, Billy told him that he planned to take Toad's ashes to Sheridan, and would not be back.

Returning the lunch supplies to the house, Billy drove to the funeral parlor. A young man dressed in a dark suit ushered him into the undertaker's office. "Mr. Hammond will be here shortly," he said. "Please have a chair and make yourself comfortable."

"Thanks," Billy replied, and sat down in a maroon, leather-upholstered chair.

The undertaker came into the room and sat behind his large, walnut desk. "Well, Mr. O'Leary, I need to ask you some questions and then we can make the arrangements. Are you a relative of Theodore Monroe, the deceased?"

"No, I didn't even know his real name until recently. He went by 'Toad'."

"Do you know his next-of-kin?"

"Toad told me he didn't have anyone."

"You told me he wanted cremation, so that is all arranged. I need to know who is responsible for the funeral charges."

"I am. But, there won't be a funeral. Toad just wanted to be cremated."

"Are you sure you don't want a service of some sort? What church did Mr. Monroe attend?'

"He never mentioned any church. A service will not be necessary. All he wanted was to be cremated and for me to take his ashes to Sheridan."

"We have several urns. I will show them to you in the coffin room. They run from fifty dollars to three hundred. The coffins are various prices too."

"He won't need a coffin because he's gettin' cremated."

"State law requires a coffin. Come with me, now, and I will show you what we have for you to choose from."

Billy was puzzled and angry, but did not argue as he followed Hammond out of the office, through a wide hallway to a door. Hammond flipped a switch before opening the door to the Coffin Viewing Room. Somber music came from a sound system. Hammond stopped at the first opened coffin. "This is our very best. It is solid brass with a Simmons innerspring mattress that comes with silk sheets and a down-pillow. It is twenty-thousand dollars. As we progress down the line, the prices diminish. Of course, the prices I am quoting you are all inclusive except for the cemetery plot."

"Mr. Hammond," Billy said. "Just show me the cheapest coffin you have. All this fancy stuff isn't goin' to make any difference to old Toad, seein' how he's already dead."

Hammond led Billy to the end of the room. "Here it is, the least expensive. It is made from pine."

"So, how much is it?"

"One thousand dollars. The price includes cremation, a viewing, and a short service."

"I just want the coffin and the cremation," Billy said.

"The price is the same whether or not you want a viewing and service."

"I think I'll inquire at the other mortuary," Billy said.

"You will find the same prices at The Palms. If you should decide to change funeral homes, I will have to charge you three hundred dollars for the hearse from the county morgue to here."

"You're goin' to make a bundle on a dead man, no matter what, aren't you." Billy said, angrily.

"The prices I have quoted you are all approved by the Wyoming Undertakers Association."

"I am sure they are. What about the urn for his ashes?"

"Step this way."

Green velvet lined shelves held a variety of urns, from highly decorative to plain. Small discrete-looking black cards with gold-colored numbers gave the prices for each urn. "Suppose I bring in a gallon jar with a top. I don't think Toad would care what kind of a container I take his ashes to Sheridan in."

"That will not be necessary. We furnish a metal box when people do not require an urn."

"That sounds like the best way to go," Billy said.

"Let's go back to the office. I think we are finished here."

Seated in his high-backed leather desk chair, Hammond took an order book from a drawer. "I am assuming you agree to our services rather than switch mortuaries."

"Yes."

Hammond wrote a list on the order blank. He put $1000.00 next to "total."

"Do you plan to pay with cash, check, or credit card, Mr. O'Leary."

"I'll get the cash from the bank."

"Our policy is payment in advance, Mr. O'Leary."

"If you can get through to him, tell Mr. Monroe that I'll be back as soon as possible," Billy said sarcastically.

Hammond smiled because he thought he had to.

Billy drove to the bank in Toad's old truck, crying a little and cussing the undertaker. Explaining to the customer service manager that he would be leaving Jackson and wanted to close the account, He waited until the woman came back with the balance. "This is your current balance, Mr. O'Leary."

Billy gulped when he saw the $16,451.84 printed on the paper tape.

"How would you like the funds?" she asked. "I can give you a cashier's check, cash, or wire the funds to a bank where you will be going."

"I would like a cashier's check for fifteen thousand, and the rest in cash."

"I'll be back in just a minute."

Astonished by the amount of money in Toad's account, Billy could only think about how surprised Primrose would be. That reminded him to make sure to write her a letter about his leaving Jackson.

Returning to the mortuary, Billy counted out ten one hundred dollar bills onto Hammond's desk. The undertaker handed him a receipt. "Mr. Monroe's ashes will be available in two days, Mr. O'Leary. You may pick them up after nine in the morning. Thank you for your business."

"Well, Mr. Hammond, I will not say, 'you're welcome', because you are runnin' the biggest rip-off I have ever experienced."

After going back to the house to tell Max he would handle the next day's lunch, he drove to the Mangey Moose. Joe Spencer greeted him with a wave of his hand. Billy sat down at the bar.

"I would like a straight shot of Jack Daniels, Joe," Billy said.

"Don't tell me you've quit drinking Budweiser."

"No. I'm havin' one Jack Daniels for old Toad. He died last night."

Billy suddenly began to weep.

"Goddam, Billy, I'm so sorry to hear that. Here. The Jack's on me."

Billy put his head down on his folded arms on the bar. His shoulders shook as he cried. Joe came out from behind the bar, and put his arm around Billy's shoulders.

"Hey, man. I'm really sorry," Joe said. "Is there anything I can do?"

Billy shook his head without raising it from his arms. In a few minutes he got himself under control. Joe patted his back, and returned to his position behind the bar.

"Well, I reckon I'd better do what I came here for," Billy said. "Here's to Toad, the old cowboy, who lived one helluva good life."

Joe filled another shot glass with Jack Daniels.

"I'll drink to Toad, too," he said, and tossed down the whiskey.

"I'll be leavin' Jackson in a couple of days, Joe. Toad asked me to take his ashes to Sheridan."

"You have to do what you have to do. I'll be sorry to see you go. Another shot?"

"No thanks. I have a letter to write and supper to eat before I come back to play."

"Take the night off if you want to, Billy."

"I'd like to play, but thanks for the offer. But, if it's all right with you, tonight will be my last night."

"Sure, Billy. I can understand that. Will you be coming back here after you go to Sheridan?"

"No," Billy replied. "A while back, an old boy told me that Taos, New Mexico is a place I might enjoy."

"I've heard there's a lot of writers and artists in Taos."

"That's what the dude said. He also told me there are some great bars to play in."

"I've never been there, but if there are writers and artists, there's bound to be some bars."

Joe stepped to the cash register, pushed the button to open the drawer, and took out a hundred dollar bill. Pushing the drawer back in, he turned back to Billy, and put the bill on the bar. "Here's your summer bonus, Billy. I don't want to forget to give it to you later."

"Thanks a lot. I have enjoyed playin' for you. Maybe, I'll get up this way again."

After writing his letter to Primrose, Billy mailed it at the post office before going to the Cowboy Bar for a prime rib sandwich. The Mangey Moose had begun to fill with customers when he arrived to play. As he got ready and tuned the banjo, he thought back to the summers he had been in Jackson, about Myra, and the many hours he had spent listening to Toad tell his stories.

The evening went well. Billy played almost constantly, taking only short breaks to rest his voice. The crowd applauded his performance of each song, and the money in his banjo case showed their appreciation beyond applause. The few remaining customers at closing time listened closely after he dedicated "Streets of Laredo" to an old cowboy named Toad.

The next afternoon, when Max and his crew returned from the river, Billy offered to give Max the chuck-box from the pickup. "You might as well have Toad's chuck-box, because I won't be needing it," Billy said.

"I appreciate that, Billy. I'll back my pickup to yours, and we can slide it over. I hired a man to cook starting tomorrow, but he doesn't have a vehicle. I'll have him use my pickup."

Max maneuvered his pickup truck around, and they slid the wooden chuck-box onto the bed. "I'll miss you, Billy," Max said.

"You have been great for the operation and I've enjoyed knowing you."

Max reached into his pocket, pulled out a roll of bills, and handed Billy a hundred dollars.

"Here's some traveling money. I hope to see you again next summer."

"Thanks Max. I don't know about next summer. It wouldn't be the same without old Toad."

"I know what you mean. Toad was sure a piece of work."

The next morning, Billy loaded his duffel bag and banjo, drove to the mortuary, and picked up the metal box containing Toad's ashes. Placing the box and Toad's old cowboy hat next to him on the seat, he drove north out of Jackson and through the Teton National Park. Marveling at the wildlife in Yellowstone, Billy stopped occasionally to watch elk, bison and bear. He watched "Old Faithful" relieve its pressure into the sky, and continued on, arriving in Cody late in the day. Consulting his map the next morning, he decided on taking route 14A that would cross over and through the Big Horn Mountains, bringing him into Sheridan from the northwest.

Remembering Toad's stories about Sheridan, Billy made sure he visited the Mint Bar. From Toad's description, he could see that the place had not changed since Toad had spent pay day nights there many years before. He ordered a shot of Jack Daniels, asked the comely bartender for directions to the cemetery, and returned to the pickup. Sleep came quickly after he curled himself up on the seat.

The sun, streaming through the windshield, awakened him. After a substantial breakfast, he found the cemetery. With the metal box, containing the ashes and his banjo, Billy followed the map to Roy Neal's headstone. It was early enough in the morning so that the graveyard was deserted except for him.

Leaning the banjo against a large granite marker, he opened the metal box and carefully scattered Toad's ashes next to Roy's grave. When he had finished, he stood there for a moment before taking up his banjo, and putting the strap over his head. As he played the melody, he sang "Streets of Laredo" through his tears. His sorrow lifted. He played and sang a song he had been composing in his mind. He called it, "Old Cowboy."

Without further tarrying in Sheridan, Billy drove south to Buffalo and on to Casper where he saw oil wells on either side of the highway. By the time he reached Cheyenne, the sun had only a couple of hours left before it would dip below the long horizon of the southern Wyoming plains.

Driving steadily the next day, he reached New Mexico at sundown. After supper in Ratón, he continued on to Eagle Nest, where he camped by the lake.

The chill of the mountain air in the morning, made him snuggle down in the bedroll until it covered his head. Hunger eventually forced him to head down to Taos. As he enjoyed breakfast at Mary's Cafe, Billy glanced around at the other customers. There were hippie types, locals dressed in a variety of styles, but nobody who looked like a tourist.

After breakfast, he left the pickup in a public parking lot, and ambled through the town, carrying his banjo. Comparing Taos with Jackson, Billy noted that there were more art galleries in Taos and the flavor of the town created by its architecture was more like Tubac than Jackson with its many log buildings. Taos was built with adobe. There were not as many bars as he expected. Toward noon, he returned to Mary's Cafe, hoping to find out from some local resident which bar he might try for a playing gig.

The lunch crowd had not yet arrived. After sitting at a table, the waitress stopped to take his order. She wore a long skirt, sandals, and a turquoise pendant hanging around her neck on a silver chain. Her black hair, in a single braid, reached her waist. Without a trace of makeup, her face had begun to reflect her outdoor lifestyle.

"I'll have coffee and a grilled cheese sandwich," Billy said. "How long have you lived here?"

"Going on three years. I live in a commune out on the mesa

near the river. We take turns working in town."

"I'm lookin' for a place to play banjo. Where would you suggest?"

"I don't do the bars, but you might try Bar Bonillas. I've heard they get good crowds on weekends."

"I think I saw it. Is it upstairs on Paseo del Norte?"

"That's it," she replied. "I'd better get your order filled."

After finishing his sandwich, Billy climbed the stairs to the bar. Bar Bonillas occupied the entire second floor of a spacious building. A burly looking Mexican man with a black, bushy moustache greeted him. "I'm lookin' for the manager," Billy said.

"I am 'Nacho' Bonillas, manager, owner, and day bartender."

"Nice to meet you. I'm Banjo Billy, and I'm lookin' for a place to play."

"Do you sing, too?"

"Yeah, I'll play somethin' for you," Billy said, and took his banjo out of the case.

After tuning the instrument, he played and sang "Blowing in the Wind" and "Proud Mary."

"Do you know any Mexican songs?"

"Not yet, but I wouldn't mind learnin' some. The trouble is I don't speak Spanish."

"It doesn't really matter here. Most of the customers are gringos. I just wondered if you knew some *corridos*. I like *corridos*. I haven't had any live music in here for a while. Most of the hippies around here are too stoned to play. I like your banjo, and you sing good too."

"What do you pay?"

"Twenty bucks a night, from seven until closing, around one in the morning. You'll make pretty good tips, too."

"When do you want me to start?"

"Tomorrow. I'll put a sign out front today. Have you got a photo I can put on the sign?"

"No, but tell me where to get one taken."

"I've got a camera. Wait here a minute. You want a drink?"

"A Budweiser would be great."

Nacho Bonillas took the bottle from the cooler, opened it and put it in front of Billy. Then he went into a back room for his camera. After taking several shots of Billy and his banjo, Nacho put the camera next to the cash register.

"My brother has his own dark room. I'll have him make us a nice enlargement for the sign."

Billy dug in his pocket for money to pay for the beer.

"It's on me."

When Billy inquired about a good place to camp, Nacho gave him directions to a stream next to the road leading to the ski resort.

"I go up there to fish once in a while," Nacho said. "Not many people camp there because there are no official campgrounds, but it's free."

"That is exactly the kind of place I am lookin' for," Billy said.

Before driving to the stream, Billy bought an inexpensive fly-rod set and worms in a styrofoam container. Wanting to discover how good the fishing would be, he purchased a three-day, non-resident fishing license. Parking the pickup next to the fast flowing stream, he then assembled the fishing gear, and baited the hook with half a worm. His thoughts jumped to Primrose and Cougar and the peach trees. "I wonder how big they are getting," he mumbled to himself. "Cougar will outgrow them easily."

Choosing an opening in the trees lining the rocky stream bed, Billy made his first cast into a pool below some boulders, where the flow hesitated before plunging downstream. After his fourth cast into the pool, he felt a slight tug on the line. Working the line with his left hand, he raised and lowered the baited hook, trying to entice the fish into striking. But, the current caught the line, and sent it downstream. After pulling in the line for another cast, he saw that most of the bait had been stolen.

Taking the other half of the worm, and threading it onto the hook, he made another cast into the pool. Another tug, and Billy pulled out a foot of slack from the reel. At the next tug, he was ready, jerking the line. The rod bent as the fish fought the pull. Billy began reeling in the line, keeping it taut so the fish could not dislodge the hook.

When the fish broke the surface, he saw a foot-long rainbow trout. Backing away from the stream, he swung him to shore and grabbed the slippery fish over its gills with his left hand. Putting the fly-rod on the ground he reached into the fish's mouth and gripped the straight part of the hook with his right thumb and index finger, then pushed it inward to free the barbed end.

Leaving the fish flapping around in the bed of the pickup, he took a small styrofoam cooler to the stream and filled it with water. After placing the trout in the cooler he returned to the stream to look for another pool. Within an hour, he had three nice trout for supper. He built a small cooking fire. He broiled the trout on the coals of the fire and relished the taste of the meal. *I sure wish Toad could be here.*

His hunger satisfied, Billy rinsed his hands in the stream, then played his banjo until he grew sleepy enough to crawl into his bedroll.

Many of the tourists left Taos after Labor Day weekend. Billy sat with Nacho Bonillas after the bar closed for the night the Saturday after Labor Day. "I need to head back to Arizona, Nacho. This has been a good place to play, and I've enjoyed the artists and writers."

"You been good for business," Nacho said, and sipped from his glass of beer. "Business will pick up again when it snows."

"It's like that in Jackson, too, but I have to get goin'."

"You gotta job here when you get back."

Thanks, Nacho. I'll see you next spring."

Returning home, he found that Cougar had grown considerably. While telling Primrose about Toad, Billy broke down in tears. She put her arms around him. Cougar came over, hugged his legs and patted them with his little hands. "Toad was a real friend," Billy said, after brushing the tears from his eyes. "I miss him too much. Why does death leave me feeling so damn empty?"

Billy surprised Primrose with the cashier's check. Two days after his return to the cabin, they drove to Tucson where they started a time deposit account in both their names. With the banking business accomplished, Billy insisted on buying a youth bed for Cougar. They gave the crib to an expectant woman who lived alone in Arivaca.

The following week, they spent cutting firewood for another winter. Cougar followed Billy everywhere. He liked listening to him play the banjo and enjoyed taking walks along the creek. For his second birthday, Primrose baked a cake in the Dutch oven, a skill she had mastered shortly after she had moved into the cabin.

When they checked their mail during the first week in April, the postmistress handed Billy a return receipt to sign. Then she gave him a large, brown envelope from a law firm in Springfield. Once they settled back in the pickup, he opened the envelope.

The cover letter, written in a cold, matter-of-fact manner, informed Billy that his father had died as the result of a massive stroke. It went on to explain that his father had bequeathed all of his worldly goods, with the exception of one hundred dollars, to the First Evangelical Church of Springfield. The one hundred dollars would be Billy's as soon as the will had gone through the probate court.

In addition to the letter, the lawyer had enclosed a copy of the will and a letter to Billy that his father had written four months prior to the stroke. In the letter, his father not only rebuked Billy for not coming home to amount to something other than a wandering banjo player, but also for having a child out of wedlock. The letter ended with, "May our Lord have mercy on your soul, Son."

Primrose read the letters, and glanced at the copy of the will.

"Some preacher really got to your father," she said.

"Yeah, and now that preacher is a half million dollars richer," Billy laughed.

"What my father never realized is, I never wanted a stinkin' dime of his money, because there would have been a chain attached to it."

"That is just one more reason I love you so much, Billy."

"When the hundred bucks gets here, if it ever does, we are goin' to have us a hundred dollar party."

With disdainful ceremony, Billy stuffed the envelope and all its contents into the fire burning merrily in the box heater.

The check arrived in the middle of August. Primrose signed for the certified letter and enclosed the envelope in one of her letters to Billy in Taos.

CHAPTER TWELVE

After a successful summer at Bar Bonillas, Billy returned to the cabin in September. As he passed through Tucson, he stopped at the pawn shop where he had retrieved his banjo after it was stolen. He found a small guitar to give to Cougar.

"Isn't Cougar too young to learn how to play it?" Primrose asked.

"I expect it will be a while before his fingers are long enough to make chords, but it will wait for him."

Billy spent a month overhauling the engine in the pickup. On the trip back to Arivaca it had begun to smoke and was burning a quart of oil every two hundred miles. When he finished rejuvenating the old pickup, it sounded like it had a new engine.

Pete showed up in late November and spent three days at the cabin on his way from Taxco to California with a large assortment of silver jewelry. He tried to entice Billy into spending the next summer in California, playing in beach resorts.

"I think I'll stick with Taos for a while," Billy said.

During the following summer, every letter from Primrose said, "Every day, Cougar asks me when is his Daddy coming home?" She also told him that the first crop of peaches had ripened on the trees. "I ate some and made four jars of jam."

The next winter, Billy began in earnest to show Cougar how to play a few chords on his guitar. The lessons did not last long, because Billy did not want sore fingers to discourage the boy from playing the instrument.

When spring arrived, Billy drove back to Taos, only to find that Bar Bonillas had been sold to two gay men from San Francisco. The new name of the place was "Lucifer's." They offered Billy a raise in his nightly pay, but he refused. Spending a night at his favorite spot next to the trout stream, he pondered where to go next. The next morning he decided to try Silverton, Colorado. After mailing a letter to Primrose telling about his change in plans, he drove north.

It quickly turned out that Silverton was not a place where he could play and make enough money to live on. The railroad company gave him permission to play for incoming passengers, but they refused to pay him a daily wage. The manager explained that by the time the passengers had reached Silverton, the railroad already had their money.

He met three trains, and played for the disembarking passengers, standing behind his open banjo case. There were a few smiles from the people focused on the main street tourist traps, but not a single bill went into the case. The following morning, he left for Durango, wishing he had listened to Pete more carefully.

After landing a gig in the Caboose Restaurant in Durango, Billy spent the summer there. He went from table to table, playing and singing his songs. The clientele liked what he performed, and as most everywhere he played, were generous with their tips. Playing through lunches and suppers, he made more money than he had in Taos.

When he returned to the cabin, Cougar's behavior took him aback. Instead of running out to meet him, Cougar sat by the door of the cabin. But, after Billy grabbed him and lifted him into the air, the little boy laughed. Later, as they ate supper, Cougar tapped Billy on his arm to get his attention.

"Daddy, why do you always go away? Don't you like us?"

"I love you," Billy said, and tousled Cougar's hair. "I go away to make money playing my banjo for Mommy and you."

Stopping off at the cabin during his annual trip from Taxco, Pete told Billy about the hotels and night clubs in San Diego. "I might give San Diego a try next spring," Billy said. "I'll look you up when I get there."

"You have my address," Pete said. "I finally found a cheap apartment, so I don't live in the camper except when I'm on the road."

Instead of driving north next May, Billy headed west to San Diego. He stayed with Pete, shared the rent for the apartment, and found Mission Bay hotels and bars lucrative places to perform. People from Arizona and New Mexico as well as Californians flocked to the even climate of the southern California beaches. The Arizonans and New Mexicans wanted to escape the heat of desert summers. Californians just went to the beaches. Billy found the tipping generous and the gig-wage better than he had ever experienced in Wyoming, New Mexico or Colorado.

Billy's conversations with Pete were often reminiscences of their experiences in Vietnam. Once in a while they both drank beer in serious quantities. At times, Billy wondered if he would ever be able to forget about the horrors of that war he had experienced. But, both veterans seemed mesmerized by their memories.

Primrose's letters spoke concern about Cougar. She told Billy about how she didn't think the boy accepted her explanations of why his Daddy wasn't at home like other fathers. When Billy returned in September, he noticed that Cougar seemed even more aloof than usual. Billy resumed the guitar lessons, even though the boy's hands needed more time to grow in order to play many of the chords. By the time he approached his tenth birthday, Cougar had learned to play the guitar, and could sing a few songs to his own accompaniment. Billy enjoyed the time together with his son.

Billy's pattern of going to San Diego for the summers and returning to the cabin during the rest of the year became established.

One day, soon after returning for the winter, Billy took the banjo from the hook on the wall of the cabin. Opening the case, he removed the instrument and tuned it to the Gibson banjo he usually played. Cougar came in from helping Primrose weed the garden. "Son, it's time for you to learn the banjo. It might be a little big for you, but you'll get used to it. I did."

He helped Cougar get the instrument situated for playing, and then began the first lesson. The boy had long fingers like Billy, but the long neck of the banjo proved more challenging than the small guitar he had become so well acquainted with.

Once the banjo lessons began, Cougar seemed less aloof from Billy. By May, father and son were playing a few duets together.

One night at supper, Billy mentioned his plan to leave for San Diego. Cougar pushed his chair back from the table, and stomped angrily out of the cabin. Billy and Primrose looked at each other.

"He's upset. The other day, he told me he wanted you to stay and play banjo together," Primrose said.

"He ought to know that I have to go to California to make money."

"Cougar only understands how he feels, Billy. He's but ten years old and money means nothing to him. He thinks money is more important to you than we are, and he's hurt."

"Goddammit, I don't know how to deal with this."

"I don't either," Primrose said. "I know that you have to do what you do. We have talked about all this before."

"If I took him with me, he might understand."

"Cougar is in school. He is doing well. What would you do with a ten-year-old while you are playing your gigs?"

"I could wait until school is out. He could find somethin' to do on the beach while I'm playin'."

"Get real, Billy," Primrose said. "You play at night. Do you really think Cougar would enjoy being alone while you are in some bar playing your music?"

"I know you're right. I just don't know what to do about this."

"Just go do what you have to do. I would rather have you the happy Banjo Billy I love, than a miserable Bill O'Leary doing something you don't want to do. Cougar will have to deal with the situation as best he can."

During his fourteenth summer, Cougar reached six feet in height. His voice had already changed to a deep, resonant baritone. Like his father, many years before, he won a talent contest sponsored by the county during the summer youth program. A

Tucson television station featured him on a program spotlighting the winners. Writing about Cougar's victory, Primrose said that she felt bad that Billy had not been around to see Cougar in his moment of triumph.

Billy wrote a letter to Cougar, congratulating him on winning the talent contest, and promising he would be home as soon as possible. Arriving at the cabin two days after the Labor Day Weekend, Billy was surprised at Cougar's rapid summer's growth. They were both the same height, but Cougar had yet to fill out his frame. Billy judged that within another year, his son would be even taller.

He had a girl friend who lived in Tubac. Yolanda and Cougar saw each other at school, and she had gone to watch him perform during the talent contest. Cougar hadn't mentioned Yolanda to Billy, but Primrose had written about her in one of her letters.

After greeting his father on his return, Cougar went to his room, which Billy had built for his son several winters earlier. Cougar had begun to shave the reddish whiskers on his chin, but he left the silky moustache. Billy noticed his son's quick exit and paused scowling before turning to Primrose.

He took Primrose into his arms. She wrapped her arms around his waist and drew him closer to her. "Cougar grew a lot," Billy said. "He's as tall as I am."

"Kids do grow. Did you see his feet?"

"I didn't notice. I saw his moustache though."

"By the look of his feet, I would say he will grow even more," Primrose said.

"I'm starting to feel small."

"There's not much you can do about that. He will level off one of these days."

"What about his girl friend, Yolanda?"

"She's a pretty girl, and much shorter than Cougar. There's a dance at the high school next Saturday. I drive him to all the dances, so you can come with us and meet her."

Billy enjoyed meeting Yolanda, and watching his son dance with her. Her long black hair rippled as she danced. The white blouse, trimmed with red and green embroidery, accentuated her copper-colored skin. Billy smiled at the way she looked adoringly up at his son. He danced with Primrose several times.

Billy was surprised when one of the students took the microphone and announced, "Our own Cougar O'Leary will now play his banjo and sing."

Cougar stepped up to the microphone, and played "On The Road Again." The applause told Billy that the students were very proud of Cougar O'Leary. Billy found his eyes fill, and he put his arm around Primrose. On the way back to the cabin, Billy complimented Cougar on his performance.

As the winter proceeded, Billy and Cougar played their banjos together after Cougar returned from school in the afternoon. The playing together brought them closer, but Billy still sensed that Cougar retained some of his aloofness.

One evening, when they had finished "Proud Mary," and were putting away their banjos, Cougar hesitated before going to his room to do homework.

"Dad, what do you think about me playing both banjo and guitar?"

"You're good at both instruments, but you can't play both at the same time."

"I know that, but there are some songs that are better on a guitar."

"Then let's go to Tucson on Saturday and I'll get you a guitar that suits you."

"Hey Dad, that'll be cool."

Cougar took his time choosing the guitar. Billy suggested he get some extra strings. The next day, they walked along the creek, and played together. They sat down among some boulders, and after playing a song together, Cougar leaned his guitar against his leg.

"There's something I want to ask you, Dad."

"What is it?"

"Last summer I asked Mom why her name wasn't O'Leary like yours and mine. She told me that you two weren't married."

"We are married in most ways, Son. We just never went through the legal part."

"Doesn't that make me a bastard?"

"I never thought about that. I've always thought about you as my son, not a bastard."

"A bastard is someone whose parents aren't married."

"I suppose that, legally, that's right."

"If you and Mom were married, would you still take off every May and stay away until fall?"

"Like I said, Son, your mother and I are married as far as we are concerned. I go off to make money playin' banjo."

"Why do you have to stay away so long? Every time the peaches ripen Mom says she wishes you could be here to taste them fresh from the trees."

"I have thought about the peaches ripening, but I play for tourists durin' the summer. There are no tourists here, so I go where they go."

"I think I would like to play for tourists, too," Cougar said.

"You can do that if you want to some day. But, right now you should finish school and maybe go on to college. We have some money for that."

"I know. Mom told me all about your friend Toad. I remember him a little, but I was pretty young when he was here."

"Well, think about goin' to college. You might not like playin' banjo for tourists."

"I love playing banjo and guitar. Winning the contest and being on TV was sure something."

"I know what you mean. It's the same thing I feel when people applaud when I finish a song."

The next winter, Billy and Cougar played more songs together. Cougar had reached six-feet-three-inches tall, and was beginning to fill out in his chest. Billy decided to ask for a gig at Gus and Andy's, with Cougar playing with him on Saturday nights.

The customers stopped talking and drinking when Billy and Cougar played "Dueling Banjos." Starting at opposite ends of the lounge, and making their way toward each other, they ended the song standing side by side. Not only did the crowd applaud, some cheered.

One Saturday the bar was full as usual. Primrose had come into town with them, and enjoyed listening to them perform. She and Billy watched from a table as Cougar played some solos on his guitar. Then, father and son played "Proud Mary" together on their banjos. The applause was deafening. Billy and Cougar joined Primrose at her table during breaks. After the last song, Billy, Primrose and Cougar went back to the cabin.

The gig lasted two weeks before a jazz combo, already scheduled, arrived in town.

The morning after their last night at Gus and Andy's, they awakened to a mackerel sky. The sun had long before risen over the mountains to the east. Primrose gathered the eggs from the hen house, and made omelets with green chile, onion and longhorn cheese. After breakfast, Billy and Cougar took their banjos out of the cases, and began playing.

"I wish we could keep playing at Gus and Andy's," Cougar said. "That was a great crowd to play for."

"They were good," Billy said. "By the way, here's your half of the tips and twenty-five out of the wages."

Billy handed Cougar a hundred and twenty-five dollars.

"Wow, Dad," Cougar said. "I didn't pay any attention to the tips. We did pretty well, didn't we?"

"We did very well, Son. That crowd liked the idea of a father and son playin' and singin' together."

"That's cool."

But, after the first of May, Billy noticed that Cougar had returned to his aloofness. He thought about trying to talk to the boy more, but the opportunity never presented itself.

He had loaded the pickup on the Sunday morning of his planned departure for San Diego, and went back into the cabin to say good-bye. Primrose, as usual on these occasions, stood by the bed teary-eyed.

"Where's Cougar," Billy asked.

"He's probably gone for a walk along the creek."

"I'll go get him and say good-bye."

"I think it's best to leave him alone," Primrose said. "I'll tell him you wanted to see him before you left."

Billy took Primrose into his arms.

"I love you, Lady," he said.

"I love you, too, Banjo Billy."

As the pickup bounced over the road to Arivaca, Billy scowled, thinking about Cougar taking off along the creek, in spite of him knowing it was time to say good bye.

He thought about the old pickup. He had overhauled the engine three times and replaced the transmission twice. As Toad had done, Billy drove on back roads as often as possible because he knew it was dangerous to go at his slow pace on the interstate highways.

When he arrived in San Diego, Pete was not there, having gone on one of his selling trips up the coast. Billy let himself into the apartment with his key. After cleaning up from the trip, he drove to Mission Bay to find a gig for the rest of the spring and summer.

During the fall of Cougar's senior year in high school, Billy noticed that the sounds coming from Cougar's room were guitar instead of banjo. He did not hear Cougar singing, only strange instrumentals that he did not recognize. When Cougar came out for supper, Billy decided to inquire. "What was that music you were playin' this afternoon?"

"'Malagueña.' I'm learning classical guitar, Dad," Cougar replied.

"Whatever made you decide on that?"

"My music teacher at the high school is a classical guitarist. He's a really cool dude and plays very well."

"Does he know you're a banjo player?"

"Oh yeah. He's heard me play lots. He says I am good enough to learn classical guitar, so he's teaching me."

"What about your banjo?"

"A bunch of us at school are forming a group. I'll be playing banjo in it. We are calling ourselves 'The Selves' because we each do a lot of solo stuff."

"Do you have any gigs?"

"Just at school dances right now, but Jorge, he's kind of the leader, is looking around."

"I'd like to hear your group play," Billy said.

"We start a week from Saturday."

Billy and Primrose attended the dance. Cougar drove in early in the van. They joined in the dancing, and enjoyed listening to "The Selves."

Before Easter, Cougar came home excited from school.

"Mom, Mr. Beltrán, my music teacher, wants to take me to Las Vegas over spring break. He wants to introduce me to the music department at the university there."

"That sounds wonderful," Primrose said. "How long will you be gone?"

"It might take a week. Mr. Beltrán said I might have to play for them. He's trying to get me a scholarship."

"Why the university in Las Vegas?" Billy asked.

"Mr. Beltrán graduated from there, and he knows the faculty. He had a scholarship when he went there."

Cougar spent the first week of his spring break going to Las Vegas with his guitar teacher. When he returned to the cabin, he told Billy and Primrose about the trip. "It was really cool. Mr. Beltrán told the chairman of the music department that he thought I could become a soloist. I filled out all the application stuff, and they will let me know in April."

"That sounds wonderful," Primrose said. "I told you that we

have money to help with your college."

"I know, Mom. But, if I can get a scholarship and play banjo in a club to make some extra money, I won't need that money."

"It's there if you need it, Cougar."

"I still don't know how you can make a livin' playin' classical guitar," Billy said.

"I can't think about that until I learn classical guitar," Cougar replied. "Mr. Beltrán plays in the Tucson Symphony besides teaching music at the high school. He seems to be happy."

Pete stopped by the cabin the day after Cougar received the letter informing him that he had won a music scholarship to the University of Nevada at Las Vegas. "That's really terrific," Pete said. He shook Cougar's hand and patted him on the back.

"Are you heading back to San Diego?" Billy asked.

"No," Pete replied. "I gave up the apartment. The jewelry business is dead on the coast. I still have most of the stuff I brought from Taxco last winter, so I'm haulin' ass to Denver. If I can't sell anything there, I'll go to Dallas."

"San Diego won't be much fun without you there," Billy said.

Billy drove to San Diego, wondering if he could find a place to stay. Disappointed that the Mission Beach Hotel, where he had previously done well getting gigs, had been sold, and renovations, still underway, kept the doors closed. After checking with other places for a gig and being told that they all had entertainment booked for the summer, he drove to La Jolla. La Jolla's a snazzy place. People have big bucks there.

Finding the same situation in La Jolla as he had discovered at Mission Beach, he decided to play on the sidewalk next to a small park. "Salting" the open banjo-case with a dollar bill, he tuned the instrument and began playing. Couples dressed in the latest fashions passed in front of him. None paused. Only glances came his way, and they were not accompanied by smiles.

During his third song, A police patrol car parked by the curb. Billy could see the officer talking into his radio before he got out of the patrol car and ambled over. Billy stopped playing. "You sound good," the officer said.

"Thanks, I try," Billy replied.

"There's an ordinance here against begging on the street or sidewalks."

"I'm not begging," Billy said. " I'm playin' banjo and singin'."

"You have your case open, and that comes under the heading of begging. It's not my law. This place is uptight about people who don't have a job."

"Dammit, officer," Billy said. "I spent two tours in Vietnam. They kept tellin' us we were there for freedom, and now, I can't play my banjo to make a livin' here. That sure as hell doesn't sound like freedom to me."

"Hey, man," the officer said. "I was in 'Nam, too. Military Police company. I sympathize with you a hundred and fifty percent, but there's nothing I can do. It's my job to enforce the laws here, even if I think a lot of them are bullshit."

"Do you know of any joint where I could get a gig?"

"There are no joints in La Jolla. This is where the 'beautiful people' hang out. I would try some of the towns up the coast."

Billy put his banjo back in the case. "I reckon you have told me enough about this place that I might as well look somewhere else."

"Good luck to you, man," the officer said. "In some ways, I wish I was going with you, but I've got a wife and two kids."

"I've got a wife and one kid in Arizona," Billy said, reddening at his lie.

"My wife would never let me loose to go anywhere. You're lucky. Take care."

"You too," Billy said.

The policeman returned to the patrol car, talked into his radio, and drove off. Billy strolled slowly back to the pickup, and drove out of La Jolla.

Billy spent the next three weeks driving from town to town, playing in bars for tips and beer and on sidewalks for tips. He wrote Primrose a letter telling her about the lack of gigs in any one place. Feeling like he wasn't welcome anywhere, he drove back to Arizona, heading for Flagstaff. At seven thousand feet elevation, Flagstaff had a reputation for summer tourists looking for vacation spots with cool temperatures.

CHAPTER THIRTEEN

Arriving in the middle of the Flagstaff Summer Music Festival, Billy landed a gig at a small college bar near the university. The Happy Pumpkin's owner, a man about Billy's age, offered twenty dollars a night and beer. "The tips will vary according to the crowd," the short, rotund owner said. "It's mostly university students and they tip best early in the month after they get their checks from home."

Billy thought he had never seen a human being who resembled a pumpkin more than the bar owner. Besides being round, he smiled almost constantly through a mouth with several gaps where teeth once were. Larry Wright also possessed a shiny, brown, bald head. Billy thought the name of the bar could not have been more appropriate.

Billy found a place to spend nights in a parking area next to Lake Mary. Just as the Happy Pumpkin's owner had said, the tips varied considerably. But, Billy was content to be in one place. He wrote Primrose to tell her he would probably stay in Flagstaff until fall.

During a break the fourth night of the gig, one of the bar's regular customers, a professor of music at the university, introduced himself to Billy.

"You are very good on the banjo," Howard Dobbs said. "How long have you been playing?"

"Since I was in high school," Billy said. "What do you play?"

"I play piano, guitar, and harp. But, I mostly teach guitar at the university."

"I have a son who is plannin' to study classical guitar at the University of Nevada at Las Vegas."

"That's great," Dobbs said. "I am acquainted with Henry Chaffee. He teaches classical guitar there and will, no doubt, be teaching your son."

Howard Dobbs came by the Happy Pumpkin almost every evening for his two drinks of bourbon whiskey before retiring to his small house two blocks away. Billy and Dobbs struck up a friendship based on their common love of music. One evening, Dobbs invited Billy to drive to Lockett Meadow, at the mouth of the Inner Basin on the San Francisco Peaks. "That sounds like a good way to spend an afternoon," Billy said. "When do you want to go?"

"Saturday is best. There aren't as many people there as on Sunday. I can only go up there on weekends."

"That's fine with me, as long as I get back here in time to play."

The next Saturday morning, Billy parked his pickup in front of Dobb's house. From Flagstaff they drove north in Dobb's Jeep past Sunset Crater, and turned west on the dirt road leading to Lockett Meadow.

The road up the mountain slope was steep and sinuous. They passed one area that had been burned a number of years before. Young ponderosa pine had been planted by the Forest Service, and those surviving grew midst a vigorous stand of grass, greened by summer rains. At last, the road leveled through an open stand of tall ponderosa where they spotted a white-tail doe and fawn bounding gracefully away from the vehicle. "I think I have seen that pair before," Dobbs said.

"Do you come up here often?" Billy asked.

"Quite a bit. I also like to drive out to Hart Prairie on the other side of the mountain. I find a lot of peace up here. It is a sacred mountain to the Navajo and Hopi. I can understand why."

The road followed the contour of the mountainous terrain, curving into the high meadow bounded by aspen groves. Dobbs parked the Jeep.

"This is sure a beautiful place," Billy remarked.

"I enjoy listening to the wind rustling through the the aspen leaves. Those large trees with initials carved into their bark are a hundred years old. The young spruce between them are starting to take over again."

"What do you mean by takin' over again?" Billy asked.

"At this elevation, Aspen come in after forest fires. They grow faster than spruce, after a hundred years or so the aspen come to the end of their life-span and the spruce take over again."

"That pond over there looks like it's man-made," Billy said.

"Sometimes you can watch the Basque shepherds bringing their sheep in to water them."

Billy and Dobbs looked at the initials carved into the bark of large aspen at one side of the meadow. "These are basque names carved back in the twenties and thirties," Dobbs said. "The sheepmen 'import' Basques to herd the sheep here because they cannot find anyone in the Southwest who is willing to spend the long and lonely hours on the mountain."

"It is sure peaceful up here," Billy said.

"I have spent a lot of time on the mountain," Dobbs said. "When I got back from Vietnam I had a lot of thinking to do."

"Like I told you before, I was there for two tours. That experience still bugs the hell out of me. I have nightmares and get scared shitless. I can't settle down even though I have a precious woman and a wonderful son."

"You might try screaming it all out up here. I did. It took a while, but now I have come to some sort of inner peace I didn't have before."

They began hiking up into the Inner Basin, once the crater of the ancient volcano that formed the mountain. Dobbs led Billy to Snowslide Spring, where the alpine flowers bloomed around the crystal clear water. "What are these scarlet flowers?" Billy asked.

"Those are called Parry's primrose," Dobbs replied. "We are lucky to see them in bloom."

"I have a primrose," Billy said. "She is beautiful, too. But, she blooms all the time."

They returned to Flagstaff in time for Billy to play at the Happy Pumpkin. As he played and sang, he found it difficult to concentrate on his music with the thoughts about the mountain invading his mind.

The next morning he decided to move his camp site closer to the mountain, and drove out to Hart Prairie, where he found a small grove of young aspen not far from the cinder-covered road. After his night's work, Billy slept in his new place. When the sun had awakened him, he started a small campfire, and made a pot of coffee.

Looking at the mountain from the prairie, he saw the peak Dobbs had told him about; Mount Humphrey, the tallest point in the State of Arizona. Large groves of aspen grew above the prairie, and to the north he saw an old ranch house built of logs. Finished with his coffee, he spent the rest of the morning roaming about the prairie and through the groves of aspen as their bright green leaves sang in the breeze.

All day, he kept thinking about what Dobbs had said about finding his inner peace on the mountain by screaming out all that bothered him about the war. After finishing playing for the night, he asked the owner of the Happy Pumpkin for a week off. Larry didn't ask any questions, but wanted to know when Billy would be back again to play. "I'll be here in a week. There's something I need to do," Billy said.

Stopping at a convenience store before driving to Lockett Meadow, he bought enough food for a week's stay on the mountain. He crawled into his bedroll on the grassy understory of a stand of tall, majestic ponderosa near the beginning of the narrow road to the meadow.

Without brewing coffee in the morning, Billy tossed his bedroll into the pickup and drove up the road in low gear. A doe and her fawn scampered away as he entered the level part of the road through the ponderosa pine. He remembered hunting back in Illinois. Now, after Vietnam, Billy had no desire to carry another rifle as long as he lived.

Arriving at the meadow as the sun poked over Sugarloaf to bathe the aspen groves in its early light, he parked, and gathered wood for a campfire. The coffee made, he sat on the tailgate sipping his first mug of the strong, hot brew as the bacon sizzled in the skillet.

After breakfast and extinguishing the campfire with water from the pond, he began the trek up into the Inner Basin carrying his banjo. Reaching the aspen grove near Snowslide Spring, he stopped to rest, sitting on a deadfall. The old crater had an eery look to it. Dobbs had told him that a forest fire had swept through the spruce in the 1890's. Like sentinels, many of the dead, gray relics still stood as young spruce and bristlecone pine had finally begun to re-forest the basin without help from man.

Billy had come up the mountain to scream. Howard Dobbs had explained what he had done and how. He had read a book by a psychiatrist who practiced in Hollywood. The man had recommended that anyone attempting to go through with his method be accompanied by a therapist. Dobbs had told Billy that he thought he could manage by himself and that the author of the book was just trying to accumulate clients.

Now, Billy had to begin. Somehow, he had to take himself away from the present and go back in time. After an hour of concentrating in his mind, his thoughts fled back to the jungles of Vietnam. He went back to the early morning when Pete had stepped on the land-mine that blew off his leg. They had been sent out on patrol. Pete had been promoted to sergeant the week before and was in the lead. It was only the day before that they had slogged their way over the same muddy trail through the jungle.

The explosion of the mine had sent the patrol to their bellies in the mud. They heard Pete scream out, and realizing that one of their own had been hit, Billy and two others got up and ran to him. "Medic!" someone began yelling. The man with the red cross on his sleeves rushed up, took one look at Pete, and began trying to stop the flow of blood from the leg that was missing a foot. "I need a stretcher," the medic had said. One of the men began trotting back to company headquarters.

Billy had knelt at Pete's side. The medic gave Pete a shot of morphine and Pete seemed to relax into slumber. The man returned with the stretcher and they strapped Pete into it. Billy lifted the head of the stretcher and the man who had brought it took the other end. The medic walked along at the side, holding a compress onto Pete's bloody stump. The medic radioed for a helicopter to evacuate Pete to the regimental hospital.

They put the stretcher down at the edge of a clearing. Minutes later they heard the thumping sound of the "Huey" as it came in low over the jungle and landed. A medic jumped out and helped load the stretcher with Pete into the belly of the air-craft. With a whirring of blades, the machine lifted off and was gone. Moments later Billy had snapped. He raked the jungle with the automatic rifle, spraying the broad-leafed trees with lead. The weapon empty, the moans of the wounded Viet Cong became audible from the jungle. Billy snapped in a clip, charged through the trees and saw one dead on the jungle floor and the wounded man next to him with his intestines falling out. Billy had then riddled the wounded man's body. The lieutenant yelled at him to hold his fire.

Suddenly, Billy rose from the deadfall by the aspen grove and began yelling out every swear word he knew, breaking the peace of the Inner Basin. Opening his eyes, he realized what he had been doing and stopped cursing. "Wow," he said out loud. "That stuff that Dobbs talked about seems to work. I was back in that goddam jungle; back to that time when Pete lost his foot. I even went into the jungle and finished that Cong off. I feel a whole lot lighter."

After a refreshing drink from Snowslide Spring, he returned to his camp. All the way back, Billy felt a sense of relief, but he knew that it was just the beginning. Every morning and some-times in the evening he felt himself wanting to scream and cry. Sometimes he directed his anger toward the war, other times toward his father. When the week had passed, he wanted to stay in Lockett Meadow in spite of being out of food supplies except coffee. "I didn't realize how heavy all this stuff I've been carrying around in my head was," he said aloud as he looked at the aspen on the perimeter of the meadow. "All that death I saw, and then

Myra, Toad and my parents..." He climbed into the pickup, and drove slowly down the twisting road to the highway.

Back at the Happy Pumpkin, he tuned the banjo to get ready for the evening. Dobbs came in. Larry poured bourbon into the iced glass and put it on the bar. Seeing Dobbs, Billy sat down next to him and asked Larry for a Budweiser.

"I did it for a week," Billy said.

"How did it go?" Dobbs asked.

"Really quite amazin'. Actually, outrageously amazin'."

"How come you're back?"

"I said I would be back in a week."

"When are you leaving again?"

"Maybe in a couple of days. I wanted to stay," Billy said.

"I know what you mean. It's a real cleansing."

"I'll say it is."

"I haven't told you what I had to deal with on the mountain," Dobbs said. "I guess I can now. I was on a patrol entering a village in the middle of the jungle. We had scattered out. Suddenly I saw a rifle barrel start to rise from a pile of brush. I fired my M-16 into the brush and the rifle dropped. I ran over to see what had been my target. I pulled the pile of brush away and saw her. I had killed a young girl. I'll bet she wasn't even fifteen years old."

"That's pretty heavy," Billy said.

"It was too much for me. I couldn't carry a weapon after that, so they sent me back to the States. Since I spent my time screaming on the mountain, I have finally been able to go out on a few dates with women."

"How long did you spend on the mountain?" Billy asked.

"A month."

"I'm going back in a couple of days."

"It takes a while," Dobbs said. "It's different for me than it is for you. For a long time, I thought my guitar could get me through it all. I guess it helped, but not like the mountain."

"Yeah," Billy said. "I think I've been playin' banjo for the same reason. It helps to lose myself in the rhythms and melodies of music and have people smilin' at me."

He tuned the banjo and played "Peach Trees."

A few days later, Billy bought enough food for two weeks on the mountain. When he returned to Flagstaff, he felt almost free, and better than he had for years. He thanked Larry for letting him play at the Happy Pumpkin and said good-bye to Howard Dobbs. He wanted to see Primrose more than anything. He had never gone home as early as the first week in August. He looked forward to surprising her. *I realize now that Primrose and Cougar are what life is all about. I know she has wanted to be married. It's in her eyes. I reckon it's time for me to think about that commitment. I'll get back in time to drive Cougar to Las Vegas to start his classes at the university.*

In order to avoid the fast traffic on the highway to Phoenix, and to escape the city, he drove the back roads through Happy Jack, Strawberry and Pine. After Payson he headed for Globe to spend the night where he and Toad had once stayed. With Toad's old cowboy hat in the passenger seat next to him, as it had been since his dear friend's death, Billy wished that the old cowboy was with him. He wanted Toad to know that he had come through all right.

After pulling in to the spot, Billy gathered some firewood and made his campfire. As he gazed at the flames, he felt himself slipping back to face his father again. He didn't scream like he did on the mountain, but found himself crying.

The fire had burned down to coals when the tears stopped. He no longer hated or resented his father. Instead, he accepted what his father had been, and felt sad that the man had never understood his son.

After sundown the August heat of southern Arizona seemed to disappear, and a cool breeze wafted in the sound of rock and roll music from a distance. Billy started toward the sound. A hundred yards down the road and around a small hill, he saw a car parked, its radio blasting out at high volume. Through the back window, he saw a teenaged couple kissing each other, oblivious to the world around them. He turned around, and ambled back to his camp. *I hope that kid never has to go to war*, he thought.

Back at his camp, Billy tossed a few sticks on the coals of the fire. As he watched them burst into flame, his thoughts returned to Toad; how his friend had been a drifter most of his life right up to the end. Gazing into the flickering flames of the campfire, he whispered, "Well, Toad, maybe you taught me something you had not figured on teaching me. Maybe I have been drifting around long enough."

The next day, late in the afternoon, Billy arrived at the cabin. After parking the pickup behind the van, he heard Primrose humming a song as she took a shower. "Hey, beautiful lady, how did you know I was coming home?" he called.

Primrose, startled at hearing a voice, poked her head out to see who had spoken. When she saw Billy, she threw open the curtain, and dripping wet, ran out into his waiting arms. "What are you doing back here so early?"

"I had to come home to see you."

After kissing each other passionately, Billy took off his clothes, and joined Primrose in the shower. "Where's Cougar?" Billy asked as Primrose soaped his chest.

"He left for Las Vegas in June. He wanted to get a job playing banjo to make money before his classes began. My two men off playing music for the summer people."

"I was lookin' forward to drivin' him to Vegas."

"That would have been good for both of you, but he took the bus. I drove him into Tucson and cried all the way back. I sure miss having him around. I'm sure glad to see you, Billy."

With the soap rinsed off their bodies, they went into the cabin, and still wet from the shower, made love.

Afterward, they sat naked at the table with two of the beers Billy had brought from Arivaca. "Damn you, Banjo Billy," Primrose said, and smiled. "Every time you leave I get so mad at you. Then every time you come home, I just want to love you to death."

"Every time I leave I start missing you before I get to the road to Arivaca. I don't stop missing you until I'm in your arms again."

"You seem different. You look different. You aren't stoned are you?"

Billy laughed.

"I'm not stoned. I haven't done a number in a long, long time. I feel changed. Now, don't get me wrong, I'll explain. I still love you. In fact, I think that after what I did on the mountain outside of Flagstaff, I am able to love you more than I thought was possible."

"How did all this changing come about, Billy?"

Billy began the story of meeting the guitar professor and what he had gone through screaming out all his anger about the war and even about his father. "I came to some conclusions about why I always had to leave and go places to play banjo. Now I can accept my father for what he was, even though I don't agree with the way he lived his life. Driving back through the ponderosa pine forest from Flagstaff, I realized that I shouldn't make judgements about Cougar wanting to learn classical guitar. He should be able to pursue whatever he wants to without me tellin' him that he can't make any money playin' classical guitar."

Billy laughed, and took a pull on his beer.

"Hell's fire, as Toad might have said, he might make more money playin' classical guitar than I ever did playin' banjo."

"In his last letter he said he had a good gig at a club and had enrolled in an English class during the summer session," Primrose said. "He seems to be doing very well."

"I wish I could have driven him to Las Vegas," Billy said.

"There's a lot of things you probably wish you had done with Cougar over the years," Primrose said. "You can't go back and relive any of it. He was once a very angry boy, but I think he has gotten over being mad at you for not being around."

"I think I'd like to go to Las Vegas," Billy said. "Do you want to go with me?"

Primrose smiled and put her hand on Billy's cheek. "I might some time. I think this would be a good chance for you and Cougar to be together as father and son."

"I want to stay here with you for a few days. I have this great feelin' inside of me that I want to make love to you every minute."

"A couple of days of that, and you will be so tired you'll want to take a trip to Las Vegas," Primrose chided, and laughed.

"Well, let's get over to the bed," he said.

"Goddamit Banjo Billy, I don't have a clue why I love you so much, but I do."

"I might even ask you to marry me."

"Wow, you really have changed," Primrose said, raising her eyebrows.

"I haven't asked you yet," Billy teased and smiled.

"What makes you think I would say yes?"

Billy changed the subject abruptly. "Are the peaches ripe yet?"

"They're pretty close to ready. Maybe a couple of weeks more."

"I'll be back to help you pick them," Billy said, and took her into his arms again.

Two days later, Billy tossed his traveling gear into the pick-up, put Toad's old cowboy hat on the passenger seat next to him, and left for Las Vegas to visit Cougar.

Primrose had told him the name of the club Cougar was playing in, but Billy had never been to Vegas and didn't know where it might be. He drove up and down the streets looking for "The Kickin' Mule." Finally he turned into a side street and saw the neon picture of a mule standing on his front feet and kicking up with his hind legs. As he drove slowly past, he saw a poster in the window announcing "Cougar O'Leary Playing Banjo and Guitar." He had a strange feeling of both fear and anticipation.

Parking the pickup in the lot next to the club, he took his banjo with him into the place. Inside there were rows and rows of slot machines, almost all being played by customers. Next were the Black-Jack and poker tables, two roulette wheels and a large craps table that was crowded with hopeful dice shooters. Over the din of the gambling activities he heard Cougar's banjo. Billy edged his way to the back of the gambling hall. On a platform behind a shiny dance floor he spotted Cougar playing to a crowd seated at tables. Stage lights shining on Cougar made the sequins on his jacket sparkle.

Billy eased himself into a chair at a small empty table next to the dance floor, propping his banjo against the other chair. As he settled himself, a waitress came and took his order.

Cougar finished his song and started another. With the lights in his eyes, he couldn't see Billy. After finishing "The Times They Are Changin," and waiting for the applause to fade, he spoke into the microphone telling his audience he would be right back after a short break. Flipping off the switch to the stage lights, he propped his banjo against the wall, and started across the dance floor.

Suddenly, he stopped as he recognized his father seated at the table. Billy rose from the chair and the two embraced.

"What are you doing here, Dad?" Cougar asked, with surprise.

"I came up to see you."

"That's great. How did you find this place?"

"Your mother gave me the name, so I just drove around until I found it."

"Have you been home?"

"Yeah, I went home early this year. I was hopin' I could drive you up here, but you had already gone."

"I wanted to find a gig."

"I am very proud of you, Son."

"Thanks, Dad. That means a lot to me."

The waitress brought another beer for Billy and one for Cougar. They chatted as they sipped their beers until it was time for Cougar to go back on stage.

"Get your banjo out, Dad. Let's show these people how we can play together. We'll do "Proud Mary" first. Wait for them to quit applauding, and then go into "Dueling Banjos."

"Son, this is your gig, not mine," Billy said.

"That doesn't matter. I'll bet the owner will get a blast out of us playing together."

"All right, Son. But, I don't want you to get into trouble."

"No problem."

Cougar returned to the platform as Billy took out his banjo from the case. He switched on the stage lights and took the microphone in his left hand.

"Ladies and gentlemen, I have a special treat for you tonight. One of the best banjo players in the country is here with me tonight. I know he is one of the best, because he taught me. I am happy to introduce, Banjo Billy O'Leary. We are going to play a couple of songs together for you. By the way, folks, Banjo Billy is my dad."

Billy got up from his chair, and carried the banjo up to the stage. They tuned their instruments together and began "Proud Mary." Cougar's voice, higher than Billy's, contrasted beautifully as they alternated on the rollin' part.

People from the gambling tables looked toward the stage as they sang and played. They joined the crowd at the lounge tables in the loud, long applause.

Billy and Cougar waited until the clapping finished, then stepped down from the stage to take their places at each end of the dance floor. Cougar began the first bar. Billy did the second. They joined each other on the third. As they dueled with their banjos they moved slowly toward each other across the floor until they turned and faced their audience. When they finished, the people stood up from their chairs applauding and yelling for them to play the song again.

Billy and Cougar glanced at each other and both shrugged at the same time. Turning around so they were back to back, they began "Dueling Banjos" for the second time. When they finished, the people stood up and applauded again. The owner of the Kickin' Mule approached Billy and Cougar. Dressed in a white western cut suit, black cowboy boots adorned with silver over the toes, and wearing a black Stetson with a silver hatband, he smiled broadly.

"You guys are great together," he said. "How about both of you guys performing here?"

"Dad, this is Mr. Mirandi," Cougar said. "He owns the Kickin' Mule."

"Danny Mirandi," said the smiling owner of the casino.

"Nice to meet you Mr. Mirandi," Billy said. "I appreciate your kind offer, but there is something I have to do."

"Well, whenever you get done with whatever it is, the offer's open. You guys are terrific."

Mirandi shook hands with Billy and Cougar before returning to his table in the lounge. Cougar announced that they were taking a short break.

Billy put his banjo back in the case, and leaned it against the wall.

"What did you mean, Dad?" Cougar asked. "What is so important that you can't stay and play with me here?"

"Son, I have been thinkin' about this since I camped up on the San Francisco Peaks outside Flagstaff. I finally made up my mind while we were playin' 'Dueling Banjos' the second time. I'm goin' home to ask your mother to marry me."

Cougar's eyes gushed tears as he put his arms around his father. "Both Mom and I have wanted that for a long time."

"I've had a bunch of demons to deal with, Son. But, I got rid of 'em. What say we play another tune for these people?"

"You name it, Dad."

"Anything except 'On The Road Again.'"

"How about that one you wrote, 'Peach Trees.' I can feel their branches touching each other."

THE END